Aravind Adiga was born in Chennai. He was educated at Magdalen College, Oxford, and Columbia University in New York, where he studied English literature. His articles on politics, business and the arts have appeared in international newspapers and magazines including *Time*, *The Financial Times*, and *The Sunday Times*. His first novel, *The White Tiger*, won the 2008 Man Booker Prize for Fiction.

# ARAVIND ADIGA

# BETWEEN THE ASSASSINATIONS

Picador

First published 2008 by Picador
an imprint of Pan Macmillan Ltd
Pan Macmillan, 20 New Wharf Road, London N1 9RR
Basingstoke and Oxford
Associated companies throughout the world
www.panmacmillan.com

ISBN 978-0-330-45054-6

*For Ramin Bahrani*

# HOW TO GET TO KITTUR

Kittur is on India's south-western coast, in between Goa and Calicut, and almost equidistant from the two. The Arabian Sea is to its west, and the Kaliamma river to its east. The terrain of the town is hilly; the soil is black and mildly acidic. The monsoons arrive in June, and besiege the town through September. The next three months are dry and cool, and are the best time to visit Kittur. Given the town's richness of history and scenic beauty, and diversity of religion, race and language, a minimum stay of a week is recommended.

# DAY ONE: THE TRAIN STATION

*The arches of the train station frame your first view of Kittur as you come in as a passenger on the Madras Mail (arrival early morning) or the West Coast Express (arrival afternoon). The station is dim, dirty, and littered with discarded lunch bags that stray dogs poke their noses into; in the evening, the rats come out.*

*The walls are covered with the image of a jolly, plump, potbellied, entirely naked man – his genitalia strategically covered by his crossed legs – who floats above a caption in Kannada that says:* A SINGLE WORD FROM THIS MAN CAN CHANGE YOUR LIFE. *He is the head of a local Jain sect that runs a free hospital and lunch-room in the town.*

*The famous Kittamma Devi temple, a modern-day structure in the style of a Tamil temple, stands on the site where an ancient shrine to the goddess is believed to have existed. It is within walking distance of the train station, and is often the first stop of visitors to the town.*

None of the other shopkeepers near the railway station would hire a Muslim, but Ramanna Shetty, who ran the Ideal Store, a tea-and-samosa place, told Ziauddin it was okay for him to stay.

Provided he promised to work hard. And keep away from all hanky-panky.

3

The little, dust-covered creature let its bag drop to the ground; a hand went up to its heart.

'I'm a Muslim, sir. We *don't* do hanky-panky.'

Ziauddin was small and black, with baby fat in his cheeks, and an elfin grin that exposed big, white, rabbity teeth. He boiled tea for the customers in an enormous, pitted stainless-steel kettle, watching with furious concentration as the water seethed, overspilled, and sizzled into the gas flame. Periodically, he dug his palm into one of the battered stainless-steel boxes by his side to toss black tea powder, or a handful of white sugar, or a piece of crushed ginger into the brew. He sucked his lips in, held his breath, and tipped the kettle with his left forearm into a strainer: hot tea dripped through the clogged pores of the strainer into small, tapering glasses sitting in the slots of a paper carton originally designed to hold eggs.

Taking the glasses one at a time to the tables, he delighted the rough men who came to the teashop by interrupting their conversation with shouts of 'One-a! Two-a! Three-a—' while slamming the glasses down in front of them. Later, the men would see him squatting by the side of the shop, soaking the dishes in a large trough filled with murky bilge water; or wrapping greasy samosas in pages ripped from college trigonometry textbooks so they could be home-delivered; or scooping the gunk of tea leaves out of the filter; or tightening, with a rusty screwdriver, a loose screw on the back of a chair. Whenever a word was said in English all work stopped: the boy would turn around and repeat the word at the top of his voice ('Sunday-Monday, Goodbye, Sexy!'), and the entire shop shook with laughter.

Late in the evening, just as Ramanna Shetty was ready to close up, Thimma, a local drunk, would roar with delight to see Ziauddin, his butt and thighs pressed against the giant ice box, shoving it back into the shop, inch by inch.

'Look at that whippersnapper!' Thimma would clap. 'The ice box is bigger than him, but what a fighter he is!'

Calling the whippersnapper close, he would put a twenty-five paisa coin in his palm. The little boy would look at the shopkeeper's eyes for approval. When Ramanna Shetty nodded, he would close his fist, and yelp in English:

'*Thanks you, sir!*'

Pressing a hand down on the boy's head one evening, Ramanna Shetty brought him in front of the drunk and asked: 'How old do you think he is? Take a guess.'

Thimma learned that the whippersnapper was nearly twelve. He was the sixth of eleven children in a farm-labouring family up in the north of the state; as soon as the rains ended his father had put him on a bus, with instructions to get off at Kittur, and walk around the market until someone took him in. 'They packed him off without even one paisa,' Ramanna said. 'This fellow was left entirely to his own wits.'

He placed a hand on Ziauddin's skull.

'Which, I can tell you, aren't much, even for a Muslim!'

Ziauddin had made friends with the six other boys who washed dishes and ran Ramanna's shop, and slept together in a tent they had pitched behind the shop. On Sundays, Ramanna pulled down the shutters at noon, and rode his blue-and-cream-coloured Bajaj scooter slowly over to the

Kittamma Devi temple, letting the boys follow on foot. When he went in to offer a coconut to the goddess, they sat on the green cushion of the Bajaj scooter, discussing the thick red words written in Kannada on the cornice of the temple.

'HONOUR THY NEIGHBOUR, THY GOD.'

'That means the person in the house next to him is your God,' one boy theorized.

'No, it means God is close to you if you really believe in him,' another retorted.

'No, it means, it means—' Ziauddin tried to explain.

But the others wouldn't let him finish: 'You can't read or write, you hick!'

When Ramanna shouted for them to come into the temple, he darted in with them a few feet, hesitated, and then ran back to the scooter: 'I'm a *Muslim*, I can't go in.'

He had said the word in English, and with such solemnity, that the other boys went silent for a moment, and then began grinning.

A week before the rains were due to start, the boy collected his bundle and said: 'I'm going home.' He was going to do his duty to his family, and work alongside his father and mother and brothers, weeding or sowing or harvesting some rich man's fields for a few rupees a day. Ramanna gave him an 'extra' of five rupees (minus ten paise each for two bottles of Thums Up he had broken), to make sure he'd return from his village.

Four months later, when Ziauddin came back, he had picked up vitiligo, and pink skin streaked his lips and speckled his fingers and earlobes. The baby fat in his face had evaporated over summer; he had returned lean and sunburnt, and with wildness in his eyes.

'What happened to you?' Ramanna demanded, after releasing him from a big hug. 'You were supposed to come back a month and a half ago.'

'Nothing happened,' the boy said, rubbing a finger over his discoloured lips.

Ramanna ordered a plate of food at once; Ziauddin grabbed it and stuffed his face like a little animal, and the shopkeeper had to say: 'Didn't they feed you anything at all back home?'

The 'whippersnapper' was displayed to all the customers, many of whom had been asking for him for months; some who had drifted to the newer and cleaner teashops opening up around the train station came back to Ramanna's place just to see the little thug. At night, Thimma hugged him several times, and then slipped him two twenty-five paise coins which he took silently, sliding them into his pants. When Ramanna saw this, he shouted to the drunk: 'Don't leave him tips! He's become a thief!'

The boy had been caught stealing samosas meant for a client, Ramanna said. Thimma asked the shopkeeper if he was joking.

'I wouldn't have believed it myself,' Ramanna mumbled. 'I saw it with my own eyes. He was taking a samosa from the kitchen, and—' Ramanna bit into a phantom samosa.

Gritting his teeth, Ziauddin had begun pushing the ice box into the shop with the back of his legs.

'But . . . he used to be an honest little fellow . . .' the drunk remembered.

'Maybe he had been stealing all along, and we just never knew it. You can't trust anyone these days.'

The bottles in the ice box jangled. Ziauddin had stopped his work.

'I'm a Pathan!' – he screamed. He slapped his chest. 'From the land of the Pathans, far up north, where there are mountains full of snow! I'm not a Hindu! I don't do hanky-panky!'

Then he walked away to the back of the shop.

'What the hell is this?' The drunk asked.

The shopkeeper explained that Ziauddin was now spouting this Pathan-Wathan gibberish all the time; he thought the boy must have picked it up from some mullah up in the north of the state.

Thimma roared. He put his hands on his hips and shouted to the back of the shop: 'Ziauddin, Pathans are white-skinned, like Imran Khan; you're as black as an African!'

The next morning there was a storm at the tea-and-samosa store. Ziauddin had been caught red-handed this time. Holding him by the collar of his shirt, and dragging him in front of the customers, Ramanna Shetty said:

'Tell me the truth – you son of a bald woman. Did you steal it? Tell me the truth this time, and I might give you another chance.'

'I am telling the truth,' Ziauddin said, touching his pink, vitiligo-discoloured lips with a crooked finger. 'I didn't touch even one of the samosas.'

Ramanna grabbed him by the shoulder, and pushed him to the ground, kicked him, and then shoved him out of the teashop, while the other boys huddled together and watched impassively, like sheep do when they watch one of their flock being shorn. Suddenly Ramanna howled: he lifted up one of his fingers, which was bleeding.

'He bit me – the animal!'

'I'm a Pathan!' Ziauddin shouted back, as he got up to his knees. 'We came here and built the Taj Mahal and the Red Fort in Delhi and so don't you dare treat me like this, you son of a bald woman, you—'

Ramanna turned to the ring of customers who had gathered around him and Ziauddin, and were staring at the two of them, trying to make up their minds as to who was right and who was wrong: 'There is no work here for a Muslim, and he has to fight with the one man who gives him a job.'

A few days later, Ziauddin was passing by the teashop, driving a cycle-rickshaw, with large canisters of milk clanging together on the blue seat.

'Look at me,' he mocked his former employer. 'The milk people trust me!'

But that job too did not last long; once again he was accused of theft. He publicly swore never to work for a Hindu again.

New Muslim restaurants were being set up at the far side of the railway station, where the Muslim immigrants were setting up their houses, and Ziauddin found work in one of these restaurants. He made omelette and toast at an outdoor grill, and shouted in Urdu and Malayalam: 'Muslim men, wherever in the world you are from, Yemen or Kerala or Arabia or Bengal, come eat at a genuine Muslim shop!'

But even this job did not last – he was charged again with theft by his employer, who slapped him when he talked back – and he was seen next in a red uniform at the railway station, carrying mounds of luggage on his head and fighting bitterly with the passengers over his wages.

'I'm the son of a Pathan; I have the blood of a Pathan in me. You hear; I'm no cheat!'

When he glared at them, his eyeballs bulged out, and the tendons in his neck stood out in high relief. He had become another of those lean, lonely men with vivid eyes who haunt every train station in India, smoking their beedis in a corner by themselves and looking ready to hit or kill someone at a moment's notice. Yet when old customers from Ramanna's shop called him by his name, he grinned, and then they saw something of the boy with the big smile who had slammed tea on their table and mangled their English. They wondered what on earth had happened to him.

In the end, Ziauddin picked fights with the other porters, got kicked out of the train station too, and wandered aimlessly for a few days, cursing Hindu and Muslim alike. Then he was back at the station, carrying bags on his head again. He was a good worker; everyone had to concede that much. And there was plenty of work now for everyone. Several trains full of soldiers had pulled up at Kittur – there was talk in the market that a new army base was being set up on the route to Cochin – and for days after the soldiers left, freight trains followed in their wake, carrying large crates that needed to be loaded off the trains constantly. Ziauddin shut his mouth, and carried the crates off the train, and out of the station, where army trucks were waiting to load them.

*

One Sunday morning, he lay on the platform of the station, asleep at ten in the morning, dead tired from the week's labour. He woke up with his nostrils itching: the smell of soap was in the air. Rivulets of foam and bubble flowed next to him. A row of thin black bodies was having a bathe at the edge of the platform.

The fragrance from their foam forced Ziauddin to sneeze.

'Hey, bathe somewhere else! Leave me alone!'

The men laughed and shouted and pointed snow-white fingers at Ziauddin: 'We're not all unclean animals, Zia! Some of us are Hindus!'

'I'm a Pathan!' he yelled back at the bathers. 'Don't talk to me like that.'

He was shouting out once again how his people had smashed Hindu temples and built the Taj Mahal and the Qutub Minar when the bathers, the thick rich lather still on their bodies, rushed forward in a crowd, saying:

'A coolie, sir? A coolie?'

A stranger had come to the platform, even though no train had pulled up. A tall, fair-skinned man holding a small black bag. He wore a clean white business shirt and grey cotton trousers and everything about him smelled of money; this drove all the porters wild, and they crowded around him, still lather-covered, like men with some horrible disease gathering around a doctor who might have a cure. But he turned down all of them; he walked straight up to where Ziauddin lay. He apparently wanted this boy alone.

'Which hotel?' Ziauddin asked, struggling up to his feet.

The stranger shrugged, as if to say: 'Your choice.'

The two of them walked towards the cheap hotels that filled the roads near the station. Stopping at a building that was full of signs – for electrical shops, chemists, pharmacists, plumbers, and saris – Ziauddin pointed out a red sign on the second floor.

**HOTEL DECENT**
**BOARDING AND LODGING**
**VERY HIGH QUALITY**
**NORTH INDIAN SOUTH INDIAN CHINESE WESTERN TIBETAN DISHES**
**TAXI PASSPORT VISA XEROX TRUNK CALL FOR ALL COUNTRIES**

'How about this one, sir? It's the best place in town.' He put a hand on his heart. 'I swear.'

Hotel Decent had a good deal with all the railway porters: a 'cut' of two and a half rupees for every customer they brought in.

The stranger lowered his voice: 'My dear fellow, is it a *good* place, though?' He emphasized the critical word by saying it in English.

'Very good,' Zia said with a wink. 'Very, very good.'

The stranger crooked his finger and summoned Zia closer to him. He spoke into Zia's ear:

'My dear fellow: I am a Muslim.'

'I know, sir. So am I.'

'Not just any Muslim. I'm a *Pathan*.'

It was as if Ziauddin had heard a magic spell. He gaped at the stranger.

'Forgive me, sir . . . I . . . didn't . . . I . . . Allah has sent you to exactly the right porter, sir! And this is not the right hotel for you at all, sir. In fact it is a very *bad* hotel. And this is not the right . . .'

Tossing the foreign bag from hand to hand, he took the stranger around the station to the other side – where the hotels were Muslim-owned, and where 'cuts' were not given to the porters. He stopped at one place and said: 'Will this do?'

**HOTEL DARUL-ISLAM**
**BOARDING AND LOGING**

The stranger contemplated the sign, the green archway into the hotel, the image of the Great Mosque of Mecca on its doorway; then he put a hand into a pocket of his grey pants, and brought out a five-rupee note.

Ziauddin squeezed his fingers back. 'It's too much sir, for one bag. Just give me two rupees.'

He bit his lip.

'No, even that is too much.'

The stranger smiled. 'An honest man.' He tapped two fingers of his left hand on his right deltoid.

'I've got a bad arm, my friend. I wouldn't have been able to carry the bag here without suffering a lot of pain.' He pushed the money into Zia's hands.

'You deserve even more.'

Ziauddin took the money; he looked at the stranger's face.

'Are you really a *Pathan*, sir?'

The boy's body shivered when he heard the stranger's answer.

'Me too!' he shouted, and then ran like mad, yelling all the way: 'Me too! Me too!'

That night Ziauddin dreamt of snow-covered mountains and a race of fair-skinned, courteous men who tipped like gods. In the morning, he returned to the guest house, and found the stranger on one of the benches outside, sipping from a yellow teacup.

'Will you have tea with me, little Pathan?'

Confused, Ziauddin shook his head, but the stranger was already snapping his fingers. The proprietor, a fat man with a clean-shaven lip and a full, fluffy white beard like a crescent moon, looked unhappily at the filthy porter, before indicating, with a grunt, that he was allowed to sit down at the tables today.

The stranger asked: 'So you're also a Pathan, little friend?'

Ziauddin nodded. He informed the stranger the name of the man who had told him he was a Pathan. 'He was a learned man, sir: he had been to Saudi Arabia for a year.'

'Ah,' the stranger said, shaking his head. 'Ah, I see. I see now.'

A few minutes passed in silence. Ziauddin said: 'I hope you're not staying here a long time, sir. It's a bad town.'

The Pathan arched his eyebrows.

'For Muslims like us, it's bad. The Hindus don't give us jobs; they don't give us respect. I speak from experience, sir.'

The stranger took out a notebook and began writing. Zia watched, but said nothing. He looked again at the stranger's handsome face, his expensive clothes; he inhaled the scent that exuded from his fingers and face, and grinned, and struck his feet together. This man is a countryman of mine, he thought. A countryman of mine!

The Pathan finished his tea. He yawned. As if he had forgotten all about Zia, he went back into his guest house and closed the door behind him.

The moment his foreign guest had disappeared into the guest house, the owner of the place caught Ziauddin's eye and jerked his head, and the dirty coolie knew that his tea was not coming. He went back to the train station, where he stood in his usual spot and waited for a passenger to approach him with steel trunks or leather bags to be carried to the train. But his soul was shining with pride, and he fought with no one that day.

The next morning, he woke up to the smell of fresh laundry over his face. 'A Pathan always rises at dawn, my friend.'

Yawning and stretching himself, Ziauddin opened his eyes: he saw a pair of beautiful pale blue eyes looking down on him: eyes such as a man might get when he looks at snow for a long time. Stumbling to his feet, Ziauddin apologized to the stranger, then shook his hand, and almost kissed his face.

'Have you had something to eat?' the Pathan asked.

Zia shook his head; he never ate before noon.

The Pathan took him to one of the tea-and-samosa stands near the station. It was a place where Zia had once worked, and the boys looked in astonishment as he sat down at the table and shouted out:

'A plate of the *best* stuff. Two Pathans need to be fed this morning!'

The stranger leaned in and said, quickly: 'Don't say it aloud. They shouldn't know *that thing* about us: it's our *secret*.'

Zia watched as the stranger thrust a note into his hands. Uncrumpling the note, the boy saw the image of a tractor and a rising red sun. Five rupees.

'You want me to take your bag all the way to Bombay? That's how far this note goes in this town.'

He leaned back while a serving-boy put down the two cups of tea, and a plate with a large samosa, sliced into two and covered with ketchup, on the table. The Pathan and Zia chewed on their halves of the samosa. He took out a piece of the samosa that had got stuck in his teeth; and then he told Ziauddin what he expected for the five rupees.

Half an hour later, Zia sat down at a corner of the train station, in front of the waiting room. When customers asked him to move luggage, he rotated his head from side to side and said: 'I've got another job today.' When the trains came into the station, he began counting them. He found it difficult to remember the number. So he moved outside, sat under the shade of the tree; each time an engine whistled past he made a scratch with his big toe on the sand outside, crossing off each batch of five. Some of the trains were packed; some had entire carriages full of soldiers with guns; and some were almost entirely empty. He wondered where they were going to, all these trains, all these people. Cochin, Trivandrum, Madras . . . he closed his eyes and dozed; the engine of a train startled him, and he scraped another notch with his big toe. When he got up for some lunch, he realized he had been sitting on part of the markings on the ground, and they were smudged under his weight; and then he had to try desperately to decipher what he had written.

In the evening, he saw the Pathan on one of the benches outside the guest house, sipping tea. The big man smiled when he saw Ziauddin; he slapped a spot on the bench three times.

'They didn't give me tea last evening,' Ziauddin complained, and explained what had happened. The Pathan's face darkened; Ziauddin saw that the stranger was righteous. He was powerful: without saying a word he turned to the proprietor and glowered; in a minute a boy came running out of the hotel holding a yellow cup and put it down in front of Zia. He inhaled the flavours of cardamom and sweet steaming milk, and said:

'Seventeen trains came into Kittur. Sixteen left Kittur. I counted every one of them just like you asked.'

'Good,' the Pathan said. 'Now tell me: how many of these trains had Indian soldiers in them?'

Ziauddin stared.

'How-many-of-them-had-Indian-soldiers-in-them?'

'All of them had soldiers . . . I don't know . . .'

'Six trains had Indian soldiers in them,' the Pathan said. 'Four going to Cochin, two coming back.'

17

The next day, Ziauddin sat down at the station half an hour before the first train pulled in. He wrote the numbers on the earth with his big toe; in between breaks for the trains he went to the snack-shop in the station.

'You can't come here!' the shopkeeper shouted. 'We don't want any trouble again!'

'You won't have any trouble from me,' Zia said. 'I'm an honest man now.' To prove his honesty, he put out a rupee note on the table of the snack-shop, and told the shopkeeper: 'Put that note into your money-box, and then give me a chicken samosa.'

In the evening Zia reported to the Pathan that eleven trains had come with soldiers.

'Good.'

The Pathan, reaching out his weak arm, exerted a little pressure on each of Ziauddin's cheeks. He put another five-rupee note out, which the boy took without hesitation.

'Tomorrow I want you to notice how many of the trains had a red cross marked on the sides of their compartments.'

Ziauddin closed his eyes, and repeated: 'With a red cross marked on them.'

He jumped up, gave a military salute, and said: '*Thanks you, sir!*'

The Pathan laughed; a warm, hearty, foreign laugh.

The next day, Ziauddin was sitting under the tree once again, scrawling numbers with his toe in three rows. One, the number of trains. Two, the number of trains with soldiers in them. Three, trains marked with red crosses.

Sixteen, eleven, eight.

Another train passed by; he looked up from the ground, squinted, then moved his toe into position over the first of the three rows.

He held his toe like that, in mid-air, for an instant, and then let it drop to the earth, taking care that it not smudge any of the numbers in the rows. The train left, and immediately behind it, another one pulled into the station, full of soldiers, but Ziauddin did not add to his tally. He just looked at the scratches he had made on the earth.

The Pathan was in the guest house when Ziauddin got there at four. The tall man's hands were behind his back, and he had been pacing around the benches. He came to the boy with quick steps.

'Did you get the number?'

Ziauddin nodded.

But when the two of them had sat down, he asked: 'What're you making me do these things for?'

The Pathan leaned all the way across the table with his weak right arm, and tried to touch Ziauddin's hair.

'A little philosopher, aren't you?'

The teashop proprietor with the beard like the moon came without prompting; he put two cups of tea down on the table, then stepped back and rubbed his palms and smiled. The Pathan dismissed him with a movement of his head. He sipped his tea; Ziauddin did not touch his.

'Do you know where those trains full of soldiers and marked with red crosses are going?'

Ziauddin looked down at his tea.

'Towards Calicut.'

The stranger brought his face closer. The boy saw things he had not seen before: scars on the Pathan's nose and cheeks, and a small rip in his left ear.

'The Indian army is setting up a base somewhere between Kittur and Calicut. For one and one reason only—' he held up a thick finger. 'To do to the Muslims of South India what they are doing to Muslims in Kashmir.'

Ziauddin was still looking at the tea. A skin of rippled brown cream was congealing on its surface.

'I'm a Muslim,' he said. 'The son of a Muslim too.'

'Exactly. Exactly. That's what's important.' The Pathan's thick fingers covered the surface of the teacup. 'Now listen, philosopher: Each time you watch the trains, there will be a little reward for you. Mind – it won't always be five rupees, but it will be something. A Pathan takes care of other Pathans. It's simple work. I have been sent to do the hard work. You'll—'

Ziauddin said: 'I'm not well. I can't do it tomorrow.'

The foreigner thought about this, and then said: 'You are lying to me. May I ask why?'

A finger passed over a pair of vitiligo-discoloured lips. 'I'm a Muslim. The son of a Muslim, too. We never lie.'

'There are fifty thousand Muslims in this town.' The foreigner's voice crackled with irritation. 'Every one of them seethes. Everyone is ready for action. I was only offering this job to you out of pity. Because I see what the kaffirs have done to you. Otherwise I would have offered the job to any of these other fifty thousand fellows.'

Ziauddin kicked his chair back and stood up.

'Then get one of those fifty thousand fellows to do it.'

Outside the compound of the guest house, he turned around. The Pathan was looking at him; he spoke in a soft voice.

'Is this any way to repay me, little Pathan?'

Ziauddin said nothing. He looked at the ground. His big toe slowly scratched a figure into the earth: a large circle. He sucked in fresh air, and released a hoarse, ravaged, wordless hiss.

Then he ran. He ran out of the guest house, ran around the train station to the Hindu side, ran straight up to Ramanna Shetty's teashop, ran around the back of the shop and into the blue tent where the boys lived; he sat there with his mottled lips pressed together and his fingers tightly clasped around his knees.

'What's got into you?' the other boys asked. 'You can't stay here, you know. Shetty will throw you out.' They hid him there that night for old times' sake. When they woke up he was gone. Later in the day he was seen once again at the railway station, fighting with his customers and shouting at them:

'—*don't* do hanky-panky!'

## HOW OUR TOWN IS LAID OUT

In the geographical centre of Kittur stands the peeling stucco façade of Angel Talkies, a pornographic cinema theatre; when townsfolk give directions, they use Angel Talkies as a reference point. The theatre divides Umbrella Street, the commercial district. A significant chunk of Kittur's economy consists of the manufacture of hand-rolled beedis; no wonder then that the tallest building in town is the Engineer Beedi Building, also on Umbrella Street, owned by Mabroor Engineer, the town's richest man. Not far from it sits Kittur's most famous ice-cream shop, The Ideal Traders' Ice Cream and Fresh Fruit Juice Parlour. The White Stallion Talkies, the town's only exclusively English language film theatre, is another nearby attraction. Ming Palace, the first Chinese restaurant in Kittur, opened on Umbrella Street in 1986. The Ganapati Temple in this street is modelled after a famous temple in Goa and is the site of an annual pooja to the elephant-headed deity. Continue on Umbrella Street north of Angel Talkies, and you will reach, via the Nehru Maidan and the train station, the Roman Catholic suburb of Valencia, whose main landmark is the Cathedral of our Lady of Valencia. The Double Gate, a colonial-era arched gateway at the end of Valencia, leads into Bajpe, once a forest, but today a fast-expanding suburb. To the south of Angel Talkies, the road goes uphill into the Lighthouse Hill, and down to the Cool-Water Well.

From a busy junction near the Well begins the road that leads to the Bunder, or the port. Further south from the

Bunder may be seen Sultan's Battery, a black fort, which overlooks the road that leads out over the Kaliamma River into Salt Market Village, the southernmost extension of Kittur.

## DAY TWO: THE BUNDER

*You have walked down the Cool-Water Well Road, past Masjid
Road, and you have begun to smell the salt in the air and note
the profusion of open-air fish stalls, full of prawns, mussels,
shrimp and oysters; you are not far from the Arabian Sea.*

*The Bunder, or the area around the port, is now mostly
Muslim. The major landmark of the Bunder is the Dargah,
or tomb-shrine, of Yusuf Ali, a domed white structure to
which thousands of Muslims from across south India make
pilgrimage each year. An ancient banyan tree growing behind
the saint's tomb and festooned with ribbons of green and
gold is believed to have the power to cure the mutilated.
Dozens of lepers, amputees, victims of partial paralysis, and
geriatrics squat outside the shrine begging alms from visitors.*

*If you walk to the other end of the Bunder, you find the
industrial area, where dozens of textile sweatshops operate
in dingy old buildings. The Bunder has the highest crime
rate in Kittur, and is the scene of frequent stabbings, police
raids and arrests. In 1987, riots broke out near the Dargah
between Hindus and Muslims, and the Bunder was shut down
for six days. The Hindus have since been moving out to Bajpe
and Salt Market Village.*

Abbasi uncorked the bottle – Johnnie Walker Red Label
blended, second-finest whisky known to God or man – and

24

poured a small peg into two glasses with Air India maharajah logos embossed on them. He opened an old fridge, brought out a bucket of ice, and dropped three cubes by hand into each glass. He poured cold water into the glasses. He found a spoon and stirred. He bent his head low, rolled his spittle into a ball and prepared to drop it into one of the glasses.

Oh, too simple, Abbasi. Too simple.

He sucked in the spittle. Unzipping his cotton trousers in three gestures, he let them slide down. Bunching the first two fingers of his right hand together, he stuck them deep into his butt; he brought the two fingers out, dipped them into one of the glasses of whisky, and stirred vigorously.

He pulled up his pants and zipped them. He frowned at the tainted glass; he wondered how to arrange the tray so that the right man took the right glass.

He came out of the pantry with the tray.

The official from the State Electricity Board, sitting at Abbasi's table, grinned. He was a fat, black man in a blue safari suit and a steel ballpoint pen in its pocket. Abbasi placed the tray with care in front of the gentleman.

'Please,' Abbasi said, with redundant hospitality; the official had already taken the glass closest to him. He began sipping and licking his lips. He finished the whisky in slow gulps, and put it down with a bang.

'Good stuff. A man's drink.'

Abbasi smiled ironically.

The official put his hands on his tummy.

'Five hundred,' he said. 'Five hundred rupees.'

Abbasi was a small man, with a streak of grey in his

beard which he did not attempt to dye over, as most middle-aged men in Kittur did; he thought the white streak gave him a look of ingenuity, which he felt he needed, because he knew that his reputation among friends was that of a simple-minded creature vulnerable to attacks of idealism.

His ancestors, who had served in the royal darbars of Hyderabad, had bequeathed him an elaborate sense of courtesy and good manners, which he had adapted for the realities of the twentieth century by adding touches of sarcasm and self-parody.

He folded his palms into a Hindu's namaste, and bowed low before the official. 'Sahib, you know we have just restarted the factory . . . there have been a lot of costs in reopening. If you could show some . . .'

'Five hundred. Five hundred rupees.'

The official twirled his glass around, and then stared at the Air India logo with one eye, as if that some small part of him were embarrassed by what he was doing. He jabbed his fingers at his mouth: 'A man has to eat these days, Mr. Abbasi. And prices are rising so fast. Ever since Mrs. Gandhi died, this country has begun falling apart.'

Abbasi closed his eyes. He reached into his desk, yanked out a drawer, took out a wad of notes, counted them off, and put the amount in front of the official. The fat man, moistening his finger after each note, counted them off one by one; taking out a blue rubber band from an inner pocket, he strapped it around the notes twice.

But Abbasi knew the ordeal was not over yet. 'Sahib, we have a tradition in this factory that we never let a guest depart without a gift.'

He rang the bell for Ummar, his manager, who came almost at once with a shirt in his hands. He had been waiting outside the whole time.

The official took the white shirt out of its cardboard box: he looked at the design on the shirt, of a golden dragon whose tail spread over into the back of the shirt.

'It's gorgeous.'

'We ship it to the United States. It's worn by men who dance professionally. They call it "ballroom dancing." They put on this shirt and swirl under red disco lights.' Abbasi held his hands over his head, and spun around, shaking his hips and buttocks suggestively; the official watched him with lascivious eyes.

He clapped, and said: 'Dance for me one more time, Abbasi.'

When that was done, he took the shirt up to his nose, and sniffed it three times.

'This pattern—' he pressed on the outlines of the dragon with his thick finger. 'It is wonderful.'

'That dragon is the reason I stopped,' Abbasi said. 'To stitch the dragon, it takes very fine embroidery work. The eyes of the women doing it get damaged. One day this was brought to my attention; I thought, I don't want to answer to Allah for the damage being done to the eyes of my workers. So I said, go home, and I closed the factory.'

The official smiled ironically. Another of these Muslims who drink whisky and quote Allah in every other sentence.

He put the shirt back in its box and tucked it under his arm. 'What made you reopen this factory, then?'

Abbasi bunched his fingers and jabbed them into his mouth. 'A man has to eat, sahib.'

They went down the stairs together, Ummar following them three steps behind. When they got to the bottom, the official saw a dark door, a portal of blackness, to his right. He took a step to the darkness. In the dim light inside the room, he saw women with white shirts on their laps, stitching threads through half-finished dragons. He wanted to go in, but Abbasi said: 'You go in on your own, sahib. I'll wait out here.'

He turned around and looked at the wall, while Ummar took the official around the factory floor, introduced him to some of the workers, and brought him back out. The official held his hand out to Abbasi just before leaving.

'I shouldn't have touched him,' Abbasi thought, the moment he closed the door.

At six p.m., half an hour after the women left the dark stitching room for the day, Abbasi closed the factory, got into his Ambassador car, and drove out from the port towards Kittur; he was thinking about only one thing.

Corruption. There is no end to it in this country. In the past four months, since he had decided to reopen his shirt factory, he had had to pay off:

The electricity man; the water board man; half the income tax department of Kittur; half the excise department of Kittur; six different officials of the telephone board; a land tax official of the Kittur City Corporation; a sanitary inspector of the Karnataka State Health Board; a health inspector of the Karnataka State Sanitation Board; a delegation of the All India Small Factory Workers' Union;

delegations of the Kittur Congress Party, the Kittur BJP, the Kittur Communist Party, the Kittur Muslim League.

The white Ambassador car went up the driveway of a large, whitewashed mansion. At least four evenings a week Abbasi came to the Canara Club, to the small air-conditioned room with the green billiards table upstairs, to play snooker and have drinks with friends. He was a good shot, and his aim deteriorated after his second whisky, so his friends liked playing long sets with him.

'What's bothering you, Abbasi?' Sunil Shetty, who owned another shirt factory down the road from Abbasi, asked. 'You're playing very rashly tonight.'

'Got another visit from the electricity department. A real bastard this time. Dark-skinned fellow. Lower caste of some kind.'

Sunil Shetty purred in sympathy; Abbasi missed his shot.

Halfway through the game, the players all moved away from the table, while a mouse scurried across the floor, running along the walls until it found a hole to vanish into.

Abbasi banged his fist on the edge of the table.

'Where does all our membership money go? They can't even keep the floors clean! You see how corrupt the management of the club is?'

After that, he sat quietly with his back to the sign that said RULES OF THE GAME MUST BE FOLLOWED AT ALL TIMES and watched the others play, while resting his chin on the end of the stick.

'You are tense, Abbasi,' said Ramanna Padiwal, who owned a silk-and-rayon store on Umbrella Street, and was the best snooker-shark in town.

To dispel this myth, Abbasi ordered a round of whisky for everyone, and they stopped playing and held their glasses wrapped in paper napkins and sipped. As always, what they began talking about first was the whisky itself.

'You know that chap who goes around from house to house offering to pay fifty rupees if you sell him your old cartons of Johnnie Walker Red Label,' Abbasi said. 'To whom does he sell those cartons in return?'

The others laughed.

'For a Muslim, you're a real innocent, Abbasi' – Padiwal, the used-car salesman, let out a laugh. 'Of course he sells them to the bootlegger. That's why the Johnnie Walker Red you buy from the store, even though it has a genuine bottle and genuine carton, is bootlegged.'

Abbasi spoke with a finger drawing circles in the air, as if attempting to unravel the knots of the problem: 'So I sold the carton to the man who will sell it to the man who will bootleg the stuff and sell it back to me?' He drew the finger back into the palm. 'That means I've cheated myself?'

Padiwal shot a look of wonderment at Sunil Shetty, and said: 'For a Muslim, this fellow is a real . . .'

It was a sentiment that was widespread among the industrialists – ever since that day when Abbasi had shut down his factory because the work was damaging the eyes of the employees. Most of the snooker-players owned, or had invested in, factories that employed women in the same manner; none had dreamed of closing down because a woman here or a woman there went blind.

Sunil Shetty said: 'The other day I read in the *Times of India* that the chief of Johnnie Walker said there is more

30

Red Label consumed in the average small Indian town than is produced in all of Scotland. When it comes to three areas—' he counted them off, 'black-marketing, counterfeiting, and corruption, we are the world champions. If they were included in the Olympic games, India would always win gold, silver and bronze in those three.'

After midnight, Abbasi staggered out of the club, leaving a coin with the guard who got up from his chair to salute him, and help him into his car.

Quite blindly drunk, he raced out of the town and up to the port, slowing down when the smell of sea breeze got to him.

Stopping by the side of the road when his house came into view, he decided he needed one more drink. He always kept a small bottle of whisky under his seat, where his wife would not find it, for just such a need; bending down, he slapped his hand around the floor of the car. His head banged into the dashboard. He found the bottle, and a glass.

After the drink, Abbasi realized he couldn't go home at once; his wife would smell the liquor on him the moment he got past the threshold. There'd be another scene. She never understood why he drank so much.

He drove up to the port. He parked the car next to a garbage dump, and walked over to a teashop. The sea was visible beyond a small beach; the smell of roasted fish wafted through the air.

A blackboard outside the teashop proclaimed, in letters of white chalk: WE CHANGE PAKISTANI MONEY AND CURRENCY. The front walls of the shop were adorned with a photograph of the Great Mosque in Mecca, and a poster of a boy with a white cap and a girl in a green burqa bowing to the Taj Mahal. Four benches had been arranged in an outdoor verandah. A dappled white-and-brown goat was tied to a pole at one end of the verandah; it was chewing on dried grass.

Men were sitting on one of the benches. Abbasi touched one man on his shoulder; he turned around.

'Abbasi.'

'Mehmood, my brother. Make some room for me.'

Mehmood, a fat man with a thin white beard and no moustache, did so, and Abbasi squeezed in next to him. Abbasi had heard that Mehmood stole cars; he had heard that Mehmood's four sons drove them to a village on the Tamil Nadu border, a village whose only business was the sale and repurchase of stolen cars.

In addition to Mehmood, Abbasi recognized Kalam, who was rumoured to import hashish from Bombay and ship it to Sri Lanka; Saif, who had knifed a man in Trivandrum; and a small, white-haired man who was only called Professor – and who was believed to be the shadiest of the lot.

These men were smugglers, car thieves, thugs, and worse; but while they sipped tea, nothing would happen to Abbasi. It was the culture of the port. A man would be stabbed in daylight, but never at night, and never while taking tea. In any case, the sense of solidarity among the Muslims at the port had deepened since the riots.

The Professor was finishing up a story of Kittur in the twelfth century, about an Arab sailor named bin Saad who sighted the town, just when he had given up hope of finding land. He had put his hands up to Allah and promised that if he arrived on land, he would never again drink liquor or gamble.

'Did he keep his word?'

The Professor winked. 'Take a guess.'

The Professor was always welcome at late-night chit-chats at the teashop because he could rattle off many fascinating things about the port; how its history went back to the Middle Ages, for instance, or how Tippu Sultan had once installed a battery of French-made canons here to scare away the British. He pointed a finger at Abbasi: 'You're not your usual self. What's on your mind?'

'Corruption,' Abbasi said. 'Corruption. It's like a demon sitting on my brain and eating it with a fork and knife.'

The others drew closer to listen. Abbasi was a rich man; he must have an intimacy with corruption that exceeded theirs. He told them about the morning.

Kalam, the drug-dealer, smiled and said: 'That's nothing, Abbasi.' He pointed an arm to the sea. 'I have a ship, half full of cement and half full of something else, that has been waiting two hundred metres out at sea for a month. Why? Because this inspector at the port is squeezing me. I pay him and he wants to squeeze me even more, too much more. So the ship is just drifting out there, half full of cement and half full of something else.'

'I thought things would get better with this fellow Rajiv Gandhi taking over,' Abbasi said. 'But he's let us all down.'

'We need one man to stand up to them,' the Professor said. 'Just one honest, brave man. That fellow would have done more for this country than Gandhi or Nehru did.'

The remark was greeted by a chorus of ayes.

'Yes,' Abbasi agreed, stroking his beard. 'And the next morning he would be floating in the Kaliamma River. Like this.'

He mimicked a corpse.

There was general agreement over this remark too. But even as the words left his mouth, Abbasi was already thinking: 'Is it really true? Is there nothing we can do to fight back?'

In the side of the Professor's trousers, he saw the glint of a knife. The effect of the whisky was wearing off, but it had carried him to a strange place, and his mind was filling with strange thoughts.

Another round of tea was ordered by the car-thief, but Abbasi, yawning, crossed his hands and shook his head.

The next day, he turned up to work at ten-forty, his head still throbbing with pain.

Ummar opened the door for him. Abbasi nodded his head, and took the mail from him. With his eyes on the floor, he moved to the stairs that led up to his office. He stopped. At the threshold of the black door that led to the factory-floor, one of the stitching women was standing and staring at him.

'I'm not paying you to waste time,' he snapped.

She turned and fled into the black doorway. He hurried up the stairs.

He put on his glasses, read the mail, read the newspaper, yawned, drank tea, and opened a book, with the logo of the Karnataka Bank on it; he went down a list of customers who had paid and not paid. He kept thinking of last evening's game of snooker.

The door creaked open; Ummar's face popped in.

'What?'

'They're here.'

'Who?'

'The government.'

Two men in polyester shirts and ironed blue bell-bottoms came into his room. One of them, a burly man with a big potbelly and a moustache like that of a wrestler in a village fair, said:

'Income Tax Department.'

Abbasi got up. 'Ummar!' he shouted. 'Get one of the women to run and bring tea from the teashop by the sea. And some of those round Bombay biscuits as well.'

The big taxman sat down at the table without being invited. His companion, a lean, dark fellow, hesitated in a fidgety kind of way, until he was cued by the other to get into a chair too.

Abbasi smiled. The taxman with the moustache talked.

'We have just walked around your factory-floor. We have just seen the women who work for you, and the quality of the shirts they stitch.'

Abbasi smiled and waited for it.

It came quickly this time.

'We think you are making a lot more money than you have declared to us.'

Abbasi's heart beat hard; he told himself, calm down. There is always a way out.

'A lot, lot, lot more.'

'Sahib, sahib,' Abbasi said, patting the air with conciliatory gestures. 'We have a custom in this shop. Everyone who comes in will take a gift before leaving.' Ummar, who knew already what he had to do, was waiting at the threshold of the office with two shirts. With a fawning smile, he presented them to the two officers. They accept the bribes without a word, the lean fellow looking at the big one for approval before snatching his gift.

Abbasi asked: 'What else can I do for you two sahibs?'

The one with the moustache smiled. His partner too smiled. The one with the moustache held up the last three fingers of his hand.

'Each.'

Three hundred per head was too low; real pros at the income tax office wouldn't have settled for anything under five hundred. Abbasi guessed that the two men were doing this for the first time. In the end, they would settle for a hundred each, plus the shirts.

'Let me offer you a little boost first. Do the sahibs take Red Label?'

The fidgety fellow almost jumped out of his seat in excitement, but the big one glared at him.

'Red Label would be acceptable.'

They've probably never got offered anything more than hooch, Abbasi realized.

He walked into the pantry, took out the bottle. He poured into three glasses with the Air India maharajah logo. He opened the fridge. He dropped six cubes of ice into each, and poured a thin stream of ice water from a bottle. He spat in two of the glasses, and arranged them furthest away on the tray.

The thought fell into his mind like a meteor from a purer heaven. *No.* Slowly it spread itself throughout his mind. No, he could not give this whisky to these men. It might be counterfeit stuff, sold in cartons bought under false premises, but it was still a thousand times too pure to be touched by their lips.

He drank one whisky, and then the second, and then the third.

Ten minutes later, he came into the room with heavy steps. He bolted the door behind him, and let his body fall heavily against it.

The big taxman turned around sharply: 'Why are you closing the door?'

'Sahibs. This is the port city of the Bunder, which has ancient traditions and customs, dating back centuries and centuries. Any man is free to come here of his own will, but he can leave with the permission of the locals.'

Whistling, Abbasi came over to the desk, and picked up the phone receiver; he shoved it, like a weapon, right in the face of the bigger taxman.

'Shall I call the income tax office right now? Shall I find out what is happening? If you have been authorized to come? Shall I?'

They looked uncomfortably. The lean man was sweating. Abbasi thought: My guess is right. They are doing this for the first time.

37

'Look at your hands. You have accepted shirts from me, which are bribes. You are holding the evidence in your hands.'

'Look here—'

'No! You look here!' Abbasi shouted. 'You are not going to leave these premises alive, until you sign a confession of what you were trying to do. Let us see how you get out. This is the port city. I have friends in four directions around here. You will both be dead and floating in the Kaliamma River if I snap my fingers now. Do you doubt my words?'

The big taxman looked at the ground, while the other fellow sweated an amazing amount in under a minute.

Abbasi unbolted the door; he held one wing open. 'Get out.' Then, with a wide smile, he bowed down to them:

'Sahibs.'

The two men scampered out without a word. He heard the thump of their feet on the staircase; and then a cry of surprise from Ummar, who was walking up the stairs with a tray of tea and Britannia biscuits.

He let his head rest on the cool wood of the table and wondered what he had done. Any moment, he was expecting that the electricity would be cut off; the income tax officials would return, with more men and an arrest warrant in their hands.

He walked round and round the room, thinking: What is happening to me? Ummar stared at him in silence.

After an hour, to Abbasi's surprise, there was no call from the income tax office. The fans were still working. The light was still on.

Abbasi began to hope. These guys were raw – tyros. Maybe they'd just gone back to office and got on with their work. Even if they had complained, the government officials were wary of the port since the riots; it was possible they didn't want to antagonize any of the Muslim businessmen here now. He looked out the window at the port: This violent, rotten, garbage-strewn port, crawling with pickpockets and knife-carrying thugs – it seemed the only place where a man was safe from the corruption engulfing Kittur.

Yes: he had done it. He had beaten the demon: he had beaten corruption for once!

'Ummar!' he shouted. 'I'm leaving early today for the club – give Sunil Shetty a call to say that he too should come today, I have great news for him!'

He came running down the stairs, and stopped at the last step. To his right, the black doorway opened into the factory-floor. In the six weeks since his factory had reopened, he had not once gone through this doorway; Ummar had handled all the affairs of the factory-floor. But now the doorway to his right, black and yawning, had become inescapable.

He felt he had no option but to go in. He realized now that the morning's events had all been, somehow, a trap: to bring him to this place, to make him do what he had avoided doing since reopening his factory.

The women were sitting on the floor of the dim room, pale fluorescent lights flickering overhead, at work stations indicated by numerals in red letters painted on the walls. They were holding the white shirts close to their eyes and stitching gold thread into them; they stopped when he came in. He flicked his wrist, to indicate they should keep working.

39

He didn't want their eyes on him: those eyes that were being damaged, while their fingers created golden shirts that he could sell to American ballroom dancers.

Damaged? No, that was not the word. That was not the reason he had shunted them to a side room.

Everyone in that room was going blind.

He sat down on a chair in the centre of the room.

The optometrist had been clear about that; the kind of detailed stitchwork needed to be done on the shirts put a scar on the women's retina. He had used his fingers to show Abbasi how thick the scar was. Two women had already gone blind; that was why he had shut down his factory. When he reopened, all his old workers came back at once. They knew their fate; but there was no other work to be had.

Abbasi closed his eyes. He wanted nothing more than for Ummar to shout that he was needed urgently upstairs.

But no one came to release him, and he sat in the chair, while women around him stitched, and their stitching fingers kept talking to him: We are going blind; look at us!

'Is your head hurting, sahib?' a woman's voice was asking him. 'Do you want me to get you some Dispirin and water?'

Without daring to look at her, Abbasi said: 'All of you please go home. Come back tomorrow. But please go home today. You'll all be paid.'

'Is sahib unhappy with us for some reason?'

'No, please. Go home now. You'll all be paid for the whole day. Come back tomorrow.'

He heard the rustle of their feet and he knew, they must be gone now.

They had left their shirts at their work stations, and he picked one up; the dragon had been half stitched on it. He kneaded the shirt between his fingers. He could feel, between his fingers, the finespun fabric of corruption.

'The factory is closed,' he wanted to shout to the dragon. 'There – you happy with me? The factory is closed.'

And after that? Who would send his son to school? Would he sit with a knife by the port and smuggle cars like Mehmood? The women would go elsewhere, and do the same work.

He slapped his hand on his thigh.

Thousands, sitting around teashops and universities and workplaces every day and every night were cursing corruption. Yet not one fellow had found a way to slay the demon without giving up his share of the loot of corruption. So why did he – an ordinary fellow given to whisky and snooker and listening to gossip from thugs – have to come up with an answer?

But just a moment later, he did have an answer.

He was offering Allah a compromise. He would be taken to jail, but his factory would go on with its work: he closed his eyes and prayed to his God to accept this deal.

An hour passed, and no one had come to arrest him.

Abbasi opened a window in his office. He could see only buildings, a congested road, and old walls. He opened all the windows, but still he saw nothing but walls. He climbed up to the roof of his building, and ducked under a clothesline to walk out into the terrace. Coming to its edge, he put his foot on the tiled roof that made an awning over the front of his shop.

From here, a man could see the limits of Kittur. At the very edge of the town, in close succession, stood a minaret, a church steeple, and a temple tower, like signposts meant to identify the three religions of the town to voyagers from the sea.

Abbasi saw the Arabian Sea leading out from Kittur. The sun was shining over it. A ship was slowly leaving the port, edging to the spot where the blue waters of the sea changed colour, and turned a deeper hue. It was about to hit a large patch of brilliant sunshine, an oasis of pure light.

## DAY TWO (AFTERNOON): LIGHTHOUSE HILL

*After a lunch of prawn curry and rice at the Bunder, you may want to visit Lighthouse Hill and its vicinity. The famous lighthouse, built by the Portuguese and renovated by the British, is no longer in use. An old guard in a blue uniform sits at the base of the lighthouse. If the visitors are poorly dressed, or speak to him in Tulu or Kannada, he will say, 'Can't you see it's closed?' If the visitors are well-dressed or speak English, he will say: 'Welcome.' He will take them into the lighthouse, and up the spiral staircase to the top, which affords a spectacular view of the Arabian Sea. In recent years, the Corporation has begun running a reading room inside the lighthouse, whose collection includes a book by Father Basil D'Essa, S.J., on the history of Kittur. The Deshpremi Hemachandra Rao Park around the lighthouse is named in honour of the freedom fighter who hung a tricolour from the lighthouse during British rule.*

It happens at least twice a year. The prisoner, handcuffs on his wrist, is taking strides towards the Lighthouse Hill police station with his head held up high and a look of insolent boredom on his face; while following him, almost scampering to catch up, are the two policemen who are holding the chains attached to the handcuffs. The odd part is that the man in handcuffs seems to be dragging along the policemen, like a fellow taking two monkeys out for a walk.

In the past nine years, the man known as 'Xerox' Ramakrishna has been arrested twenty-one times for the sale, at discounted rates, of illegally photocopied or printed books on the granite pavement in front of Deshpremi Hemachandra Rao Park to the students of St. Alfonso College. A policeman comes in the morning, when he is sitting with his books spread out on a blue bed-sheet; he puts his stick on the books and says: 'Let's go, Xerox.'

The bookseller turns around to his eleven-year-old daughter, Ritu, who sells books with him, and says: 'Go home and be a good girl, dear.' Then he holds his hands out for the cuffs.

In jail, Xerox is unchained, and put in a cell. Holding on to the bars of the cell, he regales the policemen with ingratiating stories. He may tell them a smutty tale about some college girl whom he saw that morning wearing blue jeans in the American style, or a new swear-word in Tulu he has heard on the bus while going to Salt Market Village, or perhaps, if they are in the mood for longer entertainment, he will narrate to them, as he has done so many times before, the story of what his father did all his life for a living – taking the crap out of the houses of the rich landlords, the traditional occupation of people of his caste. All day long, his old man would hang around the back wall of the landlord's house, waiting for the smell of human faeces; as soon as he smelled that smell, he came close to the house, and waited, with bent knees, like a wicketkeeper waits for the ball in cricket. (Xerox bent his knees and showed how.) Then, as soon as he heard the 'thud,' of the boom-box closing, he had to run to the wall, pull out the retractable potty through a hole in the wall, empty it into the rose-plants, wipe it clean with his loincloth and insert it back into the wall before the next person came to use the toilet. That was the job he did, his whole life, can you believe it!

The jailors will laugh.

They bring Xerox samosas wrapped in paper, they offer him chai, they consider him a decent fellow. They let him out at midday; he bows low to them and says: 'Thank you.' Then Miguel D'Souza, the lawyer for the publishers and booksellers on Umbrella Street, calls the station and yells: 'Have you let him off again? Doesn't the law of the land mean anything?' The inspector of the station, Ramesh, keeps the receiver at a distance from his ear, and reads the newspaper, looking at the Bombay stock market quotes. That is all Ramesh really wants to do in life: read the stock market quotes.

By late afternoon, Xerox is back at it. Photocopied or cheaply printed copies of Karl Marx, *Mein Kampf*, and others, are arranged on a blue cloth that is spread out on the pavement, on Lighthouse Hill, and little Ritu sits stiff-backed, with her long unbroken nose and faint moustache, watching the customers pick up the books and flip through them.

'Put that back in place,' she will say, if a customer has rejected a book. 'Put it back exactly where you picked it up from.'

'*Accounting for Entrance Exams*?' one customer shouts at Xerox. '*Advanced Obstetrics*?' another shouts.

'*The Joy of Sex*?'
'*Mein Kampf*?'
'Lee Iacocca?'
'What's your final rate?' the young man asks, flipping through the book.
'Seventy-five rupees.'
'O, you're *raping* me! It's too much.'
The young man walks away, turns around, comes back, and says, 'What's your final rate, I have no time to waste.'
'Seventy-two rupees. Take it or leave it. I've got other customers.'

The books are photocopied, or sometimes printed, in an abandoned printing press in Salt Market Village. Xerox loves being around machinery. He strokes the photocopier; he adores the machine, the way it gives off flashes of lightning as it works, the way it whirrs and hums. He cannot read English, but knows that English words have power, and that English books have aura. He looks at the image of Adolf Hitler on the cover of *Mein Kampf*, and he feels his power. He looks at the face of Kahlil Gibran, poetic and mysterious, and he feels the mystery and poetry. He looks at the face of Lee Iacocca, relaxed with his hands behind his head, and he feels relaxed. That's why he once told Inspector Ramesh: 'I have no desire to make any trouble for you or for the publishers, sir; I just love books: I love making them, holding them and selling them. My father took out crap for a living, sir: he couldn't even read or write. He'd be so proud if he could see that I made my living from books.'

Only one time has Xerox really been in trouble with the police. That was when someone called the station and said that Xerox was selling copies of Salman Rushdie's *The Satanic Verses* in violation of the laws of the Republic of India. This time when he was brought into the station in handcuffs there were no courtesies, no cups of chai.

Ramesh slapped him.

'Don't you know, the book is banned, you son-of-a-bald-woman? You think you are going to start a riot among the Muslims? And get me and every other policeman here transferred to Salt Market Village?'

'Forgive me,' Xerox begged. 'I had no idea that this was a banned book, really . . . I'm just the son of a man who took out crap, sir. He waited all day long for the boom-box to make a noise. I know my place. I wouldn't dream of challenging you. It was just a mistake, sir. Forgive me, sir.'

D'Souza, the booksellers' lawyer, heard what had happened and came to the station, a small man with black oily hair, and a neat moustache. He took a look at the banned book – a massive paperback with an image of an angel on the front – and shook his head in disbelief.

'That fucking untouchable's son, thinking he's going to photocopy *The Satanic Verses*. What balls."

He sat down at the inspector's desk and shouted: 'I told you this would happen, if you didn't punish him! You're responsible for all this.'

Ramesh glared at Xerox, who was lying on a bed penitently, as he had been ordered to do.

'I don't think anyone saw him sell it. Things will be fine.'

To calm the lawyer down, Ramesh asked a constable to go bring a bottle of Old Monk rum. The two of them sat down at the desk and talked.

47

Ramesh read out passages from the book, and said: 'I don't get what the fuss is all about, really.'

'Muslims,' D'Souza said, shaking his head. 'Violent people. Violent.'

The bottle of Old Monk arrived. They drank it in half an hour, and the constable went to bring them another. In his cell, Xerox was in bed, perfectly still, looking at the ceiling. The policeman and the lawyer kept drinking. D'Souza told Ramesh his frustrations, and the inspector told the lawyer his frustrations. One had wanted to be a pilot, soaring in the clouds and chasing stewardesses around, and the other – he had never wanted anything but to dabble in the stock market. That was all.

'Do you want to know a secret?' Ramesh asked, at midnight. He walked stealthily to the prison and showed the lawyer the secret. One of the bars of the jail was detachable. The policeman removed it, and swung it, and then put it back in place. 'That's how the evidence is hidden,' he said. 'Not that this kind of thing is done often at this station, mind you – but that's how it is done, when it is done.'

The lawyer giggled. He loosened the bar and slung it over his shoulder, and said: 'Don't I look like Hanuman now?'

'Just like on TV,' the policeman said.

The lawyer asked that the cell door be opened, and it was. The two of them saw the sleeping prisoner lying on his cot, an arm over his face to keep out the jabbing light of the naked bulb over him. A sliver of naked skin just above his groin was exposed beneath his cheap polyester shirt; a creeper of thick black hair, which looked to his two onlookers like an outgrowth from his pubic zone, was just about visible.

'That fucking son of an untouchable. See him snoring.'

'His father took out crap – and this fellow thinks he's going to dump crap on us!'

'Selling *The Satanic Verses*. He'll sell it under my nose, will he?'

'These people think they own India now. Don't they? They want all the jobs, and all the degrees at university, and all the . . .'

Ramesh pulled the pants down the legs of the snoring man, who did not wake up at once; he lifted the bar high up, while the lawyer said: 'Do it like Hanuman does, on TV!' Xerox woke up with a scream. Ramesh handed D'Souza the bar. The cop and the lawyer took turns: he smashed it into Xerox's legs, just at the knee-joint, like the monkey god did on TV, and then he smashed it into Xerox's legs, just below the knee-joint, like the monkey god did on TV, and then he smashed it into Xerox's legs, just above the knee-joint, and then, laughing and kissing each other, the two staggered out, shouting for someone to lock up the station behind them.

Periodically through the night, when he woke up, Xerox resumed his screaming.

In the morning, Ramesh came back, was told by a constable about the state of things in the prison, and said, 'Shit, it wasn't a dream then.' He ordered the constables to take the man in the prison to the Havelock Henry District Hospital, and asked for a copy of the morning paper, so he could check the stock market.

The next week, Xerox came, noisily, because he was on crutches, into the police station, with his daughter behind him.

'You can break my legs, but I can't stop selling books. I'm destined to do this, sir,' he said. He grinned.

Ramesh grinned too, but he avoided the man's eyes.

'I'm going to the hill, sir,' Xerox said, lifting up one of his crutches. 'I'm going to sell the book.'

Ramesh and the other cops gathered around Xerox and his daughter and begged. Xerox wanted them to phone D'Souza, which they did. He came with his wig, along with two assistants, also in black gowns and wigs. When he heard why the policeman had called him over, he burst into laughter.

'This fellow is just teasing you,' the lawyer told Ramesh. 'He can't possibly go up the hill with his leg like that.'

D'Souza pointed a finger at the middle region of Xerox's body.

'And if you do try to sell it, mind – it won't be just your legs that we break next time.'

A constable laughed in the background.

Xerox looked at Ramesh with his usual ingratiating smile. He bent low with folded palms and said: 'So be it.'

D'Souza sat down for a drink of Old Monk rum with the policemen, and they settled into another game of cards. Ramesh said he had lost some money on the market the past week; the lawyer sucked his teeth and shook his head, and said that everyone in a big city like Bombay was a cheat or a liar or a thug.

Xerox turned around on his crutches and walked out of the station. His daughter came behind him. They went in the direction of the hill. The climb took two hours and a half, and they stopped six times for him to drink tea, or a glass of sugarcane juice. Then his daughter spread down the blue sheet in front of Deshpremi Hemachandra Rao Park, and Xerox lowered himself. He sat on the sheet, stuck his legs out slowly, and put a large paperback down next to him. His daughter sat down too, keeping watch over the book with a stiff upright back. The book was banned throughout the Republic of India and it was only thing that Xerox intended to sell that day: *The Satanic Verses*, by Salman Rushdie.

## DAY TWO (CONTINUED): OUR SCHOOL

*A short walk from the end of the park rises a massive grey Gothic tower with a coat of arms and the motto* LUCET ET ARDET *painted on it. This is the St. Alfonso Boys' High School and Junior College, established 1858, one of the oldest educational establishments in the state of Karnataka. The Jesuit-run school is Kittur's most famous, and many of its alumni have made it into the Indian Institute of Technology, the Karnataka State Regional Engineering College, and other prestigious universities in India and abroad.*

Several seconds, perhaps even a full minute, had passed since the explosion, but Lasrado, the chemistry professor, had not moved. He was at his desk, arms apart, mouth open. Smoke was billowing from the last bench, a yellow dust like pollen had filled the room, and the stench of fireworks was in the air. The students had all left the room by now; they watched from the safety of the door.

Gomati Das, the calculus teacher, came from next door with a large part of his classroom; then came Professor Noronha, the English and Ancient History man, bringing his flock of curious eyes with him. Father Almeida, the Principal, pushed his way through the crowd, and entered the acrid classroom, a palm over his nose and mouth. He lowered his palm and shouted: 'What is the meaning of this nonsense?'

52

Lasrado was the only one left in the classroom; he stood at his desk like the heroic boy who would not jump from the burning deck. He replied in a robotic monotone.

'A bomb in class, *Father*. In the last bench. It went *opp* during the lecture. About one minute *apter* I began talking.'

Father Almeida squinted at the thick smoke, and then turned around at the boys: 'The youth of this country have gone to hell and will ruin the names of their fathers and grandfathers!'

With great care, covering his face with his arm, he walked over to the last bench, which had toppled over from the blast.

'The bomb is still smoking,' he shouted. 'Close the doors and call the police.'

He touched Lasrado on the shoulder. 'Did you hear me? We're going to close the doors and—'

Red-faced with shame, quivering with wrath, Lasrado turned suddenly, and – addressing the Principal, the teachers, the students – yelled:

'You *Puckers*! *Puckers!*'

In moments the entire Junior College had emptied out; the boys stood in the garden, or in the corridor of the Science and Natural History wing, where the skeleton of a shark that had washed up on the beach a few decades ago had been suspended from the ceiling as a scientific curiosity. Five students kept apart from everyone else, under the shade of a big banyan tree. They were distinguishable from the others by the pleated trousers that they wore, with brand-name labels visible on the rear-pockets or on the side, and by their general air of cockiness. They were Shabbir Ali, whose father owned the only video rental store in town; the Bakht twins Irfan and Rizvan, children of the blackmarketeer; Shankara P. Kinni, whose father was a plastic surgeon in the Gulf; and Pinto, the scion of a coffee estate family.

One of them had burst the bomb. Each of this group had been subjected to multiple periods of suspension from classes for bad behaviour, been kept back at least a year or two because of poor scores, and been threatened with expulsion for insubordination. If anyone would explode a bomb, it had to be one of this lot.

They seemed to think so themselves.

'Did you do it?' Shabbir Ali asked Pinto, who shook his head.

Ali looked at the others, silently repeating the question. 'I didn't do it either,' he stated at the end.

'Maybe God did it,' Pinto said, and all of them giggled. Yet the five of them were aware that everyone in the school suspected them. The Bakht twins said they would go down to the port to eat mutton biryani and watch the waves; Shabbir Ali would go to his video store, or replay a pornographic movie; Pinto would probably go along with him.

Only one of them stayed back in the school.

*

He could not leave yet; he loved this scene, this smoke and confusion. He kept his fist clenched.

He mingled among the crowd, he listened to the hubbub, he drank it like honey. Some students had gone back into the building; they stood on the balconies of the three floors

54

of the college and shouted down to those on the ground; and this added to the humming noise, as if the college were a beehive that someone had struck with a pole. He knew that it was his hubbub – the students were talking about him, the professors were cursing him. He was this morning's god.

For so many years this educational institution had spoken to him – spoken rudely: teachers had caned him, headmasters had suspended and threatened to expel him. (And, he suspected, behind his back, it had mocked him for being a Hoyka, a lower caste.)

Now he had spoken back to it. He kept his fist clenched.

'Do you think it's the terrorists . . .' he heard some boy say. 'The Kashmiris, or the Punjabis . . .'

No, you morons! – he wanted to shout out. It's me! Shankara!

There – he watched Professor Lasrado, his hair still dishevelled, in the midst of a group of his favourite students, the 'good boys,' seeking support and succour from them.

Oddly enough, he felt an urge to go up to Lasrado and touch him on the shoulder, as if to say, 'Man, I feel your grief, I understand your humiliation, I sympathize with your rage,' and thus end the long strife between him and the chemistry professor. Weirdly, he also felt the desire to be one of the students whom Lasrado trusted at such moments, one of his 'good boys.' But this was a smaller desire inside him.

The main thing was to exult. He looked at the chemistry professor and smiled.

He turned to his left; someone in the crowd had said: 'The police are coming.'

Aravind Adiga

He hurried to the backyard of the college, opened a gate, and walked down the long road of stone steps that led to the Junior School. After the new passageway had been opened through the playground, hardly anyone came down this route any more. He knew he'd be alone.

The road was called Old Court Road. The court had long relocated and the lawyers had moved, and the road had been closed down for years – after the suicide that took place here of a wandering businessman. Shankara had been coming down this road ever since he was a boy; it was his favourite part of the town. Even though he could call his chauffeur up to the college, the man was instructed to wait for him down at the foot of the hills.

The road was lined with banyan trees; but even from strolling in the shade, Shankara had worked up a terrific sweat. (He was always like that, quick to sweat, as if some irresistible heat were building up inside him.) Most boys had handkerchiefs placed in their pockets by their mothers, but Shankara had never carried one, and to dry himself, he had adopted a savage method: he tore off large leaves of a nearby tree, and scraped his arms and legs over and over again, until the skin was red and raw.

He felt dry.

About halfway down the hill, he parted a growth of trees, and walked into a bower that was completely hidden except to those who knew about it. Inside this bower, was a statue of Jesus, in dark bronze. Shankara had known of this statue for years, ever since stumbling upon it as a boy while playing hide-and-seek with his friends. There was something

56

wrong with the statue; with its dark skin, the askew expression on its lips, its bright eyes, it seemed more like an icon of the devil than of God. Even the words at the base – I AM THE RESURRECTION AND THE LIFE – seemed like a taunt to God.

He saw that there was still some of the fertilizer lying around the foot of the statue – the dregs of the same powder that he had used to detonate his bomb in the last bench. Quickly he covered the powder with dry leaves. Then he leaned against the base of the Jesus. 'Puckers,' he said – and giggled.

But as he did so, he felt as if his great triumph had been reduced to that one giggle.

He sat by the foot of the dark Jesus, and the tension and thrill slowly left him. He always relaxed around images of Jesus. There was a time when he had thought about converting to Christianity; among Christians there are no castes. Every man was judged by what he had done with his life. But after the way the Jesuit priests had treated him – caning him once on a Monday morning in the assembly grounds for insubordination, in full view of the entire school – he had sworn never to become a Christian. There was no better institution to stop Hindus from converting to Christianity than the Catholic boys' school.

Waving goodbye to the Jesus, and making sure again there was no fertilizer left around the base of the statue, he continued downhill.

His driver, a small black man in a bedraggled khaki uniform, was waiting for him, halfway down the road.

'What are you doing here?' he shouted. 'I told you, wait at the bottom of the hill for me; never to come up this road!'

The driver bent low with folded palms.

'Sir . . . don't be angry . . . I heard . . . a bomb . . . your mother asked me to make sure you were . . .'

How quickly news had spread of the bombing. It was bigger than him; it was taking on a life of its own.

'It's just a small matter,' he told the driver, as they walked down. Was that a mistake, he wondered – should he have exaggerated the event instead?

He hated the irony. His mother had sent the driver to look for him, as if he were a little baby boy – he, who had exploded the bomb! He grit his teeth. The driver opened the door of the white Ambassador car for him, but instead of going in, he began shouting.

'You bastard! Son of a bald woman!' He paused for breath, and then said: 'You *pucker*! You *pucker*!'

He began laughing hysterically as he got into the car; the driver stared at him, uncomprehendingly.

On the way back, he thought, any other master can expect loyalty from his driver. Yet Shankara expected nothing; he worried that the driver belonged to a higher caste.

As they paused at a red light, he heard two ladies in the adjacent Ambassador talking about the bomb blast. '. . . the police have sealed off the entire school and college now. No one can leave.'

It occurred to him he had had a lucky escape; another moment, and he would have fallen into the trap of the police.

When he got to his mansion, he ran in through the back door, bounded up the steps to his room. He had thought, at one point, of sending a manifesto to *The Dawn Herald*: 'The man Lasrado is a fool, and the bomb was burst in his class to show the whole world that.' He could not believe it was still on his desk; he tore it up at once. Then, unsure if the pieces could be pieced together and the message recreated, he thought about swallowing them all. Then decided to swallow some pieces with key words – 'rado,' 'bo,' 'm,' 'class to.' The rest he set fire to, with his pocket lighter.

Besides, he thought, slightly sick from the sensation of paper settling into his stomach, it was not right to send that message out, because ultimately his anger was not solely at Lasrado, it went much deeper. If the police asked him for a statement, what he would say was this:

'I have burst a bomb to end the 5,000-year-old caste system that still operates in our country. I have burst a bomb to show that a man should not be judged, as I have been, merely by the accident of his birth.'

And the lofty sentences made him feel better. He was sure he would be treated in a different way in jail, as a martyr of some kind. The Hoyka self-advancement committees would take out marches for him, and the police would not dare touch him. Perhaps, when he was released, great crowds would wave for him – he would be launched on a political career.

Now he felt he had to send an anonymous letter to the newspaper at all costs. He took a fresh piece of paper and pen and began writing it out, even as his stomach was churning from the pieces of letter he had just swallowed.

There! He was done. He read it over. 'The Manifesto of a Wronged Hoyka. Why the Bomb was Burst Today!'

But then he held it back. It was well-known he was a Hoyka. Everyone knew it. They gossiped about it, and their gossip was like that faceless buzz that had come out of the black doors of the classrooms today. Everyone in his school, in this whole town, knew that as rich as Shankara Prasad was, he was only a Hoyka. If he sent that letter, they would know it was he who had exploded the bomb.

He jumped. It was only the scream of the vegetable seller, who had brought his cart right outside his house: 'tomatoes, tomatoes, ripe red tomatoes, come get your tomatoes.'

He wanted to go down to the port, book into a cheap hotel, and say he was someone else. No one would ever find him there.

He paced around his room, and then went back and slammed his door; he dived into his bed and pulled the sheet over him. Inside the darkness of the bedsheet he could still hear the vendor shouting: 'tomatoes, ripe red tomatoes, hurry before they all rot!'

*

In the morning, his mother was watching an old black-and-white Hindi film which she had rented from Shabbir Ali's father's video store. This was how she spent every morning these days, in this addiction to old films.

'Shankara, I heard there was some brouhaha in school,' she said, turning around when she heard him come down the steps. He ignored her and sat at the table. He could not remember the last time he had spoken a word to his mother.

'Shankara,' his mother said, putting the toast down on the table before him. 'Your Urmila Aunty is coming. Please stay around.'

He bit into the toast, saying nothing to his mother. He found her possessive, and pesky, and hectoring and bossing him around to do this and do that. But he also knew that she was in awe of her half- Brahmin son; she also felt beneath him, because she was a full-blooded Hoyka.

'Shankara! Please tell me: will you stay around?'

Dropping his toast onto his plate, he got up and went up the stairs.

'Shan-ka-ra! Come back!'

Even as he cursed her, he understood her fears. She did not want to face the Brahmin woman alone. Her sole claim to acceptance, to respectability, was the production of a male child, an heir – and if he wasn't in the house, then she had nothing to show. She was just a Hoyka trespassing into a Brahmin's household.

He thought: It is her own fault if she feels wretched in their presence. Again and again he had told her, Mother, ignore our Brahmin relatives. Don't humiliate yourself once more in front of them. If they don't want us, let us not want them.

But she could not do that; she still wanted to be accepted. And the ticket of acceptance was Shankara. Not that he himself was fully acceptable to the Brahmins. They saw him as the product of a buccaneering adventure on the part of his father; they associated him (he was sure) with a range of corruptions. Mix one part premarital sex and one part caste violation in a black pot and what do you get? This cute little satan – Shankara.

Some Brahmin relatives, like Urmila Aunty, had come to see him for years, although they never seemed to enjoy fondling his cheeks, or sending flying kisses his way, or doing the other repulsive things aunties did to nephews. He got the feeling, around her, that he was being tolerated.

Fuck, he did not like being tolerated.

He had the driver take him to Umbrella Street, gazing blankly as the car passed its furniture shops and sugarcane juice stands. He got off at the White Stallion Talkies. 'Don't wait for me; I'll call you when I'm done with the movie.'

As he was climbing up the steps, he saw the owner of a store nearby waving at him vigorously. A relative, on his mother's side. The man flashed him enormous smiles; then he began gesturing for him to come sit down in his shop. Shankara was always treated as someone special among his Hoyka relatives; because he was half-Brahmin, and hence so much higher than them in the caste scale; or because he was so rich, and hence so much higher than them in the class scale. Swearing to himself, he kept going up the stairs. Didn't these Hoykas understand? There was nothing he hated more than their grovelling to him, because of his half-Brahmin-ness. If they had been contemptuous of him, if they had forced him to crawl into their shops to expiate the sin of being half-Brahmin, then wouldn't he have come to see them every day!

There was another reason for him not to visit that relative. He had heard a rumour that the plastic surgeon Kinni had kept a mistress in this part of town – another Hoyka girl. He suspected that the relative would know of this woman, that he would be thinking constantly, this fellow Shankara – poor, poor Shankara, little does he know of his father's treachery. Shankara knew all about his father's treachery – this father, whom he had not seen for six years, who no longer even wrote or called on the phone, although he still sent packages of candies and foreign-made chocolates.

Yet, somehow, he felt his father knew what life was about. A Hoyka mistress near the theatre, and another beautiful Hoyka woman for a wife. Now he was leading a life of ease and luxury in the Gulf, fixing the noses and lips of rich Arab women. Another mistress there, for sure. Fellows like his father belonged to no caste or religion or race; they lived for themselves. They were the only real men in this world.

The box office was shuttered. NEXT SHOW 8.30 P.M. He came down the stairs quickly, avoiding eye-contact with his relative. Walking a couple of streets in a hurry, he sat down at the Ideal Traders' Ice Cream Shop and ordered a custard-apple milkshake.

He sucked it in quickly, and with the sugar in his brain he leaned back and chuckled and said:

'Pucker!'

So he had done it; he had humiliated Lasrado for having humiliated him.

'One more custard-apple shake!' He shouted. 'With double ice cream!'

Shankara had always been one of the 'bad ones' at school. Since the age of eight or nine, he had been in trouble. But

63

the most trouble he had ever had was with this chemistry teacher with the speech impediment. One morning, Lasrado had caught him smoking a cigarette at the sugarcane juice stand outside the college.

'Smoking *bepore* the age of twenty will arrest your – development as a normal human being,' Mr. Lasrado had shouted. '*Ip* your pather were here, and not in the *Gulp*, he would do exactly what I am doing now . . .'

For the rest of that day, Shankara was made to kneel outside the Chemistry class. He knelt with his eyes to the ground, and thought, over and over again: 'He is doing this to me because I am a Hoyka. If I were a Christian or a Bunt he would never have hurt me like this.'

That night, he lay in bed, and the thought had come to him: 'Since he has hurt me, I will hurt him back.' And it came to him, so clearly and succinctly, like a bolt of sunlight, like a credo for his whole life. The initial euphoria turned into a restlessness, and he turned from side to side in the bed, saying, Mustafa, Mustafa. He had to meet Mustafa now.

The bomb-maker.

He had heard the name several weeks ago, at Shabbir Ali's place.

They had just – all five of the 'bad boys' gang' – watched another porno at Shabbir Ali's place that night. The woman had been entered from her arse; the big black man had stuck his cock into her again and again. Shankara had no idea it could be done that way too; nor did Pinto, who kept squealing for pleasure. Shabbir Ali watched his friends' amusement with a kind of whimsical detachment; he had seen this video many times, and it no longer excited his lust. He lived in such familiarity with evil that nothing excited him anymore – neither scenes of fornication nor rape nor even bestiality; he had almost returned to a state of innocence.

After the video, the boys lay on Shabbir Ali's bed, threatening to jerk off right there, while their host warned them not to even think of it.

A condom appeared in their midst, and then they stuck fingers into it.

'Who's this for, Shabbir?'

'My girlfriend.'

'Shut up, you homo.'

'You're the homo!'

The others talked about sex, and Shankara, staring at the ceiling, pretending to be immersed in himself, listened. He felt he was always being kept out of such discussions, because the others knew he was a virgin. There was a girl in the college who 'talked' to men. Shabbir Ali had 'talked' to her; he implied that he had done much more. Shankara had tried to keep up the pretence that he too had 'talked' to women; maybe even screwed a whore on Old Court Road. Still, he knew that the others saw through him.

Ali began passing things around the room; after the condom, a dumb-bell that he kept under his bed. A copy of *Hustler* magazine. *Playboy* magazine. The official NBA magazine.

'Guess what this is,' he said. It was something small and black, with a timer attached to it.

65

'It's a detonator,' he said, after no one could guess.

'What does it do?' Shankara asked, getting up on the bed and holding the thing to the light.

'It detonates, you idiot.' There was laughter around the room. 'You use it in a bomb.'

'It's the easiest thing on earth, to make a bomb,' Shabbir said. 'Take a bag of fertilizer, and then put this detonator in it, and that's it.'

'Where would you get the detonator?' Someone, not Shankara, asked. 'Mustafa gave it to me,' he said, almost in an aside to the other two.

Mustafa, Mustafa. Shankara clung tightly to the name.

'Where does he live?' One of the twins asked.

'Down by the port. In the market. Why?' Shabbir Ali poked his questioner. 'You planning on making a bomb?'

'Why not?'

More giggling. And Shankara had said nothing more that evening, repeating Mustafa, Mustafa to himself, terrified he would forget that name unless he said nothing else all evening.

*

As he was stirring his third custard-apple shake, two men came and sat down next to him: two policemen. One ordered an orange juice, and the other wanted to know how many types of tea they had at the shop. Shankara got up; then sat down. He knew they would start talking about him. His heart beat faster.

'The bomb as it is, was nothing. It flopped. Only the detonator went off, and it sent the fertilizer swirling all around. That idiot who made it thought making a bomb is just putting a detonator in a bag of fertilizer. It's a good thing, otherwise some of those boys would have been killed.'

'What is the youth of this country coming to?'

'These days, it's all sex, sex, and violence. The whole country is going the Punjab way.'

One of the cops caught him staring, and stared back. He turned his eyes away. *Maybe I should have stuck around with Urmila Aunty. Maybe I should have kept indoors today. Just to be safe.*

But what guarantee that she – even though she was his aunty – wouldn't betray him? You never knew what Brahmins were up to. As a boy, he had been taken to a marriage of the Brahmin relatives. His mother never came along to such events, but his father put him in the car, and then told him to play with his cousins. The Brahmin boys invited him to join a competition. An inch of salt sat on a slab of vanilla ice cream; the challenge was for someone to eat that slab. 'You idiot,' one of the others shouted, when Shankara put his spoon down, a scoop of salty ice cream in his mouth. 'It was just a joke! No one would actually do such a thing!'

As the years passed, he found that it was always the same. Once, a Brahmin boy in school had invited him home. He took a chance, he liked the fellow, he said yes. The boy and his mother invited Shankara into the drawing room. It was a 'modern' family – one that had lived abroad. He saw small Eiffel Towers and porcelain milkmaids in the drawing room, and he felt reassured that he would not be ill-treated here.

He was given tea and biscuits, and made to feel perfectly at home. But when he left, he turned around, and saw his friend's mother taking a cleaning-rag in her left hand. She had begun wiping the spot on the sofa clean where he had been sitting.

His caste seemed to be the knowledge of people who had no business knowing it. One day, when he had gone to play cricket at Nehru Maidan, an old man had stood watching him from the wall of the playground. In the end, he called Shankara to him, and examined his face, neck, and wrists for several minutes. Shankara had stood helpless during the examination: he just watched the wrinkles radiating from the old man's eyes.

'You're the son of Vasudev Kinni, and the Hoyka woman, aren't you?'

He insisted that Shankara walk along with him.

'Your father always was a headstrong man. He would never agree for an arranged marriage. One day he found your mother, and he told all the Brahmins, To hell with you. I am marrying this beautiful creature, whether you like it or not. I knew what the consequence would be; you would be a bastard. Neither a Brahmin nor a Hoyka. I told your father this. He did not listen.'

The man patted him on the shoulder. The unselfconscious way in which he was touching Shankara suggested that he was not a bigot, not a caste-obsessed man, but someone just speaking the sad truth of life.

'You too belong to a caste,' said the old fellow. 'The Brahmo-Hoykas, in between the two. They are mentioned in the scriptures, and we know that they exist somewhere. They are a separate people entirely from other humans. You should talk to them, and marry one of them. That way everything will be normal again.'

'Yes, sir,' Shankara said, not knowing why he said it.

'Today, there is no such thing as caste,' the man said, with regret. "Brahmins eat meat. Kshatriyas get educated and write books. And lower-castes convert to Christianity and Islam. You heard what happened at Meenakshipuram, didn't you? Colonel Gadaffi is trying to destroy Hinduism, and the Christian priests are hand in glove with him.'

They walked along for a while, until they came to the bus stand.

'You must find your own caste,' said the man. 'You must find your people.' He lightly embraced Shankara, and boarded the bus. He began to jostle with young men for a seat on the bus. Shankara felt sorry for this old Brahmin. He had never in his life had to catch a bus; there was always the chauffeur.

Shankara thought: he is of a caste higher than me, but he is poor. What does this thing mean then, caste?

Is it just a fiction for old men like him? If you just said to yourself, Caste is a fiction, would it vanish like smoke; if you said, 'I am free,' would you realize you had always been free?

\*

He had finished his fourth custard-apple shake. He felt sick.

As he walked out from the ice-cream shop, all he wanted to do was to go visit Old Court Road. To sit by that statue of the dark Jesus.

He looked around to see if the police were following him. Of course on a day like this he could not go anywhere near the Jesus statue. It was suicide. They would be watching all routes into the school.

He thought of Daryl D'Souza. That was the man to go to! In fifteen years in the schooling system, Daryl D'Souza was the only one who had ever been decent to Shankara.

Shankara had first seen the professor at a political rally. This was the 'The Hoyka Pride and Self-Expression Day Rally' held at the Nehru Maidan – the greatest political event in the history of Kittur, the newspaper would say the next day. Ten thousand Hoykas had filled the cricketing grounds to demand their rights as a full-fledged community, and to ask retribution for the five thousand years of injustice done to them.

The warm-up speaker went on about the language issue. The official language of the town should be declared Tulu, and not Kannada, which was the Brahmin language.

A thunderclap of applause followed.

The professor, although not a Hoyka, was an invitee as a sympathetic outsider; he was sitting next to the chief guest, Kittur's Member of Parliament, a Hoyka, the pride of his entire community. A three-time member of parliament, and also a junior member of the Cabinet of India – a sign to the entire community of how high they could aim.

Eventually, after many more rounds of preliminary speakers, the Member of Parliament got up. He began shouting right away.

'The Hoykas were not even allowed into the temple in the old days, did you know? The Brahmin stood at the door, saying, You low-caste!'

He paused, to let the insult reverberate among his listeners.

'Low-caste! Go back! But these days, do the Brahmins dare do that to us? Do they dare call us "low-caste"? We are 90 per cent of this town! We are the majority! If they hit us, we will hit them back! If they shame us, we will—'

After the speech, someone recognized Shankara. He was taken into a small tent where the Member of Parliament was relaxing after the speech, and introduced as the plastic surgeon Kinni's son. The great man, who was sitting on a wooden chair, and drinking whisky, put down his glass hard, making the whisky spill over. He took Shankara's hand in his hand and made him squat on the ground next to him.

'In the light of your family situation, your high status in society, you are the future of the Hoyka community,' the Member of Parliament said. He inhaled deeply, then burped.

'Yes, sir.'

'You understand what I said?' the great man asked.

'Yes, sir.'

'The future is ours. We are 90 per cent of this town. All that Brahmin shit is finished,' he said – flicking his wrist.

'Yes, sir.'

'If they hit you, you hit them back. If they . . . if they . . .' The great man made circles with his hand, to finish the slurred statement.

Shankara wanted to shout out in joy. 'Brahmin shit!' Yes, that was exactly how he would put it himself; and here was a member of parliament, a Cabinet minister in the government of Rajiv Gandhi, talking as he would!

Then an aide led Shankara out of the tent. 'Sir,' the aide squeezed Shankara's bicep. 'If you can make a small donation towards this evening's function. Just a small amount—'

Shankara emptied his pockets. Fifty rupees. He gave it all to the aide, who bowed deeply, and called him once more the future of the Hoyka community.

Shankara watched. Already thousands of men were getting into lines, where the beer and small quarter-litre bottles of rum were being distributed. He saw all this with disapproval. He didn't like the idea that he was part of 90 per cent of his town. Now all at once it seemed to him that the Brahmins were defenceless – a poor, former elite of Kittur who now lived in constant fear of being robbed of their homes and their wealth by the Hoykas, the Bunts, the Konkanas, and everyone else in town. The sheer averageness of the Hoykas – whatever they did became the average at once, by definition – repulsed him.

The next morning, he thought he had been too harsh in criticizing the Hoykas. He remembered the professor who had been up on stage, and found out from his chauffeur where he lived. He walked for a few minutes up and down the front gate of the professor's house, wondering if he dared go in. Finally he opened the gate, walked up, and pressed the front doorbell.

The professor opened the door. Shankara said: 'Sir, I am a Hoyka. You are the only man in this town whom I trust. I wish to talk with you.'

Professor D'Souza and he sat in his living room and had a long talk.

'Who is that Member of Parliament? What is his caste?' the professor asked.

The question confused Shankara.

'He is one of us, sir. A Hoyka.'

'He's not,' the professor said. 'He is a Kollaba. Have you heard the term? There is no such thing as a Hoyka, my dear fellow. The caste is sub-divided into seven smaller castes. The Member of Parliament is a Kollaba, the top of the seven castes. The Kollabas have always been millionaires. They have exploited the other six Hoyka castes for years. And now once again, this man is playing the Hoyka card to get himself re-elected, so he can sit in an office in New Delhi and take large parcels filled with cash from businessmen.'

Seven sub-castes? The Kollabas? Shankara had never heard of this. He gaped.

'This is the big problem with you Hindus,' the professor said. 'You are mysteries to yourselves.'

Shankara felt ashamed to be a Hindu; what a repulsive thing, this caste system that his ancestors had devised. But at the same time he was annoyed at Daryl D'Souza. Who was this man to lecture him on caste? How dare the Christians do this? Hadn't they been Hindus too, at some point? Shouldn't they have stayed Hindus and defeated the Brahmins from within, instead of taking the easy option by converting?

He crushed his anger into a smile.

'What do we do about the caste system, sir? How do we get rid of it?'

'One solution is what the Naxalites have done, just to blow up the upper castes entirely,' said the professor. He had a quaint, woman-like habit of dipping his large round biscuit in milk, and then hurrying to eat it before it got too soggy and dissolved in the milk. 'They blow up the entire system; that way you can start from scratch.'

'From scratch' – the American idiom excited Shankara. 'I too think we should start from scratch, sir. I think we should destroy the caste system and start from scratch.'

'You are a nihilist,' the professor said, with an approving smile. He bit his soggy biscuit.

They had not met after that; the professor had been travelling, and Shankara had been too shy to barge in again. But he had never forgotten the conversation. Now, wandering around town in a daze, the sugar from the custard-apple shakes upsetting his stomach, he thought: 'He's the only man who'd understand what I've done. I'll confess everything to him.'

\*

The professor's house was packed with students. A reporter from *The Dawn Herald* was there, asking the big man questions. He had a black tape-recorder on th desk. Shankara, who had come by autorickshaw to the professor's house, waited with the students and watched the wheels of the tape move.

'It is an absolute act of nihilism on the part of some student,' the professor was saying. 'He should be caught, and thrown into jail.'

'Sir, what does this episode say about the moral standards of today's youth, sir?'

'This is an example of the nihilism of our youth,' said Professor D'Souza. Shankara watched the black wheels of the tape. 'They are lost and directionless. They have . . .' a pause '. . . lost the moral standards of our nation. Our traditions are being forgotten.'

He felt himself choking with rage.

He stormed out.

He caught an autorickshaw to Shabbir Ali's house, and rang the bell. A bearded man in a North Indian-style kurta, with his chest hair sticking out, opened the door. It took Shankara some time to recognize him as Shabbir Ali's father, a fellow he had never before seen at home.

'He is not seeing any of his friends,' he said. 'You fellows have corrupted my son.' And he slammed the door in Shankara's face.

So, the great Shabbir Ali, the man who 'talked' to women and played with condoms, was locked up in his house! By his father! Shankara wanted to laugh.

When he got out of the house, he was tired of moving in autorickshaws; so he called home from a pay-phone, and asked for the car to be sent to Shabbir Ali's front gate to pick him up.

He ran up the steps and bolted his room. He lay in bed. He picked up the phone at random. He stayed with it for an hour. Then it worked. In Kittur, that was all you had to do to enter someone else's world.

He was listening to a 'cross-connection.'

The phone line crackled and came to life. There was a husband, and a wife talking. They were speaking in a language he couldn't understand; he thought it might be Malayalam. He wondered what they were talking about – was the man complaining about his health, was she asking about more money for the household? Why were they on the phone, he wondered? Was the man living outside Kittur? Whatever their situation was, whatever they were saying in that foreign language, he felt the cosiness, the intimacy of their conversation. It would be nice to have a wife or a girlfriend, he thought. Not to be so alone all the time. Even a single real friend. Even that would have kept him from exploding that bomb, and getting into all this trouble.

The man's tone of voice changed suddenly. He began whispering.

'I think someone's breathing on the line,' the man said – or so Shankara imagined he said.

'Yes, you're right. Some pervert is listening to us,' the woman replied – or so Shankara imagined she said.

Then the man hung up.

I have the worst of both the castes in my blood, Shankara thought, lying in bed. I have the anxiety and fear of the Brahmin, and I have the propensity to act without thinking of the Hoyka. In me the worst of the two has mixed and produced this monstrosity, which is my personality.

He was going mad. Yes, he was convinced of that. He wanted to get out of the house again. He worried that the driver was noticing his restlessness.

He went out the backdoor, and slipped out of the house without the driver observing him.

'But he probably doesn't suspect me,' he thought. 'He probably thinks I'm a useless rich brat, like Shabbir Ali.'

All these rich fellows like Shabbir Ali, he told himself bitterly, lived out a kind of code. They talked things, but did not do them. They had condoms at home, but did not use them; they kept detonators but did not explode them. Talk, and talk, and talk. That was their life. It was like that incident with the salt on the ice cream again. The salt was smeared on the slab of vanilla and left there in the open; but no one was meant to lick it! That was only a joke! It was meant to be talk only, all this bomb-exploding stuff. If you knew the code, you would know it was just talk. He did not know about the code, because he did not belong – either to the Brahmins, or to the Hoykas, or to the gang of spoiled brats.

He was in a secret caste – a caste of the Brahmo-Hoykas, of which he had found only one representative so far, himself, and which put him apart from all the other castes of humankind.

\*

He took another autorickshaw to the primary school, and from there, making sure no one was watching him, walked up Old Court Road with his head to the ground and his hands in his pockets.

He parted the trees, came to the statue of Jesus, and sat down. The smell of fertilizer was still strong in the air. Closing his eyes, he tried to calm himself down. Instead, he began to think about the suicide that had taken place, on this road, many years ago. He had heard about it from Shabbir Ali. A man had been found hanging from a tree on this road – perhaps even at this spot. A suitcase lay at his feet, smashed open.

Inside, the police found three gold coins, and a note. 'In a world without love, suicide is the only transformation possible.' Then there was a letter, addressed to a woman in Bombay.

Shankara opened his eyes. It was as if he could see the man from Bombay, hanging in front of him, his feet dangling in front of the black Jesus.

He wondered: was that going to be his fate? Would he end up, condemned and hanged?

He remembered again the fateful events. After he had had the talk at Shabbir Ali's house, he went down to the port. He asked for Mustafa, describing him as a man who sold fertilizers; he was pointed to a market. He found a row of sellers of vegetables, he asked for Mustafa, and was told, 'Go upstairs.' He climbed stairs. He found himself in a pitch-black space where a thousand men seemed to be coughing at once. He began to cough. As his eyes got used to the dark he realized he was in a pepper market. Giant gunnybags of the stuff had been stacked up, and coolies who were coughing incessantly were hauling them around. Then the darkness ended, and he was in an open courtyard. Once again he asked:

'Where is Mustafa?'

He was directed by a man lying on a cart of vegetables into an open door.

He went in, and found three men sitting around a round table and playing cards.

'Mustafa's not in,' said a man with narrow eyes. 'What do you want?'

'A bag of fertilizer.'

'Why?'

'I am growing lentils,' Shankara said. The man laughed.

'What kind?'

'Beans. Green gram. Horse gram.'

He laughed again. He put his cards down, went into a room and hauled out an enormous gunny-bag, and put it down by Shankara's feet.

'What else do you need to grow your beans?'

'A detonator,' Shankara said.

The men at the table put down their cards together.

In the inner room of the house, he was sold a detonator; he was told how to turn the dial and set the timer. It would cost more than Shankara had on him at that moment, so he came back the next week with the money, and took the bag and the detonator back with him by autorickshaw, and got off at the base of Old Court Road. He had hidden it all behind the statue of Jesus.

One Sunday, he went around the school. It was like the movie *Papillon*, one of his favourites, in the scene where the hero plans on how to escape from jail – as exciting as that. He was seeing his school for the first time, with all the keenness of a fugitive's eye. After that, on that fateful Monday, he took the bag of fertilizer with him to school, and attached the detonator to it, turned the timer to one hour, left it in the last row, and sat down in class.

Then he waited, counting off the hour minute by minute, like the hero in *Papillon*.

*

The phone began ringing at midnight.

It was Shabbir Ali.

'Lasrado wants to see us all in his office, man! Tomorrow, first thing in the morning!'

Shabbir rattled off the facts. Five or six of them had to turn up in class the next day. The police would be present.

'He's going to have a lie detector present,' Shabbir paused.

Then he shouted: 'I know you did it! Why don't you confess? Why don't you confess at once!'

Shankara's blood went chill. 'Fuck you!' He yelled back, and slammed the phone down. But then he thought, my god, so Shabbir knew all along. Of course! Everyone knew all along. All the four of the bad boy's gang; and by now they must have told the whole town. He thought, yes, let me confess. It would be best. Perhaps the police would give him some credit for having confessed himself. He dialled '100', which he thought was the police number.

'I want to speak to the Deputy Inspector General at once, please.'

'Ha?'

The voice was followed by a shriek of incomprehension.

Thinking he'd get better results, he spoke in English. He said: 'I want to confess. I planted the bomb.'

'Ha?'

'The Bomb. It was me.'

'Ha?'

Another pause. The phone was transferred.

He repeated his message to another person on the other line.

Another pause.

'Sorrysorrysorry?'

He slammed the phone in anger. Damn Indian police – can't even answer a phone call; how the hell were they going to catch him?

The phone rang; Irfan, calling on behalf of the twins.

'Shabbir just called us; he says we did it, man. I didn't do it! Rizwan didn't do it, either! Shabbir is lying!'

Then he understood: Shabbir had called everyone, and accused them all – hoping to get a confession! Relief mingled with anger. He had almost been trapped! Now the anxiety that the police might trace the call to '100' back to his phone. He needed a plan, he thought, desperately. Yes, he got it; he would say, if they asked, that he was calling to report Shabbir for the crime. 'Shabbir is a Muslim,' he would say. 'He wanted to do this to punish India for Kashmir.' Suddenly it occurred to him that Shabbir, being a Muslim, probably did want to punish India for Kashmir – and he felt a flare of white rage at his old friend.

That Muslim bastard!

Lasrado was in the principal's office the next morning, sitting down next to Father Almeida, who was at his desk. The two men were staring at the five suspects.

'I have *scientipic* evidence,' Lasrado said. '*Pinger*-prints survive on the black stub of the bomb that did not explode.' He sensed incredulity among the accused, so he added: '*Pingerprints* have survived even on the loaves of bread *lept* behind in the *Paroah's* tomb. They are indestructible. We will find the *pucker* who has done this, rest assured.'

He pointed a finger.

'And you, Pinto, a Christian boy – shame on you!'

'I didn't do it, sir,' Pinto said.

Shankara wondered. Should he also throw in an interjection of his innocence, just to be safe?

Lasrado looked piercingly, waiting for the guilty party to turn himself in. Minutes passed. Shankara understood: he has no fingerprints. He has no lie-detector. He is desperate. He has been humiliated, mocked, and rendered a joke in the college, and he wants revenge.

'You *Puckers*!' he shouted. And then, again, in a voice: 'Are you *lapping* at me? Are you *lapping* because I cannot say the letter "*epp*?"'

Now the boys could barely control it; they were about to laugh. Shankara saw that even the principal, having turned his face to the ground, was trying to control his laughter. Lasrado knew this; you could see it on his face. Shankara thought: this man has been mocked his whole life because of his speech impediment. That's why he has been such a jerk in class. And now his entire life's work had been destroyed by this bomb; he will never be able to look back on his life with the false pride other professors do; never be able to say, at his farewell party, 'My students, although I was strict, loved me.' Always there would be someone whispering at the back – yes, they loved you so much they exploded a bomb in your class!

At that moment, Shankara thought, I wish I had just left this man alone. I wish I had not humiliated him, as so many have humiliated me, and my mother.

'I did it, sir.'

Everyone in the room turned to Shankara.

'I did it,' he said. 'Now stop bothering these other boys and punish me.'

Lasrado banged his hand on the desk. 'Mother-*pucker*, is this a joke?'

'No, sir.'

'*Op* course it is a joke!' Lasrado shouted. 'You are mocking me! You are mocking me in public!'

'No, sir . . .'

'Shut up!' Lasrado said. 'Shut up!' He flexed a finger and pointed it at everyone in the room.

'*Puckers! Puckers!* Get out!'

Shankara walked out with the four innocent ones. He could see that they too did not believe his confession: they thought he was mocking the teacher to his face.

'You went too far there,' Shabbir Ali said. 'You really have no respect for anything in this world, man.'

Shankara waited outside the college, smoking a cigarette. He was waiting for Lasrado. When the door to the staff room opened, and the chemistry professor walked out, Shankara threw the cigarette to the ground and stubbed it out with a scratch of his shoe. He watched his teacher for a while. He wished there were some way he could go up to him and say he was sorry.

## DAY TWO (EVENING): LIGHTHOUSE HILL (THE BASE OF THE HILL)

*You are on a road surrounded by ancient banyan trees; the smell of neem is in the air, and an eagle glides overhead. Old Court Road – a long, desolate road with a reputation as a hang-out for prostitutes and pimps – leads down from the top of the hill to St. Alfonso Junior and Middle School for Boys.*

*Next to the school you will find a whitewashed mosque dating back to the time of Tippu Sultan; a local legend says that Christians from Valencia suspected of being British sympathizers were tortured in its premises. The mosque is at the centre of a legal tussle between the school authorities and a local Islamic organization, both of which claim possession of the land it stands on. Muslim students from the school are allowed, every Friday, to leave classes for an hour to offer namaaz at this mosque, provided they bring a signed note from their fathers, or in the case of children with fathers working in the Gulf, from a male guardian. A bus stand in front of the mosque receives express-buses that go to Salt Market Village.*

*At least four stalls selling sugarcane juice and Bombay-style bhelpuri and charmuri have set up shop outside the mosque, to cater to the bus-stand passengers.*

A flurry of alarm-bells rang at ten minutes to nine, warning that this was no ordinary morning. It was a Morning of Martyrs, the thirty-seventh anniversary of the day Mahatma Gandhi had sacrificed his life so that India might live.

Thousands of kilometres away, in the centre of the nation, in cold New Delhi, the President was about to bow his head before a sacred torch. Tearing through the massive Gothic edifice of St. Alfonso Junior Boys' School – through thirty-six classrooms with vaulted ceilings, two outdoor lavatories, a chemistry-cum-biology laboratory, and a refectory where some of the priests were still finishing breakfast – the alarm-bells announced it was time for the school to do the same.

In the staff room, Mr. D'Mello, assistant headmaster, closed his copy of the newspaper noisily, like a pelican folding its wings. Tossing the paper on a sandalwood table, Mr. D'Mello struggled against his paunch to get up. He was the last to leave the staff room.

Six hundred and twenty-three boys, pouring out of classrooms and merging in one long line, proceeded into the assembly square. In ten minutes they were a geometrical pattern, a tight grid around the flagpole at the centre of the square.

Next to the flagpole was a greasy old wooden platform. Next to the platform was Mr. D'Mello, sucking the morning air into his lungs and shouting:

'A-ten-shannn!'

The students shuffled in concert. *Thump!* Their feet knocked the chatter out of the square. Now the morning was ready for the sombre ceremony.

The chief guest had fallen asleep. From the top of the flagpole, the national tricolour hung, limp and crumpled, entirely uninterested in the events organized for its benefit. Alvarez, the old school peon, tugged on a blue cord to goad the recalcitrant lump into a respectable tautness.

Mr. D'Mello sighed and gave up on the flag. His lungs swelled up again:

'Sa-loot!'

The wooden platform began to creak noisily: Father Mendonza, school headmaster, was on it. At a sign from Mr. D'Mello, he cleared his throat into the booming mike, and began a speech on the glories of dying young for your country.

A series of black boxes amplified his nervous voice across the whole square. The grid of boys listened spellbound to their headmaster. The Jesuit told them the blood of Bhagat Singh and Indira Gandhi fertilized the earth on which they stood, and they brimmed with pride.

Mr. D'Mello, squinting fiercely, kept a close watch on the little patriots. He knew that the whole humbug would end any moment. After thirty-three years in an all-boys' school, no secret of human nature was hidden from him.

The headmaster lumbered along to the crucial part of the morning's speech.

'It is customary on Martyr's Day for the government to issue every school in the state with Free Film Day tickets for that Sunday,' he said. An electric current jolted the square. The boys became breathless with anticipation.

'But this year—' the headmaster's voice quivered. 'I regret to announce there will be no Free Film Day.'

For a moment, no noise. Then, the whole square let out one big, aching, disbelieving groan.

'The government made a terrible mistake,' the headmaster said, trying to explain to them. 'A terrible, terrible mistake . . . They have asked you to go to a House of Sin . . .'

Mr. D'Mello wondered what the headmaster was prattling on about. It was time to end the speech, and send the brats back to class.

'I cannot even find the words to tell you . . . it is a terrible mix-up. I am sorry. I . . . am . . .'

Mr. D'Mello was looking for Girish, when a movement in the back of the square caught his eye. Trouble had begun. The assistant headmaster, who was obstructed by his massive paunch, struggled to get down from the podium; then, with surprising litheness, he slid through the rows of boys and honed in on the danger zone. Students turned around on their toes to watch him as he pushed his way to the end of the grid. His right hand trembled.

A brown dog had climbed up from the playground below the assembly square, and was loping about the back of the grid. Some trouble-makers were inducing it to draw nearer with winks and clicks of their tongue.

'Stop that at once!' D'Mello – he was gasping for breath already – stamped his foot in the direction of the dog. The mollycoddled animal mistook the fat man's advance for another blandishment. The teacher lunged at the dog, and it pulled back, but as he stopped to pant, it rushed back at him.

The boys were laughing openly now. Waves of confusion spread throughout the square. Over the speaker system the headmaster's voice wobbled, a hint of desperation.

'. . . you boys have no right to misbehave . . . the Free Film Day is a privilege, not a right . . .'

*'Stone it! Stone it!'* – someone shouted at D'Mello.

The panicky teacher obeyed. *Whack!* The stone caught the dog on the belly. The animal yelped in pain – he saw a gleam of betrayal in its eyes – before it bounded out of the school square and ran down the steps of the playground.

A sensation of sickness tightened in Mr. D'Mello's gut. The poor animal had been hurt. When he turned around, he saw a sea of boys grinning. One of them had goaded him on to stone the animal; he swung around, picked a boy at random – only stopping a split second to make sure that it wasn't Girish – and slapped him hard, twice.

*

When Mr. D'Mello walked into the staff room, he found all the other teachers gathered around the sandalwood table. The men were dressed alike, in light-coloured half-sleeve shirts, closely checked, with brown or blue pants that widened into bell-bottoms, while the few women wore peach or yellow polyester-and-cotton blended saris.

Mr. Rogers, the biology-cum-geology teacher, was reading aloud a schedule of the Free Film Day from an open copy of the Kannada newspaper.

*Film One: Save the Tiger*

*Film Two: The Importance of Physical Exercise*

*Bonus Reel: The Advantages of Native Sports (with special attention to Kabbadi and Kho-Kho)*

Beneath that harmless listing, came the bombshell.

*Where to send your son or daughter on Free Film Day (1985):*

*1. St Milagres Boys' High School; Surnames A to N, White Stallion Theatre, O to Z Belmore Theatre*

*2. St. Alfonso Boys' High School; Surnames A to N, Belmore Theatre, O to Z Angel Talkies.*

'Half our school!' Mr. Rogers's voice was whistle-like with excitement. 'Half our school to Angel Talkies!'

Young Mr. Gopalkrishna Bhatt, only a year out of the teachers' college in Belgaum, liked to supply the chorus for such occasions. He raised his arms fatalistically:

'What a mix-up! Sending our children to *that* place!'

Mr. Pundit, senior Kannada language teacher, scoffed at the naivety of the multitude. He was a short silver-haired man with startling opinions.

'Can't you see what's happened – it's no mix-up, it's deliberate! The Angel Talkies has bribed all those bloody politicians, so they'd send our boys to a House of Sin!'

Now the teachers were split into those who thought it was a mix-up, and those who thought it was a deliberate ploy to corrupt the youth.

'What do you think, Mr. D'Mello?' young Mr. Bhatt shouted out.

Instead of replying, Mr. D'Mello loudly dragged a cane chair from the sandalwood table towards an open window at the far end of the staff room. It was a sunny morning: he had a blue sky, rolling hills, a private vista of the Arabian Sea.

Behind him his colleagues' patter continued without a break. *Filth, smut, traitors; filth, smut, traitors.*

89

The sky was a light blue halo, a thing meant for meditation. A few perfectly formed clouds, like wishes that had been granted, floated through the azure. The slab of Heaven deepened in colour as it stretched to the horizon and touched a crest of the Arabian Sea. Mr. D'Mello invited the morning's beauty into his agitated brain.

'What a mix-up, eh, Mr. D'Mello?'

Gopalkrishna Bhatt hopped onto the window ledge, blocking the view of the sea. Dangling his legs gleefully, the young man flashed a gap-toothed smile at his senior colleague.

'The only mix-up, Mr. Bhatt,' said the assistant headmaster, 'was made on 15 August 1947, when we thought this country could be run by a people's democracy instead of a military dictatorship.'

The young teacher nodded his head. 'Yes, yes, how true. What about the Emergency, sir – wasn't that a good thing?'

'We threw that chance, away,' Mr. D'Mello said. 'And now they've shot dead Indira Gandhi – the only politician we ever had who knew how to give this country the medicine it needed.' He closed his eyes again, and concentrated on an image of an empty beach, to forget Mr. Bhatt's presence.

Mr. Bhatt said: 'Your favourite's name is in the paper this morning, Mr. D'Mello. Page 4, near the top. You must be a proud man.'

Before Mr. D'Mello could stop him, Mr. Bhatt had begun reading:

*The Mid-Town Rotary Club announces the Winners of its Fourth Annual Inter-School English Elocution Contest.*

*Theme: Science – A Boon or Curse for the Human Race?*
*First Prize: Harish Pai, St. Milagres High School (Science*
*as a Boon) Second Prize: Girish Rai, St. Alfonso High School*
*(as a Curse)*

The Assistant Headmaster pulled the newspaper out of the hands of his junior colleague. 'Mr. Bhatt—' he snarled. 'I have often said this publicly: I have no "favourites" among the boys.'

He closed his eyes, but now his peace of mind was gone.

'Second prize' – the words stung him once again. He had worked with Girish all evening on the speech – its contents, its delivery, his posture at the mike, everything! And only second prize? His eyes filled up with tears. The boy had got into a habit of losing these days.

There was commotion in the staff room now, and through his closed eyes Mr. D'Mello knew that the headmaster had come, and all the teachers were running around him to flatter him. He stayed in his seat, though he knew his peace would not last long.

'Mr. D'Mello—' came the nervous voice. 'It is a terrible mix-up . . . one half of the boys won't get to see the free film this year.'

The headmaster was staring at him from the sandalwood table. Mr. D'Mello ground his teeth. He folded his copy of the newspaper violently; he took his time getting up, and he took his time turning around. The headmaster was mopping his forehead. Father Mendonza was a very tall, very bald man, with strands of heavily oiled hair combed over his naked pate. His large eyes stared out through thick glasses

91

and an enormous forehead always glittered with beads of sweat, like a leaf spotted with dew after a shower.

'May I make a suggestion, Father?'

The headmaster's hand paused with his handkerchief on his brow.

'If we don't take the boys to Angel Talkies, they'll see it as a sign of weakness. Their rebellion will only grow.'

The headmaster bit his lips.

'But . . . the dangers . . . one hears of terrible posters . . . of evils that cannot be put into words . . .'

'I will take care of the arrangements,' Mr. D'Mello said, gravely. 'I will take care of the discipline. I give you my pledge.'

The Jesuit nodded hopefully. As he left the staff room, he turned to Gopalkrishna Bhatt Junior, and the depth of gratitude in his voice was unmistakable:

'You too should go along with the assistant headmaster when he takes the boys to Angel Talkies . . .'

*

Father Mendonza's words echoing in his mind, he walked to his first class of the morning at 11 a.m. *Assistant Headmaster.* He knew that he had not been the Jesuit's first choice. The insult still smarted after all this time. The post was his by right of seniority. For thirty years he had taught Hindi and arithmetic to the boys of St. Alfonso, and maintained order in the school. But Father Mendonza, who had recently come down from Bangalore with an oily comb-over and six trunks full of 'modern' ideas, stated his preference for someone 'smart' in appearance. Mr. D'Mello had a pair of eyes and a mirror at home. He knew what that remark meant.

He was an overweight man entering the final phase of middle age, he breathed through his mouth, and rushes of hair poked out his nose. The centrepiece of his body was a massive potbelly, a hard knot of flesh pregnant with a dozen cardiac arrests. To walk, he had to arch his lower back, tilt his head, and screw his brow and nose together in a foul-looking squint. 'Ogre,' the boys chanted as he passed. 'Ogre, Ogre, Ogre!'

At noon, he ate a dish of red fish curry out of a stainless-steel tiffin-carrier, by his favourite window in the staff room. The smell of the curry did not please his fellow teachers, so he ate alone. Done, he slowly took his tiffin-carrier to the public tap outside. The boys stopped their games. Since it was out of the question for him to bend forward (the paunch, of course), he had to fill his tiffin-carrier with water and raise it to his mouth. Gargling loudly, he belched out a saffron torrent several times. The boys shrieked with pleasure each time. When he was back in the staff room, they crowded by the tap: little skeletons of fish had piled up at its base, like deposits of a nascent coral reef. Awe and disgust commingled in the voices of the boys, and they chanted, in a voice that grew louder and louder: 'ogreogreogre!'

'The main problem with selecting Mr. D'Mello as my assistant is that he has an excessive penchant for old-fashioned violence,' the young headmaster wrote to the Jesuit Board. Mr. D'Mello caned too often. Sometimes, even as he wrote on the blackboard, his left hand would reach for the duster. He would turn around and send it flying at the last row, and there would be a scream and the bench would topple over under the weight of diving boys.

He had done worse. Father Mendonza reported in detail a shocking story he had heard. Once, many years ago, a small boy had been talking in the front row, right before D'Mello's eyes. The teacher said nothing. He just sat still, and let his anger stew. Suddenly, it was said, there was a moment of blackness in his brain. He snatched the boy from his seat and hoisted him into the air and took him to the back of the class: he shut him in a cupboard. The boy beat on the insides of the cupboard with his fists for the rest of the class. 'I can't breathe in here!' he shouted. The beating inside the cupboard grew louder and louder; then fainter, and fainter. When the cupboard was finally opened, a full ten minutes later, there was a stench of fresh urine, and the boy fell out in an unconscious heap.

Then there was the little matter of his past. Mr. D'Mello had been in training to be a priest for six years in the Valencia Seminary, before leaving suddenly, and on bad terms with his superiors. The rumour was that he had challenged the holy Dogma, and declared that he thought the notion of the Transubstantiation as laid down by the Vatican to be inaccurate – and so walked out, leaving behind six years of his life. Other rumours were that he was a free-thinker, who did not attend church service regularly.

The weeks went on. The Jesuit Board inquired by mail if Father Mendonza had made a decision yet. The young headmaster confessed he had had no time for that. Every morning the padre found that his first duty was to discipline a long line of recalcitrants. The same faces appeared morning after morning. Talking in class. Disfiguring school property. Pinching studious boys.

One day, a foreigner, a Christian woman from Britain who was a generous donor to worthy causes in India, paid a visit to the school. Father Mendonza oiled his surviving strands of hair with special care that morning. He solicited Mr. Pundit's assistance in guiding the British lady around the school. With great courtesy, the Kannada teacher explained to the foreigner the proud history of St. Alfonso, its celebrated alumni, its role in civilizing the savage nature of this part of India, once a bare wilderness overrun by elephants. Father Mendonza began to feel that Mr. Pundit was as smart a fellow as he was likely to find in this part of the world. Then, all at once, the foreigner began shrieking. The fingers of her hand spread out with horror. Julian D'Essa, the coffee-plantation scion, was standing on the last bench of a giggling classroom, exposing his privates to the world. Mr. Pundit rushed at the crazy boy, but the damage had been done. The Jesuit saw the foreign donor step back from him with terror-struck eyes: as if *he* were the exhibitionist.

An old member of the Board called Father Mendonza from Bangalore that evening to console him. Did the 'reformer' finally see the truth? Modern ideas of education were fine in Bangalore. But in a backwater like Kittur, miles and miles and miles away from civilization?

'To manage a school filled with six hundred little animals' – the old member of the Board told the sobbing young headmaster – 'you need an ogre now and then.'

Two months after arriving at St. Alfonso, Father Mendonza called Mr. D'Mello over to his office one morning. He told Mr. D'Mello that he had no option but to ask him to serve as the assistant headmaster. To handle a school like this, the Jesuit declared, he needed a man like Mr. D'Mello.

\*

*Stop for a moment*, D'Mello told himself. *Catch your breath.* He was about to go into the classroom – about to begin war. The plan had worked well so far; he had come the way of the rear entrance. A surprise attack. He had figured that the news of Mendonza's change of mind on Angel Talkies was common knowledge by now. The boys had construed it as cowardice on the part of the school authorities. The danger was highest now, but also the opportunity to teach them a lingering lesson.

The class was quiet – too quiet.

D'Mello went in on tiptoe. The last row, where the tall, over-developed, boys sat, was clumped together, a soundless knot around a magazine. D'Mello hovered over the boys. The magazine was the usual kind of magazine. 'Julian,' he said gently.

The boys turned around, and the magazine dropped to the floor. Julian stood up with a grin. He was the tallest of the tall, the most over-developed of the over-developed. A triangle of chest hair jutted out of his open shirt already, and when he rolled up a sleeve and made a muscle, D'Mello could see his biceps swelling into pale, thick tubers. As the son of a coffee-planting dynasty, Julian D'Essa could never be expelled from the school. But he could be punished. The little demon looked up at D'Mello, with a lecherous grin pasted on his face. In his mind Mr. D'Mello heard D'Essa's voice; it goaded him on to do his worst: *Ogre! Ogre! Ogre!*

He heaved the boy out of the seat by his collar. Rip – the collar came off the shirt. D'Mello's shaking elbow straightened out – it connected with the side of the boy's face.

'Get out of the class, you animal . . . and kneel down . . .'

After shoving Julian out of the class, he put his hands on his knees and caught his breath. He picked up the magazine and flipped its pages about for public view.

'So this is the sort of thing you boys want to read, huh? Now you want to go to Angel Talkies? You think you'll see the posters on the wall: those Murals of Sin?'

He walked around the class with his shaking elbow and thundered: Even the lechers were ashamed to go into Angel Talkies. They covered themselves in blankets and pushed rupee notes shamefully to the desk attendants. Inside, the walls of the theatre were carpeted with posters of X-rated films, purveyors of every known depravity. To see a movie in such a theatre was a corruption of body and soul alike.

He hurled the magazine to a wall. Did they think he was frightened to beat them? No! He was not one of these 'new-fashioned' teachers trained in Bangalore or Bombay! Violence was his staple, and his dessert. Spare the rod, and spoil the child.

He collapsed onto his chair. He was horribly out of breath. A dull pain spread its roots across his chest. He saw with satisfaction that his speech had had a little effect. The boys were sitting without a squeak. The sight of Julian with his torn collar kneeling outside the class had a quieting effect. But Mr. D'Mello knew it was just a matter of time, just a matter of time. At the age of fifty-seven he had no more illusions about human nature. Lust would inflame the boys' hearts with rebellion again.

He ordered them to open the Hindi textbooks. Page 168. 'Who will read the poem out?'

The class was silent around one raised arm.

'Girish Rai, read.'

A boy who wore comically large spectacles got up from the first bench. His hair was thick and parted down the middle; his small face was overpowered by pimples. He did not need the textbook, for he knew the poem by heart:

*Nay, said the flower*
*Cast me, said the flower,*
*Not on the virgin's bed*
*Nor in the bridal carriage*
*Nor in the merry village square.*

*Nay, said the flower*
*Cast me but on that lonely path*
*Where the heroes walk*
*For their nation to die.*

The boy sat down after reading. The entire class was silent, humbled for a moment by the purity of his enunciation in Hindi, that alien language. 'If only all of you could be like that boy,' Mr. D'Mello said softly.

But he had not forgotten that his favourite had let him down in the Rotary competition. Ordering the class to copy the poem out six times in their notebooks, he ignored Girish for two or three minutes. Then he summoned him with his fingers.

'Girish,' his voice faltered. 'Girish . . . why didn't you get first prize in the Rotary competition? How will we ever get to Delhi unless you win more first prizes?'

'Sorry, sir . . .' the boy said. He hung his head in shame.

'Girish . . . lately you haven't been winning so many first prizes . . . is something the matter?'

There was a worried look on the boy's face. Mr. D'Mello panicked.

'Is someone troubling you? One of the boys? Has D'Essa threatened you?'

'No, sir.'

He looked at the tall boys in the back seat. He turned to his right, and took a look at the kneeling D'Essa, who was grinning hard. The assistant headmaster came to a quick decision.

'Girish . . . tomorrow . . . I don't want you to go to Angel Talkies. I want you to go to Belmore Talkies.'

'Why sir?'

Mr. D'Mello recoiled.

'What do you mean why? Because I say so, that's why!' he yelled. The class looked at them; had Mr. D'Mello raised his voice at his favourite?

Girish Rai reddened. He seemed on the verge of tears, and Mr. D'Mello's heart melted. He smiled and patted the small boy on his back.

'Now, now, Girish, don't cry . . . I don't care about the other boys. They've been to the talkies many times – they've read magazines. There isn't anything left to be corrupted. But not you. I won't let you go there. Go to Belmore.'

Girish nodded, and went back to his seat in the front bench. He was still on the verge of tears. Mr. D'Mello felt his heart melting out of pity; he had been too harsh on the poor boy.

When the class ended, he went up to the front bench and tapped on the desk: 'Girish – do you have any plans for this evening?'

*

What a terrible day, what a terrible day. Mr. D'Mello was walking along the mud road that led from the school to his home in the teacher's colony. That awful *whack* of the stone echoed over and over again in his head . . . the look in that poor animal's eyes . . .

He walked back with his poetry books beneath his armpits. His shirt was now speckled with red curry, and the tips of his collars were curled in, like sunburnt leaves. Every few minutes, he stopped to straighten his aching back and catch his breath.

'Are you ill, sir?'

Mr. D'Mello turned around: Girish Rai, with a huge khaki schoolbag strapped to his back, was following him.

Teacher and pupil walked a few feet side by side, and then Mr. D'Mello stopped. 'Do you see that, boy?' he pointed.

Halfway between the school and his house ran a brick wall with a wide crack yawning down the middle. The wall and the crack in it had been there for years, in that road where no detail had significantly changed since Mr. D'Mello had moved to the neighbourhood thirty years ago to take up the quarters assigned to him as a young teacher. Three lamp-posts in an adjacent road were visible through the crack in the wall, and for nearly twenty years now, Mr. D'Mello had stopped every evening and squinted hard at the three lamp-posts. For twenty years, he had been searching the lamp-posts for the explanation of a mystery. One morning, about two decades ago, when there was a heavy rain pouring down, while passing the crack with an umbrella he had seen a sentence in white chalk marked on all three lamp-posts.

'Nathan X must die.'

He passed through the crack in the wall to the three lamp-posts, and scraped the words with his umbrella, to decipher their mystery. What did the three signs mean? An old man pulled along a cart of vegetables. He tried asking him who Nathan X was, but the vegetable-man just shrugged. Ernest D'Mello stood there, with the mist in the trees, and wondered.

The next morning the signs were gone. Intentionally wiped out. When he got to school, he scanned the obituary column of the newspaper, and couldn't believe his eyes – a man called 'Nathan Xavier' had been murdered last night at the port! He was convinced initially that he had seen some secret society planning a murder. A darker anxiety beset him soon. Maybe Chinese spies had written those words? Years had passed, but the mystery remained, and he thought about it each time he saw that crack.

'Do you think Pakistani spies did it, sir?' Girish said. 'Did they kill Nathan X?'

Mr. D'Mello grunted. He felt he shouldn't have revealed that memory to Girish; he had compromised himself. Teacher and student walked on.

Mr. D'Mello watched the rays of sunset fall through the banyan leaves in large splotches of gold on the ground, like the puddles left behind by a child on the way out from a bath. He looked to the sky, and involuntarily spoke a line of Hindi poetry: *The golden hand of the sun as it grazes the clouds* . . .

'I know that poem, sir,' a little voice said. Girish Rai repeated the rest of that couplet: '. . . *is like a lover's hand as it grazes its beloved.*'

They walked on.

'So you have an interest in poetry?' D'Mello asked. Before the boy could reply, he confessed another secret to him. In his youth he had wanted to be a poet – a nationalist writer, no less, a new Bharathi or Tagore.

'Then why didn't you become a poet, sir?'

He laughed. 'In this little hole of Kittur, my learned friend, how could a man make a living from poetry?'

The lamp-posts turned on, one by one. It was almost night now. In the distance Mr. D'Mello saw a lighted door, his quarters. As they got closer to the house, he stopped talking. He could hear the brats from here. What have they smashed today, he wondered to himself.

Girish Rai watched.

Mr. D'Mello took off his shirt, and left it on a hook on the wall. The boy saw the assistant headmaster in his singlet, slowly setting himself down on a rocking chair in his living room. Two girls in identical red frocks were running circles around the room, bellowing their lungs out. The old teacher ignored them completely. He stared at the boy for a while, again wondering why, for the first time in his career as a teacher, he had invited a student home.

'Why did we let the Pakistanis get away, sir?' Girish blurted out.

'What do you mean, boy?' Mr. D'Mello screwed his nose and brow together and squinted.

'Why did we let the Pakistanis get away in 1965? When we had them in our clutches? You said it in class one day, but you didn't explain.'

'Oh, that!' Mr. D'Mello slapped his hand on his thigh with relish. Another of his favourite topics. How the government botched up in 1965. The Indian tanks had rolled into the outskirts of Lahore when our own government had cut the ground beneath their feet. Some bureaucrat had been bribed; the tanks came back.

'Ever since Sardar Patel died, this country has gone down the drain,' he said, and the little boy nodded. 'We live in the midst of chaos and corruption; we can't fight it. We can only do our job, and go home,' he said, and the little boy nodded.

The teacher breathed out contentedly. He was deeply flattered; in all these years at the school, no student had ever felt the same outrage he had, at that colossal blunder of '65.

Lifting himself off the rocking-chair, he pulled a volume of Hindi poetry out of a bookshelf. 'I want this back, huh? And in perfect shape. Not one scratch or blotch on it.'

The boy nodded. He looked around the house furtively. The poverty of his teacher's house surprised him. The wall of the living room was bare, save for a lighted picture of the Sacred Heart of Jesus. The paint was peeling, and stout-hearted Geckos ran all over the wall.

As Girish flicked through the book, the two girls in red dresses took turns at shrieking into his ears, before screaming away into another room.

A woman in a flowing green dress, patterned with white flowers, came towards the boy with a glass of red cordial. The boy was confused by her face and could not answer her questions. She looked very young. Mr. D'Mello must have married very late in life, the boy thought. Perhaps he had been too shy to go near women in his young days.

D'Mello frowned, and drew nearer to Girish.

'Why are you grinning? Is there something funny?'

Girish shook his head.

The teacher continued. He spoke of other things that made his blood boil. Once India had been ruled by three foreigners: England, France, and Portugal. Now their place was taken by three native-born thugs: Betrayal, Bungling, and Backstabbing. 'The problem is here—' he tapped his ribs. 'There is a beast inside us.'

He began to tell Girish things he had told no one – not even his wife. His innocence about the true nature of schoolboys had lasted just three months into his life as a teacher. In those early days, he confessed to Girish, he stayed back after class to read the collection of Tagore's poetry in the library. He read the pages carefully, stopping sometimes to close his eyes and fantasize he had been alive during the freedom struggle – in any one of those holy years when a man could go to a rally and see Gandhi spinning his wheel and Nehru addressing a crowd.

When he got out of the library his head would be buzzing with images from Tagore. At that hour, electrolyzed by the setting sun, the brick wall surrounding the school was a long plane of beaten gold. Banyan trees grew along the length of the wall; inside their deep, dark canopies, tiny leaves glittered in long strings of silver, like rosaries held by the meditating tree. Mr. D'Mello stopped. The whole earth seemed to be singing out Tagore's poetry. He passed by the playground, which was set into a pit below the school. Debauched shouts jarred his reveries.

'What is that shouting in the evenings?' he naively asked a colleague. The older teacher helped himself to a pinch of snuff. Inhaling the vile stuff from the edge of a stained handkerchief, he had grinned.

''tripping. That is what is going on.'

'*tripping?*

The more experienced teacher winked.

'Don't tell me it didn't happen when you were in school . . .'

From D'Mello's expression he gathered that this was, indeed, not the case.

'It's the oldest game played by boys,' the old teacher said. 'Go down, and see for yourself. I don't have the language to describe it.'

# Aravind Adiga

He went down the next evening. The sounds got louder and louder as he descended the steps into the playground.

The next morning, he called all the boys involved – all of them, even the victims – to his desk. He kept his voice calm with an effort. 'What do you think this is, a moral school run by Jesuits, or a whorehouse?' He hit them with such violence that morning.

When he was done, he noticed that his right elbow was still shaking.

That evening, there was no noise from the playground. He recited Tagore out aloud to protect himself from evil:

*Where the head is held high and the mind is without fear . . .*

A few days later, passing the playground, he saw his right elbow trembling again in recognition. The old, familiar, black noise was rising up from the playground.

'That was when the scales fell from my eyes,' Mr. D'Mello said. 'I had no more illusions about human nature.'

He looked at Girish with concern. The little boy was stirring a large grin into the red cordial.

'They haven't done it to you, have they, Girish – when you play cricket with them in the evening? `Tripping?'

(Mr. D'Mello had already let D'Essa and his over-developed gang know: if they ever tried *that* on Girish, he would skin them alive. They would see what an ogre he really was.)

He watched Girish with anxiety. The boy said nothing.

Suddenly he put his cordial down, stood up, and advanced to his teacher with a folded piece of paper. The assistant headmaster opened it, prepared for the worst.

106

It was a gift: a poem, in chaste Hindi.

Monsoon
*This is the wet and fiery season,*
*When lightning follows after thunder.*
*Each night, the sky shakes, and I wonder,*
*What could be the reason*
*God gave us this wet and fiery season?*

'Did you write this yourself? Is this what you were blushing about?'

The boy nodded happily.

Good Lord! – he thought. In thirty years as a teacher no one had done this to him.

'Why is the rhyming scheme uneven?' D'Mello frowned. 'You should be careful about such things . . .'

The teacher pointed out the flaws of the poem one by one. The boy nodded his head attentively.

'Shall I bring you another one tomorrow?' he asked.

'Poetry is good, Girish, but . . . are you losing interest in quizzes?'

The boy nodded.

'I don't want to go anymore, sir. I want to play cricket after class. I never get to play, because of the—'

'You have to go to the quizzes!' Mr. D'Mello got up from his rocking chair. He explained: Any outlet for fame in this small town should be seized at once. Didn't the boy understand?

'First go to the quizzes, become famous, then you'll get a big job, and then you can write poetry. What will your cricket get you, boy? How will it make you famous? You'll never write poetry if you don't get out of here, don't you understand?'

Girish nodded. He finished his cordial.

'And, tomorrow, Girish . . . You're going to Belmore. I don't want any more discussion on that.'

Girish nodded.

After he left, Mr. D'Mello, sat on the rocking-chair, and thought for a long time. It was no bad thing, he was thinking, Girish Rai's newfound interest in poetry. Perhaps he could look out for a poetry contest for Girish to enter. The boy would win, of course – he would come back heaped in gold and silver. *The Dawn Herald* might put a picture of him on the back page. Mr. D'Mello would stand with his arms proudly on Girish's shoulders. 'The teacher who nourished the budding genius.' They would conquer Bangalore next, the teacher-and-pupil team that won the all-Karnataka state poetry contest. After that, what else – New Delhi! The President himself would award the two of them a medal. They would take an afternoon off, and visit the Taj Mahal together. Anything was possible with a boy like Girish. Mr. D'Mello's heart leapt up with joy, as it had not done for years, since his days as a young teacher. Just before he went to sleep in his chair he pressed his eyes shut and prayed fervently: 'Lord, only keep that boy pure.'

\*

Next morning, at ten minutes past ten, by the express order of the state government of Karnataka, a throng of innocent schoolboys from St. Alfonso's with surnames from O to Z rushed into the welcoming arms of a theatre of pornography. An old stucco angel crouched over the doorway of the theatre, showering its dubious benediction on the onrushing boys.

Once they got inside, they found they had been tricked.

The walls of Angel Talkies – those infamous murals of depravity – had been covered in black cloth. Not a single picture was visible to the human eye. A deal had been struck between Mr. D'Mello and the theatre management. The children would be shielded from the Murals of Sin.

'Do not stand close to the black cloth!' Mr. D'Mello shouted out. 'Do not touch the black cloth!' He had got everything planned out. Mr. Alvarez, Mr. Rogers, and Mr. Bhatt went among the students to keep them away from the posters. Two attendants from the theatre – presumably the dispensers of tickets to the blanket-covered men – helped in the arrangements. The boys were split into two groups. One group was marched to the upstairs auditorium, one herded downstairs. Before they could react, the boys would be sealed off inside the auditoriums. And so it was done: the plan worked perfectly. The boys were in Angel Talkies, and they were going to watch nothing but the government film; Mr D'Mello had won.

The lights were cut out inside the auditorium; a buzz of excitement from the boys. The screen glowed.

A scratched and fading reel came to life.

SAVE THE TIGER!

Mr. D'Mello stood behind the seated boys along with the other teachers. He wiped his face with relief. It looked like everything was going to be okay, after all. After leaving him alone in peace for a few minutes, young Mr. Bhatt came up to the assistant headmaster, and tried to make small-talk.

Ignoring young Mr. Bhatt, he kept his eyes on the screen. Photos of tiger-cubs frolicking together flashed on, and then a caption said: 'If you don't protect these cubs today, how can there be tigers tomorrow?'

He yawned. Stucco angels stared at him from the four corners of the auditorium, long peels of faded paint sticking up from their noses and ears, like heat-blisters. He hardly went to the films any more. Too expensive; he had to get tickets for the wife and the two little screamers too. But as a boy, hadn't films been his whole life? This very theatre, Angel Talkies, had been one of his favourite haunts; he would cut class and come here and sit alone and watch movies and dream. Now look at it. Even in the darkness the deterioration was unmistakable. The walls were foul, with large moisture-stains. The seats had holes in them. The simultaneous advance of decay and decadence: the story of this theatre was the story of the whole country.

The screen went black. The audience tittered. 'Silence!' Mr. D'Mello shouted.

The title-shot of the 'bonus reel' came on.

THE IMPORTANCE OF PHYSICAL WELL-BEING IN THE DEVELOPMENT OF CHILDREN

Images of boys showering, bathing, running and eating, each appropriately captioned began flashing one by one. Mr. Bhatt came up to the assistant headmaster once again. This time he whispered deliberately:

'It's your turn to go now, if you want.'

Mr. D'Mello understood the words, but not the hint of secrecy in the young man's voice. At his own suggestion, the teachers were taking turns to patrol the black-clothed corridor to make sure none of the over-developed boys slipped out to take a peek at the pornographic images. It had just been Gopalkrishna Bhatt's turn to patrol the Murals of Sin. For a moment he was lost – then it all made sense. From the way the young man was grinning, Mr. D'Mello realized that he had taken a quick peek himself. He looked around: each of the teachers was suppressing a grin.

Mr. D'Mello walked out of the auditorium with contempt for his colleagues.

He walked past the black-cloth-covered walls without feeling the slightest urge. How could Mr. Bhatt and Mr. Alvarez have been so base to have done it? He walked past the whole length of the black cloth without the least temptation to lift up the black cloth.

A light flickered on and off in a stairwell that led to an upper gallery. The walls of this gallery too were covered with black cloth. Mr. D'Mello dropped his mouth open and squinted at the upper gallery. No, he was not dreaming. Up there, he could make out a boy, his face averted, walking on tiptoe towards the black cloth. Julian D'Essa, he thought. Naturally. But then the boy's face came into view, just as he lifted up a corner of the black cloth and peered.

'Girish! What are you doing?'

At the sound of Mr. D'Mello's voice the boy turned. He froze. Teacher and student stared at each other.

'I'm sorry, sir . . . I'm sorry . . . they . . . they . . .'

There was giggling behind him; and suddenly he vanished, as if someone had dragged him away.

Mr. D'Mello rushed up the stairs at once, to the upper gallery. He could climb only two steps. His chest burned. Stomach heaving and hands clutching the balustrade, he rested there for a moment. The naked bulb in the stairwell sputtered on and off, on and off. The assistant headmaster felt dizzy. In his chest the heartbeat felt fainter and fainter, a dissolving tablet. He tried to call to Girish for help, but the words would not come out. Reaching a hand for help, he caught a corner of the black cloth on the wall. It ripped, and split open: hordes of copulating creatures frozen in postures of rapes, unlawful pleasures and bestialities, swarmed out and danced around his eyes in a taunting cavalcade, and a world of angelic delights that he had scorned until now flashed at him. He saw everything, and he understood everything, at last.

Young Mr. Bhatt found him like that, on the stairs, dead of a heart attack.

## THE HISTORY OF KITTUR

*(abridged from the book* A Short History of Kittur *by Father Basil D'Essa, S.J.)*

The word 'Kittur' is a corruption either of 'Kiri Uru,' 'Small Town,' or of 'Kittamma's Uru' – Kittamma being a goddess, specializing in repelling smallpox, who had a temple dedicated to her near the present-day train station. A Syrian Christian merchant's letter of 1091 recommends to his peers the excellent natural harbour of the town of Kittur, on the Malabar Coast. During the entire twelfth century, however, the town appears to have vanished; Arab merchants who came to Kittur in 1141 and 1190 record seeing only a wilderness. In the fourteenth century a dervish named Yusuf Ali began curing lepers in the Bunder; when he died, his body was entombed in a white dome, and the structure – the Dargah of Hazrat Yusuf Ali – has remained an object of pilgrimage to the present day. In the late fifteenth century, 'Kittore, also known as the citadel of elephants' is listed in the tax-collection records of the Vijayanagara rulers as one of the provinces of their empire. In 1649, a four-man Portuguese missionary delegation led by Fr. Cristofo d'Almeida, S.J., trekked down from Goa to Kittur; it found 'a deplorable mess of idolators, Jews, Mohameddans, and elephants.' The Portuguese drove out the Mohammedans, pulverized the idols, and distilled the wild elephants into a rubble of dirty ivory. Over the next hundred years, Kittur – now renamed Valencia – passed back and forth between the Portuguese, the Marathas, and the kingdom of Mysore. In

1780, Hyder Ali defeated an army of the East India Company near the Bunder; by the treaty of Kittur, signed that year, the Company renounced its claims on 'Kittore, also called as Valencia or The Bunder.' The Company violated the treaty after Hyder Ali's death in 1782, by setting up a military base near the Bunder; in retaliation, Tippu, the son of Hyder Ali, constructed the Sultan's Battery, a formidable fortress of black stone, mounted with French guns. After Tippu's death in 1799, Kittur became Company property, and was annexed to the Madras Presidency. The town, like most of South India, took no part in the great anti-British mutiny of 1857. In 1921, an activist of the Indian National Congress put up a tricolour on the old lighthouse: the freedom struggle had come to Kittur.

## DAY THREE: ANGEL TALKIES

*Nightlife in Kittur is centred on Angel Talkies. Every Thursday morning, the walls of Kittur are plastered with hand-painted posters featuring a sketch of a hefty woman brushing her hair with her fingers; below, is the title of the movie: HER NIGHTS, WINE AND WOMEN, MYSTERIES OF GROWTH, UNCLE'S FAULT. The words 'Malayalam Colour' and 'Adults Only' are prominently featured on the posters. By 8 a.m., a long line of unemployed men has queued outside Angel Talkies, waiting for the first glimpse of the new screening. Show times are 10 a.m., noon, 2 p.m., 4 p.m. and 7 p.m. Seat prices range from Rs 2.20 for a seat up the front to Rs 4.50 for a 'family circle' seat up in the balcony. Not far from the theatre is The Hotel Woodside, whose attractions include a famous Paris cabaret, featuring Ms. Zeena from Bombay, every Friday, and Ms. Ayesha and Ms. Zimboo from Bahrain, every second Sunday. A travelling sexologist, Dr. Kuruvilla, MBBS, MD, Mch, MS, DDBS, PCDB, visits the hotel the first Monday of every month. Less expensive and seedier in appearance than the Woodside are a nearby series of bars, restaurants, hostels, and apartments. Thanks to the presence of a YMCA in the neighbourhood, however, men of decency have the option of a moral and clean hostel.*

The door of the YMCA swung open at two in the morning; a short figure walked out.

He was a small man with a gigantic protruding forehead, which gave him the look of a professor in a caricature. His hair, thick and wavy and unruly like a teenager's, was oiled and pressed down firmly; it was greying around the temples and in the sideburns. He had walked out of the YMCA looking at the ground; and now, as if noticing for the first time that he was in the real world, he stopped a moment, looked this way and that, and then walked towards the market.

A series of whistles assaulted him at once. A policeman in his uniform, cycling down the street, slowed down and put a foot on the pavement.

'What is your name, fellow?'

The man who looked like a professor said:

'Gururaj Kamath.'

'And what work do you do that makes you walk alone at night?'

'I look for the truth.'

'Now don't get funny, all right?'

'Journalist.'

'For which paper?'

'How many papers do we have?'

The policeman, who may have been expecting to find some irregularity associated with this man, and hence expecting either to bully or to blackmail him, both acts which he enjoyed, looked disappointed, and then rode away. He had hardly gone down the road when a thought hit him and he stopped again and turned around to the little man.

'O, Gururaj Kamath. You wrote the column on the riots, didn't you?'

'Yes,' the little man said.

The policeman looked down to the ground.

'My name is Aziz.'

'And?'

'You've done every minority in this town a great service, sir. My name is Aziz. I want to . . . to thank you.'

'I was only doing my job. I told you: I look for the truth.'

'I want to thank you anyway. If more people did what you do, there won't be any more riots in this town, sir.'

Not a bad fellow after all, Gururaj thought, as he watched Aziz cycle down the road. Just doing his job.

He continued his walk.

No one was watching him, so he let himself smile with pride.

In the days after the riots, the voice of this little man had been the voice of reason in the midst of chaos. In precise, biting prose he had laid out for his readers the destruction caused by the Hindu fanatics who hacked down the shops of Muslim shopkeepers; in his calm, unemotional voice he had blasted bigotry and stood up for the rights of religious minorities. He had wanted nothing more from his columns but to help the victims of the riots: instead, Gururaj found himself something of a celebrity now in Kittur. A star.

A fortnight ago, he had suffered the biggest blow of his life. His father had passed away from pneumonia. The day after Gururaj returned to Kittur from his ancestral village, having shaved his head and sat by the water-tank in his ancestral temple to recite Sanskrit verses along with a priest and bid his father's soul goodbye, he discovered that he had been promoted to Deputy Executive Editor, the number two position at the newspaper where he had worked for twenty years.

It was life's way of evening things out, Gururaj told himself.

The moon shone brightly, with a large halo around it. He had forgotten how beautiful a nocturnal walk could be. The light was strong and clean, and it laminated the earth's surface; every object carved sharp shadows in it. He thought it might be the day after a full moon.

Even at this hour of the night, work was still going on. He heard a low, continuous sound, as if it were the audible respiration of the night-world: an open-back truck was collecting mud, probably for some construction site. The driver was asleep at the wheel, and his arm was sticking out of one window, and his feet out the other one; as if ghosts were doing the work, morsels of mud came flying into the truck from behind. The back of his shirt became damp, and he thought: 'But I will catch a cold. I should go back.' That thought made him feel old, and he decided to go on; he took a few steps to his left and began walking right down the centre of Umbrella Street; it had been a childhood fantasy of his to walk down the middle of a big road, but he had never been able to sneak away from his father's watchful eyes long enough to fulfil this fantasy.

He came to a stop, dead in the middle of the road. Then he walked fast to a side alley.

Two dogs were mating in the side-alley. He crouched and tried to see exactly what was happening.

After completing the act, the dogs split up. One went down the alley and the other came Gururaj's way, running with postcoital vigour, and almost brushing his pants. He followed.

It came back to the main road, and sniffed at a newspaper. The mutt bit the newspaper; it ran back into the alley, and Gururaj ran behind it. Deeper and deeper the dog ran into the side-alleys, the editor following. Finally, it dropped its bundle; it turned around, snarled at Gururaj, and tore the newspaper to shreds.

'Good dog! Good dog!'

Gururaj turned sharply to his right to confront the speaker. He found himself looking at an apparition; a man in khaki, carrying an old World War II-era rifle, with a yellowish, leathery face covered with small slits. His eyes were narrow and slanting. Drawing closer, Gururaj thought: Of course. He's a Gurkha.

The Gurkha was sitting on a wooden chair out on the pavement, with a bank's rolled-down shutter behind him.

'Why do you say that?' Gururaj shot back. 'Why are you praising the dog for defacing a paper?'

'The dog is doing the right thing. Because not a word in the newspaper is true.'

The Gurkha – Gururaj took him for an all-night security guard for the bank – got up from his chair and took a step to the dog.

At once it dropped the paper and ran away. Picking up the torn and mangled and saliva-stained paper with care, the Gurkha turned the pages.

Gururaj winced.

'Tell me what you're looking for. I know everything that's in that newspaper.'

The Gurkha let the dirty paper go.

'There was an accident last night. Near Flower Market Street. A hit and run.'

'I know the case,' Gururaj said. It had not been his story, but he read the proofs of the entire paper every day. 'An employee of Mr. Engineer's was involved.'

'The newspaper said that. But it was not the employee who did it.'

'Really?' Gururaj smiled. 'Then who did it?'

The Gurkha looked right into Gururaj's eyes. He smiled, and then pointed the barrel of the ancient gun at him. 'I can tell you, but I'll have to shoot you afterwards.'

Looking at the barrel of the rifle, Gururaj thought: 'I'm talking to a madman.'

The next day, Gururaj was in his office at six a.m. First to get there, as always. He began by looking at the telex machine, at the reels of badly smudged news it was printing out from Delhi and New York and other cities he would never go to in his life. At seven he turned the radio on, and began jotting down the main points of the morning's column.

At eight o'clock, Ms. D'Mello came in. The hammering of a typewriter broke the peace of the office.

She was writing her usual column, 'Twinkle Twinkle'. It was the daily beauty column; a women's hair-salon owner sponsored it, and Ms. D'Mello answered a set of questions about hair care that had come in by mail, offering advice and gently goading the letter-writers in the direction of the hair-salon owner's products.

Gururaj never spoke to Ms. D'Mello. He resented the fact that his newspaper ran a paid-for column, a practice he considered profoundly unethical. But there was another reason to be rude to Ms. D'Mello: she was an unmarried woman, and he didn't want anyone to assume that he might have the slightest interest in her.

Relatives and friends of his father had told Guru for years he ought to move out of the YMCA and marry, and he had almost given in, thinking the woman would be needed to nurse his father because of his growing senility, when the need for a wife was removed entirely. Now he was determined not to lose his independence to anyone.

By eleven, when Gururaj came out of his room again, the office was smoky – the only repulsive aspect of his workplace for him. The reporters were at their desks, drinking tea and smoking. The teleprinter machine, off to the side, was vomiting out a mass of smudged and misspelled news reports from Delhi.

After lunch, he sent the office-boy to find Menon, a young journalist and a rising star at the paper. Menon came to his room with the top two buttons of his shirt open, and a shiny gold necklace flashing from his neck. 'Sit down,' Gururaj said.

He showed him two articles in the newspaper on the car-crash on Flower Market Street, which he had dug out of the archives that morning. The first (he pointed to it) had appeared before the trial; the second after the verdict.

'You wrote both articles, didn't you?'

Menon nodded.

'In the first article, the car that hits the dead man is a red Maruti Suzuki. In the second, it is a white Fiat. Which one was it, really?'

Krishna checked the two articles.

'I just filed according to the police reports.'

'You didn't bother looking at the vehicle yourself, I take it?'

As he went to sleep that night, he set the alarm for two o'clock.

He woke up with his heart racing fast; he turned on the lights, left his room, and squinted at his clock. It was twenty minutes to two. He put on his pants, patted his wavy strands of hair back into place, and almost ran down the stairs and out the gate of the YMCA, and in the direction of the bank.

The Gurkha was there at his chair, with his ancient rifle.

'Listen here, did you see this accident with your own eyes?'

'Of course not. I was sitting right here. This is my job.'

'Then how the hell did you know the cars had been changed in the police—'

'Through the grapevine.'

The Gurkha talks softly. He tells the newspaper editor that there is a network of nightwatchmen who pass information around Kittur; every nightwatchman comes for a cigarette to the next and tells him something, and he goes to the next one for a cigarette. In this way, word gets around. Secrets get spread. The truth – what really happened in daytime – is preserved.

This is insane, this is impossible – Gururaj wipes the sweat off his forehead.

'So what actually happened – Engineer hit a man on his way back home?'

'Left him for dead.'

'It can't be true.'

The Gurkha's eyes flashed. 'You've lived here long enough, sir. You know it *can be.* Engineer was drunk; he was coming back from his mistress' home; he hit the fellow like some stray dog, and drove away, leaving him there, with his guts out on the street. In the morning the newspaper boy found him like that. The police know perfectly well who drives drunkenly down that road at night. So the next morning two constables go to his house. Hasn't even washed the blood off the front wheels of the car.'

'Then why—'

'He is the richest man in this town. He owns the tallest building in this town. He cannot be arrested. He gets one of the employees in his factory to say he was driving the car when it happened. The guy gives the police a sworn affidavit. I was driving under the influence of alcohol on the night of 12 May when I hit the victim. Then Mr. Engineer gives the judge six thousand rupees, and the police something less, perhaps four thousand or five, because the judiciary is of course more noble than the police, to keep quiet. Then he wants his Maruti Suzuki back, because it's a new car and a fashion statement and he likes driving it, so he gives the police another thousand to change the identity of the killer car to a Fiat, and he has his car and he's driving around town again.'

'My god.'

'The employee got four years. The judge could have given him a harsher sentence, but he felt sorry for the bugger. Couldn't let him off for free, of course. So—' (he brought down an imaginary gavel) '—four years.'

'I can't believe it,' Gururaj said. 'Kittur isn't that kind of place.'

The foreigner narrowed his cunning eyes, and smiled. He looked at the glowing tip of the beedi for a while, and then, offered the beedi to Gururaj.

In the morning Gururaj opened the only window in his room. He looked down on Umbrella Street, on the heart of the town where he was born, and where he had grown to maturity and where he would almost certainly die. He thought sometimes he knew every building, every tree, every tile on the roof of every house, in Kittur. Glowing in the morning light, Umbrella Street seemed to say, No, the Gurkha's story can't be true. The clarity of the stencilling on an advertisement, the glistening spokes of the cycle-wheel being ridden by the man delivering newspapers, said: No, the Gurkha is lying. But as Gururaj walked to his office, he saw the dense dark shade of the banyan tree lying on the road, like a patch of night left unswept by the morning's broom, and his soul was in turmoil again.

Work began. He calmed down. He avoided Ms. D'Mello.

In the evening, the editor-in-chief of the newspaper called him to his room. He was a plump old man, with sagging jowls and thick white eyebrows that looked like frosting and hands that trembled as he drank his tea. The tendons on his neck stood out in deep relief, and every part of his body seemed to be calling out for retirement.

If he did retire, Gururaj would inherit his chair.

'Regarding this story you've asked Menon to reinvestigate . . .' the editor-in-chief said, sipping the tea. 'Forget it.'

'There was a discrepancy about the cars—'

The old man shook his head. 'The police made a mistake on the first filing, that was all.' His voice changed into the quiet, casual tone Gururaj had come to recognize as final. He sipped more tea, and then some more.

The slurping sound of tea being sipped, the abruptness of the old man's manner, the fatigue of so many nights of broken sleep, got on Gururaj's nerves and he said:

'A man might have been sent to jail for no good reason; a guilty man might be walking free. And all you can say is, let's drop the matter.'

The old man sipped his tea; Gururaj thought he could detect his head moving, as if to nod in the affirmative.

He went back to the YMCA, walked up a flight of stairs to his room. He lay down on the bed with his eyes open. He was still awake at two in the morning, when the alarm went off. When he went out, he heard a whistling sound at once; the policeman, passing by him, waved heartily, as if to an old friend.

The moon was shrinking fast; in a day or two there would be total darkness at night. He walked the same way now, as if it were a ritual formula: first slowly, then crossing to the centre of the road, and then dashing into the side alley until he got to the bank. The Gurkha was at his chair, his rifle on his shoulder, a glowing beedi in his fingers:

'What does the grapevine tell you tonight?'

'Nothing tonight.'

'Then tell me something from a few nights ago. Tell me what else the paper has published that is wrong.'

'There was the riots. The newspaper got that wrong, completely.'

Gururaj thought his heart would skip a beat. 'How so?'

'The newspaper said that it was Hindus fighting Muslims, see?'

'It was Hindus fighting Muslims. Everyone knows this.'

'Ha.'

The next morning Gururaj did not turn up at the office. He went straight down to the port, the first time since coming there in the aftermath of the riots to talk to shopkeepers. He traced every restaurant and fish market that had been burned down in the riots.

He walked back to his newspaper, rushed into the office of the editor-in-chief and said:

'I heard the most incredible story last night about the Hindu-Muslim riots. Shall I tell you what I heard?'

The old man sipped his tea.

'I heard that the Member of Parliament, along with the mafia of the port, instigated the riots. And I heard that the goons and the MP have transferred the property to the hands of their own men, under the name of a fictitious trust called the New Kittur Port Development Trust. The violence was planned. Muslim goons burned Muslim shops and Hindu goons burned Hindu shops. It was a real estate transaction masquerading as a religious riot.'

The editor stopped sipping.

'Who told you this?'

'A friend. Is it true?'

'No.'

Gururaj smiled, and said: 'I didn't think so, either. Thanks.' He walked out of the room while his boss watched him with concern.

The next morning, he got into his office late once again. After a few minutes, the office-boy turned up at his desk and shouted:

'Chief wants to see you.'

'Why didn't you turn up at the City Corporation Office today?' The old man asked him, sipping another cup of tea. 'The mayor asked for you to be there; he released a statement on Hindu-Muslim unity and attacking the BJP that he wanted you to hear. You know he respects your work.'

Gururaj pressed his hair down into place; he had not oiled it this morning and it was unruly.

'Who cares?'

'Excuse me, Gururaj?'

'You think anyone in this office doesn't know that all this political fighting is just make-believe? That in reality the BJP and the Congress cut each other deals, and share the bribe money they take on construction projects in Bajpe? You and I have known this for years that this is true and yet we pretend to report things otherwise. Doesn't this strike you as bizarre? Look here. Let's just write nothing but the truth and the whole truth in the newspaper today. Just today. One day of nothing but the truth. That's all I want to do. No one may even notice. Tomorrow we'll go back to the usual lies. But for one day I want to report, write, and edit the truth. One day in my life I'd like to be a journalist. What do you say to that?'

The editor-in-chief frowned, as if thinking about it, and then said: 'Come to my home after dinner tonight.'

At nine o'clock, Gururaj walked up to Rose Lane, to a home with a big garden and a blue statue of Krishna with a flute in a niche in the front, and rang the bell.

The editor let him into the drawing room, and closed the door. He asked Gururaj to sit down on a brown sofa.

'You'd better tell me what's bothering you.' Gururaj told him.

'Let's assume you have proof of this thing. You write about it. You're not only saying that the police force is rotten, but also that the judiciary is corrupt. The judge will call you for Contempt of Court. You will be arrested – even if what you are saying is true. You and I and people in our press pretend that there is freedom of press in India but we know the truth.'

'What about the Hindu-Muslim riots? Can't we write about the truth about that, either?'

'What is the truth about it, Gururaj?'

Gururaj told him the truth, and the editor-in-chief smiled. He put his head in his hands and, in a voice that seemed to rock the entire night, he laughed his heart out. The tendons on his neck sagged and rose and sagged again.

'Even if what you're saying is indeed the truth,' the old man said, regaining control of himself, 'and observe that I neither admit nor contradict any of it, there would be no way for me to publish it.'

'Why not?'

The editor smiled.

'Who do you think owns this newspaper?'

'Ramdas Pai,' Gururaj said, naming a businessman in Umbrella Street whose name appeared as proprietor on the front page.

The editor shook his head. 'He doesn't own it. Not all of it.'

'Who does?'

'Use your brains.'

Gururaj looked at the editor-in-chief with new eyes. The old man seemed to have a nimbus around him, of all the things he had learned over the length of his career and could never publish; this secret knowledge glowed around his head like the halo around the nearly full moon. This is the fate of every journalist in this town and in this state and in this country and maybe in this whole world, Gururaj thought.

'Had you never guessed any of this before, Gururaj? It must come from the fact you are not yet married. Not having had a woman, you have never understood the ways of the world.'

'And you have understood the ways of the world too well.'

The two men stared, each feeling tremendously sorry for the other.

The next morning, as he walked to the office, Gururaj thought: it is a false earth I am walking on. An innocent man is behind bars, and a guilty man walks free. Everyone knows that this is so and not one has the courage to change it.

From then on, Gururaj walked every night down the dirty stairwell of the YMCA, gazing blankly at the profanities and graffiti scribbled on the wall, and walked down Umbrella Street, ignoring the barking and skulking and copulating stray dogs, until he got to the Gurkha, who would lift his old rifle up in recognition and smile. They were friends now.

The Gurkha told him how much rottenness there could be in a small town: who had killed whom in the past few years; how much the judges of Kittur had asked for in bribe money, how much the police chiefs had asked. They talked until it was nearly dawn, and it was time for Gururaj to leave, so he could get some sleep before going to work.

One night, he hesitated: 'I still don't know your name.'

'Ram Bahadur.'

Gururaj waited for him to ask him his name; he wanted to say, 'Now that my father has died, you are my only friend, Ram Bahadur.'

The Gurkha sat with his eyes closed.

At four in the morning, walking back to his flat, he was thinking: who is this man, this Gurkha? From some reference he made to being a manservant in the house of a retired general, Gururaj deduced that he had been in the army, in the Gurkha regiment. But how he ended up in Kittur, why he didn't go back home to Nepal, all this was still a mystery. Tomorrow I should ask him all this. Then I can tell him about myself.

There was an Ashoka tree near the entrance to his YMCA, and Gururaj stopped to look at the tree. The moonlight lay on it, and it seemed different somehow tonight; as if it were on the verge of growing into something else.

\*

'They are not my fellow-workers; they are lower than animals.'

He couldn't stand the sight of them; he averted his eyes, and scurried into his room and slammed his door shut as soon as he got to the office. Although he kept editing the copy given to him, he could no longer bear to look at the newspaper. What especially terrified him was catching his own name in print; for this reason he asked to be relieved from What formerly was his greatest pleasure, writing his column, and insisted only on editing. Although he used to stay till midnight in the old days, he left the office at five o'clock every evening, hurrying back to his apartment to fall on his bed.

At two o'clock sharp, he woke up. To save himself the trouble of finding his pants in the dark, he had taken to sleeping in all his clothes. He almost ran down the stairs and pushed open the door of the YMCA, so he could get to the Gurkha.

Then one night, at last, it happened. The Gurkha was not sitting outside the bank. Someone else had taken his chair.

'What do I know, sir?' the new nightwatchman said. 'I was appointed to this job last night; they didn't tell me what happened to the old fellow.'

Gururaj ran from shop to shop, from house to house, asking every nightwatchman he met what had happened to the Gurkha.

'Gone to Nepal,' one nightwatchman finally told him. 'Back to his family. He was saving money all these years, and now he's left.'

Gururaj took the news like a physical blow. Only one man had known what was happening in this town, and that one man had vanished to another country. Seeing him pant for air, the nightwatchmen gathered around him, made him sit down, and brought him cool, clean water in a plastic bottle. He tried explaining to them what had happened between him and the Gurkha all these weeks, what he had lost.

'That Gurkha, sir?' One watchman shook his head. 'Are you sure you talked about these things with him? He was a complete idiot. His head had been damaged in the army.'

'What about the grapevine? Is it still working?' Gururaj asked. 'Will one of you tell me what you hear now?'

The guards stared. In their eyes, he could see doubt turning into a kind of fear. 'They seem to think I'm mad,' he thought.

He wandered at night, passing by the dim buildings, by the sleeping multitudes. He passed by large, still, black buildings, with hundreds of bodies inside lying in a stupor. 'I am the only man who is awake now,' he told himself. Up on a hill to his left, he saw a large housing block burning with light. Seven windows were lit up, and the building blazed; it seemed to him to be a living creature, a kind of monster of light, giving off light from its entrails.

Gururaj understood: the Gurkha had not abandoned him at all. He had not done what everyone else in his life had done to him. He had left something; a gift. Gururaj would now hear the grapevine on his own. He lifted his arms to the building burning with lights; he felt full of occult power.

One day as he came into work, late again, he heard a whisper behind him: 'It happened to the father too, in his last days . . .'

He thought: 'I must take more care that others do not notice this change that is happening inside me.'

When he came to his office, he noticed the office-boy was removing his nameplate from the office. 'I am losing everything I worked so hard for so many years,' he thought. But he felt no regret or passion; it seemed as if things were happening to someone else. He saw the new nameplate on the office:

KRISHNA MENON
DEPUTY EDITOR
DAWN HERALD
KITTUR'S ONLY AND FINEST NEWSPAPER

'Gururaj! I didn't want to do it, I—'

'No explanation is necessary. In your position, I'd have done the same.'

'Do you want me to speak to someone, Gururaj? We can arrange it for you.'

'What are you talking about?'

'I know you have no father now . . . But we can arrange a wedding for you, with a girl of a good family.'

'What are you talking about?'

'We think you are ill. You ought to know that many in this office have been saying that for some time. I insist that you take a week off. Or two weeks. Go somewhere on holiday. Go to the Western Ghats and watch the clouds for a while.'

'Fine. I'll take three weeks off.'

For three weeks he slept through the day and walked through the night. The late night police sentry no longer said 'hello, editor' like before, and Gururaj could see the man's head, as he cycled past, turning around to keep staring at him. The nightwatchmen also stared at him oddly; and he grinned – Even here, even in this Hades of the middle of the night, I have become an outsider, a man who frightens others. The thought excited him.

He bought a child's square blackboard one day, and a piece of chalk. That night he wrote at the top of the blackboard:

THE TRUTH ALONE SHALL TRIUMPH. A NOCTURNAL NEWSPAPER

Sole correspondent, editor, advertiser, and subscriber: Gururaj Manjeshwar Kamath, Esq.

Copying out the headline from the morning's newspaper—

'BJP City Councillor blasts Congressman'

He rubbed and scratched and rewrote it:

2 October 1989

BJP City Councillor, who needs money in a hurry to build a new mansion on Rose Lane, blasts the Congressman. He will tomorrow receive a brown bag full of cash from the Congress party, and then stop blasting the Congressman.'

Then he lay in bed and closed his eyes.

One night he thought: 'There is only one night of my vacation left.' The dawn was breaking already, and he hurried back to the YMCA. He stopped. He was sure that he was seeing an elephant outside the building of the YMCA. Was he dreaming? What on earth would an elephant be doing, at this hour, in the middle of his town? It was outside the bounds of reason. Yet it looked real and tangible to his eyes; only one thing made him think it was not a real elephant – it was absolutely still. All elephants move and make some noise all the time, so you are not seeing an elephant. He closed his eyes and walked up to the YMCA; and when he opened them again he was staring at a tree. He touched the bark, and thought:

'This is the first hallucination I have had in my life.'

When he came back to the office the next day, everyone said Gururaj was back to his old self. He had missed his office life; he had wanted to come back.

'Thank you for your offer to arrange a marriage,' he told the editor-in-chief, when they shared a coffee. 'But I'm married to my work anyway.'

Sitting in the newsroom with young men just out of college, he edited stories with all his old cheer. After all the young men were gone, he stayed back, digging through the archives. He had come back to work with a purpose. He was going to write a history of Kittur. An infernal history of Kittur – in it every event in the past twenty years would be reinterpreted. He took out old newspapers, and carefully read the front page. Then, a red pen in his hand, he scratched out and rewrote words, which fulfilled two purposes – one, it defaced the newspapers of the past, and two, it allowed him to figure out the true relationship between the words, and the characters in the news-events. At first, designating Hindi

– the Gurkha's language – as the language of the truth, he rewrote the Kannada-language headlines of the newspaper in Hindi; then he switched to English, and finally he adopted a code in which he substituted each letter of the Roman alphabet for the one immediately after it – he had read somewhere that Julius Caesar had invented the same code for the Romans – and, to complicate matters further, he inserted symbols of his own design for certain words; for instance, a triangle with a dot inside to represent the word 'Bank.' The element of irony dominated other symbols he invented; for instance, a Nazi Swastika for the 'Congress party,' and the Nuclear Disarmament symbol for the 'BJP,' and so on. One day, looking back over his past week's notes, he found that he had forgotten half the symbols, and he no longer understood what he had written. Good, he thought; that is the way it should be. Even the writer of the truth should not know the truth entirely. Every true word, upon being written, is like the full moon, and daily it wanes, and then passes entirely into obscurity. That is the way of all things.

When he was done reinterpreting each day's newspaper, he cut out the words 'The Dawn Herald' from the headline and wrote in their place: THE TRUTH ALONE SHALL TRIUMPH.

'What the hell are you doing to our newspapers?'

It was the editor-in-chief. He and Menon had sneaked up on Gururaj at the office.

The editor-in-chief turned page after page of defaced newspaper in the archives without a word, while Menon tried to take a peek from over his shoulder. They saw pages covered in squiggles, red-marks, slashes, triangles, pictures of girls with pigtails and bloody teeth, and images of copulating dogs. Then the old man slammed the archive shut.

'I told you to get married.'

Gururaj smiled. 'Listen, old friend, those are symbolic marks. I can interpret—'

The editor-in-chief shook his head.

'Get out of this office. At once. I'm sorry, Gururaj.'

Gururaj smiled, as if to say, no explanation was necessary. The editor-in-chief's eyes were teary, and his sagging neck muscles moved up and down as he swallowed again and again. The tears came to Guru's eyes as well. He thought: How hard it has been for this old man to do this. How hard he must have protected me. He imagined closed-door meetings where all his colleagues had been baying for his blood, and this decent old man alone had defended him to the end. 'I am sorry, my friend, for letting you down,' he wanted to say.

That night, Gururaj walked about telling himself he was happier than he had ever been in his life. He was a free man now. When he got back, just before dawn, to the YMCA, he saw the elephant again. This time it did not melt into an Ashoka tree, even when he came close by. He walked right up to the beast, saw its constantly flapping ears, which had the colour and shape and movement of a pterodactyl's wing; he walked around, and saw that from the back, each of its ears had a fringe of pink, and was striped with veins. How can this wealth of detail be unreal? he thought. This creature was real, and if the rest of the world could not see it, then the rest of the world was the poorer for that.

Just make one sound! He pleaded with the elephant. So I know for sure that I am not deluded, that you are for real. The elephant understood; it raised its trunk and roared so loudly that he thought he had been deafened.

'You are free now,' the elephant said, in words so loud they seemed like newspaper headlines to him. 'Go and write the true history of Kittur.'

Some months later, they got news of Gururaj again. Four young reporters went to investigate.

They muffled their giggles and pushed open the door to the municipal reading room in the lighthouse. The librarian had been waiting for them; he ushered them in with a finger on his lip.

The journalists found Gururaj sitting on a bench, reading a newspaper, it partially covering his face. The old editor's shirt was tattered, but he seemed to have gained weight, as if idleness had suited him.

'He won't say a word anymore,' the librarian said. 'He'll just sit there till sunset, holding the paper up. The only time he said anything was when I told him I loved his articles on the riots, and then he shouted at me.'

One of the young journalists put his finger on the newspaper and lowered it slowly; Gururaj offered no resistance. The journalist shouted, and stepped back.

There was a moist dark hole in the inner sheet of the paper. Pieces of newsprint stuck to the corners of Gururaj's mouth, and his jaw was moving.

# THE LANGUAGES OF KITTUR

Kannada, one of the four major languages of South India, is the official language of the state of Karnataka, in which Kittur is located. The local paper, *The Dawn Herald*, is published in Kannada. Although understood by virtually everyone in the town, Kannada is the mother-tongue of only some of the Brahmins. Tulu, a regional language that has no written script – although it is believed to have possessed a script centuries ago – is the lingua franca. Two dialects of Tulu exist. The 'upper-caste' dialect is still used by a few Brahmins, but is dying out as the Tulu-speaking Brahmins switch to Kannada. The other dialect of Tulu, a rough, bawdy language cherished for its diversity and pungency of expletives, is used by the Bunts and Hoykas – this is the language of the Kittur street. Around Umbrella Street, the commercial centre of town, the language changes to Konkani: this is the language of the Gaud-Saraswat Brahmins, originally from Goa, who own the shops here (although Tulu and Kannada-speaking Brahmins began intermarrying in the 1960s, the Konkani-Brahmins have snubbed all marriage proposals from outsiders so far). A very different dialect of Konkani, corrupted with Portuguese, is spoken in the suburb of Valencia by the Catholics who live there. Most of the Muslims, especially those in the Bunder, the port area, speak a dialect of Malayalam as their mother-tongue; a few of the richer Muslims, being from the old Hyderabad kingdom, speak Hyderabadi Urdu as their native language. Kittur's large migrant worker population, which floats around the town from construction site to construction site, is Tamil-speaking. English is understood by the middle class.

## DAY FOUR: THE COOL-WATER WELL JUNCTION

*The old Cool-Water Well is said never to dry up, but is now sealed, and serves only as a traffic roundabout. The streets around the Well house a number of middle-class colonies. Professional people of all castes – Bunts, Brahmins, and Catholics – live side by side here, although the Muslim rich keep to the port. The Canara Club, the most exclusive club in town, is located here, in a large white mansion with lawns. The neighbourhood is the 'intellectual' part of town: it boasts a Lion's Club, a Rotary Club, a Freemason's Lodge, a Baha'i educational group, a Theosophist Society, and a branch of the Alliance Française of Pondicherry. Of the numerous medical institutions located here, the two best-known are the Havelock Henry General Hospital and Dr. Shambhu Shetty's HAPPY SMILE orthodontic clinic. The St. Agnes Girls' High School, Kittur's most sought-after girls-only school, is not far from the junction. The poshest part of the Cool Water-Well Junction area is the hibiscus-lined street known as Rose Lane. Mabroor Engineer, the richest man in town, and Anand Kumar, the MP from Kittur, have mansions here.*

'It's one thing to take a little ganja, roll it inside a chapatti and chew it at the day's end, just to relax the muscles – I can

forgive that in a man, I really can. But to smoke this drug –
this *smack* – at seven in the morning, and then lie in the
corner with your tongue drooping out, I tolerate that in no
man at my construction site. You understand me? Or do you
want me to repeat this in Tamil or whatever language your
people speak?'

'I understand, sir.'

'What did you say? What did you say, you son-of . . .?'

Holding her brother by the hand, Soumya watched the
foreman chastise her father. The foreman was young, so much
younger than her father – but he wore a khaki uniform that
the construction company had given him, and twirled a cane-
stick in his left hand, and she saw that the workers, instead
of defending her father, were listening quietly to the foreman.
He was up on a blue chair on an embankment of mud; a gas
lamp buzzed noisily from a wooden pole driven into the
ground next to the chair. Behind him was the crater around
the half-demolished house; the inside of the house was filled
with rubble, its roof had mostly fallen in, and its windows
were empty. With his baton and his uniform, and his face
harshly illuminated by the incandescent paraffin-lamp, the
foreman looked like a ruler of the underworld, at the gate of
his kingdom.

A semicircle of the construction workers had formed
below him. Soumya's father stood apart from the others,
looking furtively at Soumya's mother, who was muffling her
sobs in a corner of her sari. In a tear-racked voice she said: 'I
keep telling him to give up this *smack*. I keep telling—'

Soumya wondered why her mother had to complain
about her father in front of everyone. Raju pressed her hand.

'Why are they all scolding Daddy?'

She pressed back. Quiet.

All at once the foreman got out of his chair, took a step down the embankment, and raised his stick over Soumya's father. 'Pay attention, I said' – he brought his stick down.

Soumya closed her eyes and turned her face.

The workers had gone back to their tents, which were scattered about the open field around the dark, half-demolished house. Soumya's father was lying on his blue mat, apart from everyone else; he was snoring already, his hands crossed over his eyes. In the old days she would have gone to him and snuggled into the side of his body.

Soumya went up to her father. She shook him by his big toe; he did not respond. She went to where her mother was making rice, and lay down.

Mallets and sledgehammers woke her up in the morning. Thump! Thump! Thump! Bleary-eyed, she wandered up to the house. Her father was up on the bit of the roof that remained, sitting on one of the black iron crossbeams; he was cutting it with a saw. Two men swung at the wall below with sledgehammers, and clouds of dust rose up from their blows, and covered him as he sawed. Soumya's heart leapt up.

She ran to her mother and shouted:

'Daddy's working again!'

Her mother was with the other women; they were coming down from the house, carrying large metal saucers filled to the brim with rubble on their heads. 'Make sure Raju doesn't get wet,' she said, as she passed Soumya.

Only then did Soumya notice it was drizzling.

Raju was lying on the blanket where his mother had been; she woke him up, and took him into one of the tents. Raju began whimpering, saying he wanted to sleep some more. She went to the blue mat; her father had not touched the rice from last night. Mixing the dry rice with the rainwater, she squeezed it into a gruel, and stuffed morsels into Raju's mouth. He said he didn't like it, and bit her fingers each time she fed him.

The rain grew stronger, and she heard the foreman roaring out: 'Sons of bitches, don't slow down!'

The moment the rain stopped, Raju wanted to be pushed on the swing. 'It's going to start raining again,' she said, but he wouldn't change his mind. She carried him in her arms to the old truck-tyre swing near the compound wall, and put him on it, and gave him a push, shouting: 'One! Two!'

As she was doing this, a man appeared before her.

His dark, wet skin was coated in white dust, and it took an instant for her to recognize him.

'Sweetie,' he said, 'you must do something for Daddy.'

Her heart was beating too fast for her to say a word. She wanted him to say, 'sweetie' not like he was saying it now – as if it were just a word, air that he were breathing out – but like before, when it came from his heart, when it was accompanied by his pulling her into his breast and hugging her deeply and whispering madly into her ear.

He continued speaking, in the same strange, slow, slurred way, and told her what he wanted her to do; then he walked back to the house.

143

She found Raju, who was cutting an earthworm into smaller bits with a piece of glass he had stolen from the demolition site, and said: 'We have to go.'

Raju could not be left alone even though he would be a real nuisance on a trip like this. Once she had left him alone and he had swallowed a piece of glass.

'Where are we going?' he asked.

'To the port.'

'Why?'

'There is a place by the port, a garden, where Daddy's friends are waiting for him to come. Daddy cannot go there – because the foreman will hit him again. You don't want the foreman to beat Daddy again in front of the world, do you?'

'No,' Raju said. 'And when we get to this garden, what do we do?'

'We give Daddy's friends at this garden ten rupees, and they will give us something daddy *really* needs.'

'What?'

She told him.

Raju, already shrewd with money, asked: 'How much will it cost?'

'Ten rupees, he said.'

'Did he give you ten rupees?'

'No. Daddy said we'll have to get it ourselves. We'll have to beg.'

As the two of them walked down Rose Lane, she kept her head to the ground and looked. Once she had found five rupees on the ground – yes, five! You never know what you'll find in a place where rich people live.

They moved to the side of the lane; a white car paused for a moment to go over a bump on the road, and she shouted at the driver:

'Where is the port, uncle?'

'Far from here,' he shouted back. 'Go to the main road, and take a left.'

The tinted windows in the back of the car were rolled up, but through the driver's window Soumya caught a glimpse of a passenger's hand covered with gold bangles; she wanted to knock on the window. But she remembered the rule that the foreman had laid down for all the workers' children. No begging in Rose Lane. Only on the main road. She controlled herself.

All the houses were being demolished and rebuilt in Rose Lane. Soumya wondered why people wanted to tear down these fine, large, whitewashed houses. Maybe houses became uninhabitable after some time, like shoes.

When the lights on the main road turned red, she went from autorickshaw to autorickshaw, opening and closing her fingers.

'Uncle, have pity, I'm starving.'

Her technique was solid. She had got it from her mother. It went like this: even as she begged, for three seconds she kept eye contact; her eye would begin to wander to the next autorickshaw. 'Mother, I'm hungry' (rubbing her tummy) 'give me food' (closing her fingers and bringing it to her mouth rapidly).

'Big Brother, I'm hungry.'

'Grandpa, even a small coin would—'

While she did the road, Raju sat on the ground and was meant to whimper when anyone well-dressed passed by. She did not count much on him; at least if he sat down he would stay out of other kinds of trouble, like running after cats, or trying to pet stray dogs that might be rabid.

Towards noon, the roads filled up with cars. The windows had been rolled up against the rain, and she had to raise both her hands to the glass, and scratch like a cat, to get attention. The windows in one car were rolled down, and she thought her luck had improved.

A woman in one of the cars had beautiful patterns of gold painted on her hands, and Soumya gaped at them. She heard the woman with the gold hands say to someone else in the car:

'There are beggars everywhere these days in the town. It never used to be this way.'

The other person leaned forward and stared for a moment. 'They're so *black* . . . Where are they from?'

'Who knows?'

Only fifty paise, after an hour of work.

Next she tried to get on the bus when it stopped at the red light, and beg there, but the conductor saw her coming and stood at the door: 'Nothing doing.'

'Why not, uncle?'

'Who do you think I am, a rich man like Mr. Engineer? Go ask someone else, you brat!'

Glaring at her, he raised his red cord of his whistle over his head as if it were a whip. She scrambled out.

'He was really a cock-sucker,' she told Raju, who had something to show her: a plastic wrapper, full of round buttons of air that could be popped.

Making sure the conductor couldn't see, she got down on her knees and put it right in front of the wheel. Raju crouched: 'No, it's not right. The wheels won't go over it,' he said. 'Push it to the right a little.'

When it moved again, the wheels of the bus went over the plastic perforation, and they exploded, and some of the passengers were startled, and the conductor poked his head out the window to see what had happened. The two children ran away.

It began raining again. The two of them crouched under a tree; the coconuts came crashing down, and a man who had been standing with an umbrella jumped like a frog, and swore at the tree, and ran. She giggled, but Raju was worried they would get hit by a falling coconut.

When the rain stopped, she found a twig and scratched on the ground, drawing a map of the city, as she imagined it. Here, was Rose Lane. Here, was where they had come, still close to Rose Lane. Here – was the port. And here – the garden within the port.

'Do you understand all of this?' She asked Raju. He nodded, excited by the map.

'To get to the port, we have to go—' she drew another arrow, 'through the big hotel.'

'And then?'

'And then we go to the garden in the port . . .'

'And then?'

'We find the thing Daddy wants us to get.'

'And then?'

The truth was, she had no idea if the hotel was on the way to the port or not: but the rain had driven away the vehicles from the road, and the hotel was the only place where she might be able to beg for the money right now.

'You have to ask for money in English from the tourists,' she teased Raju as they walked to the hotel. 'Do you know what to say in English?'

They stopped outside the hotel to watch a group of cows bathing in a puddle of water. The sun was shining on the water, and the black coats of the crows turned glossy as scintilla of water flew away from their shaking bodies. Raju declared it was the most beautiful thing he had ever seen.

The man with no arms and legs was sitting in front of the hotel; he yelled curses from the other side of the road.

'Go away, you devil's children! I told you never to come back here!'

She shouted back: 'To hell with you, monstrosity! We told *you*: never come back here!'

He was sitting on a wooden board with wheels. Whenever a car slowed down at the traffic light in front of the hotel, he rolled up on his wooden board and begged from one side; she begged from the other side of the car.

Raju, sitting on the pavement, yawned.

'Why do we need to beg? Daddy is working today. I saw him cutting those things—' he moved his legs apart and began sawing an imaginary crossbeam below him.

'Quiet.'

Two taxis slowed down near the red light. The man with no arms and legs rushed on his wooden board to the first taxi; she ran to the second one, and put her hands into the open window. A foreigner was sitting inside. He stared at her with an open mouth: she saw his lips making a perfect pink 'O.'

'Did you get any money?' Raju asked, when she came back from the car with the white man.

'No. Get up,' she said, and dragged the boy to his feet.

By the time they had crossed two red lights, however, Raju had it all figured out. He pointed to her clutched fist.

'You got money from the white man. You have the money!'

She went to one autorickshaw parked by the side of the road: 'Which way is the port?'

The driver yawned. 'I don't have any money. Go away.'

'I'm not asking for money. I'm asking for directions to the port.'

'I told you, I'm giving you nothing!'

She spat at his face. Then grabbed Raju by the wrist; they ran like mad.

The next autorickshaw driver they asked was a kind man. 'It's a long, long way. Why don't you take a bus? The no. 343 will get you there. Otherwise, it'll be a couple of hours at least, by foot.'

'We don't have money, uncle.'

He gave them a rupee coin, and asked: 'Where are your parents?'

They got into a bus, and paid the conductor. 'Where are you getting off?' he shouted.

'The port.'

'This bus doesn't go to the port. You need the no. 343. This is the number—'

They got out and walked.

They were near the Cool-Water Well Junction now. They found the one-armed, one-legged boy working there, as always; he went hopping about from car to car, begging before she could get there. Someone had given him a raddish today, so he went about begging with a large white raddish in his hand, tapping it on the windscreens to get the attention of the passengers.

'Don't you dare do any begging here, you sons of bitches!' he shouted at them, waving the raddish threateningly.

The two of them stuck their tongues out at him, and shouted: 'Freak! Disgusting freak!'

Raju began crying after an hour, and refused to walk anymore, so she picked in a rubbish can for some food. There was a carton with two biscuits, and they split the biscuits.

They walked some more. After a while, Raju's nostrils began bubbling.

'I can smell the port from here.'

She could, too.

They walked faster. They saw a man painting a sign in English by the side of the road; two cats fighting on the roof of a white Fiat car; a horse-cart, loaded with chopped wood; an elephant, walking down the road with a mound of neem leaves; a car that was smashed up in an accident; and a dead crow, belly-up with its claws drawn stiffly into its chest, whose belly was open, and swarming with black ants.

Then they were at the port.

The sun was setting over the sea, and they went past the packed markets, looking for an open park.

'There are no parks here, by the port. That's why the air is so bad here,' an old Muslim man, a seller of peanuts, told them. 'You've got the wrong directions.'

Looking at their crestfallen faces, he offered them a handful of peanuts to munch on.

Raju whined. He was hungry . . . to hell with the peanuts! He shoved them back at the Muslim man, who called him a devil.

That got Raju so angry he left his sister and ran, and she ran after him until Raju came to a stop.

'Look!' He shrieked, pointing a finger at a row of mutilated men with bandages on their limbs, sitting in front of a building with a white dome.

Gingerly they walked around the lepers. And then she saw a man lying down on a bench, with his palms crossed over his face, breathing heavily. She came near the bench, and found, right at the water's edge, fenced off by a small stone wall, a little green park.

Raju was quiet now.

When they got to the park, there was shouting. A policeman was slapping a very dark man. 'Did you steal the shoes? Did you?'

The dark man shook his head. The policeman hit him harder. 'Son of a bald woman, you take these drugs, and then you steal things, and you – son of a bald woman, you—!'

Three white-haired men, sitting in a bush to her side, gestured to Soumya to come and hide with them. She took Raju into the bush, and they waited there for the policeman to leave.

She whispered to the three white-haired men: 'I'm the daughter of Ramachandran, the man who smashes rich people's houses in Rose Lane.'

None of three knew her father. 'What do you want, little girl?'

She said the word, as well as she could remember: '. . . *smack*.'

One of the men, who appeared to be their leader, frowned: 'Repeat it.'

He nodded when she said it the second time. Taking out a pouch made of newspaper-skin from his pocket, he tapped it: white powder, like crushed chalk, poured out. He then took out a cigarette from his pocket, sliced it open, tapped out the tobacco, filled the white powder inside it, and rolled it close. He held the cigarette up in the air, and gestured with his other hand to Soumya.

'Twelve rupees.'

'I've got only nine,' she said. 'You'll have to take nine.'

'Ten.'

She gave them the money; she took the cigarette. A horrible doubt seized her.

'If you're robbing me, if you're cheating me – Raju and I'll come back with Daddy – and beat you all.' The three men crouched together. They began shivering, and they were laughing together. Something was wrong with them. She grabbed Raju by the wrist and they ran.

Glimpses of the scene to come flashed through her mind. She would show Daddy what she had brought for him from so far away. 'Sweetie,' he would say – the way he used to say it – and hold her in a frenzy of affection, and the two would go mad with love for each other.

Her left foot began to burn after a while, and she flexed her toes and stared at them. Raju insisted on being carried; fair enough, she thought – that little fellow had done well today.

It began raining again. Raju cried. She had to threaten to leave him behind three times; once she actually left him and walked a whole block before he came running after her, telling her of a giant dragon that was chasing him.

They got on to a bus.

'Tickets,' the driver shouted, but she winked at him and said: 'Brother, let us on for free, please . . .'

His face softened, and he let them stay near the back.

It was pitch black when they got back to Rose Lane. They saw the lamps in all the mansions lit up. The foreman was sitting under his gas lamp, talking to one of the workers. The house looked smaller: all the crossbeams had been sawed off.

'Did you go begging in this neighbourhood?' the foreman shouted, when he saw the two of them.

'No, we didn't.'

'Don't lie to me! You were gone all day – and doing what? Begging on Rose Lane!'

She raised her upper lip in contempt.

'Why don't you ask if we begged here, before accusing us of something!'

The foreman glared at them, but kept quiet, defeated by the girl's logic.

Raju ran ahead, screaming for his mother. They found their mother asleep, alone, in her rain-dampened sari. Raju ran up to her, butted his head into her side, and began rubbing against her body for warmth, like a kitten; the sleeping woman groaned and turned over to the other side. One of her arms began swatting away Raju's face.

'Amma,' he said, shaking her. 'Amma! I'm hungry! Soumya gave me nothing to eat all day! She made me walk and walk and take this bus and that, and no food! A white man gave her hundred rupees but she never gave me anything to eat or drink.'

'Don't lie!' Soumya hissed. 'What about the biscuits?'

But he kept shaking her: 'Amma! Soumya gave me nothing to eat or drink all day!'

The two children began wrestling each other. Then a hand lightly tapped Soumya's shoulder.

'Sweetie.'

When he saw their father, Raju began to simper; he turned and ran away to his mother. Soumya and her father walked to a side.

'Do you have it, sweetie? Do you have the thing?'

She drew air. 'Here,' she said, and let the packet into his hands. He took it to his nose, sniffed, and then put it under his shirt: she saw his hands reach through his sarong into his groin. He took his hand out. She knew it was coming now: his caress.

He caught her wrist; his fingers cut into her flesh.

'What about the hundred rupees the white man gave you? Where is the money?'

'He didn't give me a hundred rupees, Daddy. I swear. Raju is lying, I swear.'

'Don't lie. Where is the hundred rupees?'

He raised his arm. She began screaming.

When she came to lie down next to her mother, Raju was still complaining that he had not been fed all day long, and forced to walk from here to there. He saw the red marks on her face and neck, and went silent. She fell to the ground, and went to sleep.

**KITTUR** Total Population (1981 census): 193,432 residents
Caste and religious breakdown (as % of total population):
Hindus:
Forward castes
    Brahmins: Kannada-speaking: 4 per cent
    Konkani-speaking: 3 per cent
    Tulu-speaking: less than 1 per cent
    Bunts: 16 per cent
    Other upper castes: 1 per cent
Backward castes
    Hoykas: 24 per cent
    Miscellaneous backward castes and tribals: 4 per cent
Dalits: 9 per cent
Minorities:
Muslims
    Sunni: 14 per cent
    Shia: 1 per cent
    Ahmediya, Bohra, Ismaili: less than 1 per cent
Catholics: 14 per cent
Protestants (Anglicans, Pentecostals, Jehovah's Witnesses, Mormons): 3 per cent
Jains: 1 per cent
Other religions (including Parsi, Jew, Buddhist, Brahmo Samaji, and Baha'ii): less than 1 per cent
89 residents declare themselves to be without religion or caste.

# DAY FIVE: VALENCIA (TO THE FIRST CROSSROAD)

*Valencia, the Catholic neighbourhood, begins with Father Stein's Homeopathy Hospital, which is named after a German Jesuit missionary who began a hospice here. Valencia is the largest neighbourhood of Kittur; most of its inhabitants are educated, employed, and owners of their homes. The handful of Hindus and Muslims who have bought land in Valencia have never encountered any trouble, but Protestants looking for a home here have sometimes been attacked with stones and slogans. Every Sunday morning, men and women in their best clothing stream into the Cathedral of our Lady of Valencia for mass. On Christmas Eve, virtually the entire population crams into the Cathedral for midnight mass; the singing of carols and hymns goes on for hours.*

When it came to troubles seen and horrors experienced, Jayamma, the advocate's cook, wanted it known that her life had been second to none. In a space of twelve years her dear mother had given birth to eleven children. Nine of them had been girls. Yes, nine! Now *that's* trouble. By the time Jayamma was born, number eight, there was no milk in her mother's breasts – they had to feed her an ass's milk in a plastic bottle. An ass's milk, yes! Now *that's* trouble. Her father had saved enough gold only for six daughters to be married off; the last three had to stay barren virgins for life. Yes, for life. For forty years she'd been put on one bus or the other, and sent from one town to the next to cook and clean in someone else's house. To feed and fatten someone else's children. She wasn't even told where she'd be going next; it'd be night, she'd playing with her nephew – that roly-poly little fellow Brijju – and what would she hear in the living room but her sister-in-law tell some stranger or the other, 'It's a done deal, then. If she stays here, she eats food for nothing; so you're doing us a favour, believe me.' The next day Jayamma would be put on the bus again. Months would pass before she saw Brijju again. This was Jayamma's life, an instalment-plan of troubles and horrors. Who had worse to complain about on this earth?

At least one horror was coming to an end. Jayamma was about to leave the advocate's house.

She was a short, stooped woman in her late fifties, with a glossy silver head of hair that seemed to give off light. A large black wart over her left eyebrow was the kind that gets taken for an auspicious sign when found on infants. There were always pouches of dark skin under her eyes, shaped like garlic cloves, and her eyeballs were rheumy from chronic sleeplessness and worry.

She had packed up her things: one big brown suitcase, the same one she had come there with. Nothing more. Not a paisa had been stolen from the advocate, although the house was sometimes in a mess, and there sure had been the opportunity. But she had been honest. She brought the suitcase to the front porch, and waited for the advocate's green Ambassador. He had promised to drop her off at the bus station.

'Goodbye, Jayamma. Are you leaving us for real?'

Shaila, the little lower-caste servant-girl in the advocate's house – and Jayamma's principal tormentor of the past eight months – grinned. Although she was twelve, and ready for marriage next year, she looked only seven or eight. Her dark face was caked with Johnson's baby powder, and she batted her eyelids mockingly.

'You lower-caste demon!' Jayamma hissed. 'Mind your manners!'

An hour later, the advocate's car pulled into the garage.

'Don't you know yet?' he said, when Jayamma came towards him with her bag. 'I told your sister-in-law we could use you a bit longer, and she agreed. I thought someone would have informed you.'

He slammed his car-door shut. Then he went to take his bath, and Jayamma took her old brown suitcase back into the kitchen and began preparing for dinner.

*

'I'm never going to leave the advocate's house, am I, Lord Krishna?'

The next morning, the old woman was standing over the gas burner in the kitchen, stirring the lentil stew. As she worked, she sucked air in with a hiss, as if her tongue were on fire.

'For forty years I've lived among good Brahmins, Lord Krishna: homes in which even the lizards and the toads had

159

been Brahmins in a previous birth. Now you see my fate, to be stuck among Christians and meat-eaters in this strange town, and each time I think I'm leaving, I'm told by my sister-in-law to stay some more . . .'

She wiped her forehead, and went on to ask: what had she done in a previous life – had she been a murderess, an adulteress, a child-devourer, a person who was rude to holy men and sages – to have been fated to come here, to the advocate's house, and live next to a lower caste?

She sizzled onions, chopped coriander and threw them into the broth, then stirred in red curry powder and Monosodium glutamate from little plastic packets.

'Hai! Hai!'

Jayamma started, and dropped her ladle into the broth. She went to the grille that ran along the rear end of the advocate's house, and peered.

Shaila was at the outer wall of the compound, clapping her hands, while next door in the Christian neighbour's backyard, thick-lipped Rosie, a cleaving knife in her hand, was running after a rooster. Slowly unbolting the door, Jayamma crept out into the backyard, to take a better look. 'Hai! Hai! Hai,' Shaila was shouting in glee, while the rooster clicked and clucked, and jumped on the green net over the well, where Rosie finally caught the poor thing, and began slicing its neck. The rooster's tongue stuck out; its face turned red, and its eyes almost popped out. 'Hai! Hai! Hai!'

Jayamma ran through the kitchen, straight into the dark prayer room, and bolted the door behind her. 'Krishna . . . my Lord Krishna . . .'

The prayer room doubled as a storage room for rice, and also as Jayamma's private quarters. The room was seven feet by seven feet; the little space in between the shrine and the rice bags, just enough to curl up in and go to sleep at night, was all Jayamma had asked from the advocate. (She had refused point-blank to take up the advocate's initial suggestion that she share a room with the lower caste in the servants' quarters.)

She reached into the prayer shrine, and took out a black box whose cover she opened slowly. Inside was a silver idol of a child god – crawling, naked, and with shiny buttocks – the god Krishna, Jayamma's only friend and protector.

'Krishna, Krishna,' she chanted softly, holding the baby god in her hands again, and rubbing its silver buttocks with her fingers. 'You see what goes on around me – me, a high-born Brahmin woman!'

She sat down on one of three rice bags lined up against the wall of the prayer room, and surrounded by yellow moats of DDT. Folding her legs up on the rice-bag, and leaning her head against the wall, she took in deep breaths of the DDT – a strange, relaxing, powerfully addictive aroma. She sighed; she wiped her forehead with the edge of a vermilion sari. Spots of sunlight, filtering through the plantain trees outside, played along the ceiling of the little room.

Jayamma closed her eyes. The fragrance of DDT made her drowsy; her body uncoiled, her limbs loosened, she was asleep in seconds.

When she woke up, fat little Karthik, the advocate's son was shining a torchlight on her face. This was his way of rousing her from a nap.

161

'I'm hungry,' he said. 'Is anything ready?'

'Brother!' The old woman sprang up in one bound. 'There's black magic in the backyard! Shaila and Rosie have killed a chicken – and they're doing black magic.'

The boy turned the torchlight off. He looked at her sceptically.

'What are you talking about, you old hag?'

'Come,' the old cook's eyes were large with excitement. 'Come!'

She coaxed the little master down the long hallway into the servants' quarters.

They stopped by the metal grille which gave them a view of the backyard. There were short coconut trees, and a clothesline, and a black wall beyond which began the compound of their Christian neighbour. There was no one around. A strong wind shook the trees, and a loose sheet of paper was swirling around the backyard, like a dervish. The boy saw the white bedsheets on the clothesline swaying eerily. They too seemed to suspect what the cook suspected.

Jayamma motioned to Karthik: be very, very quiet. She pushed the door to the servants' quarters. It was bolted shut.

When the old woman unlocked it, a stench of hair oil and baby powder wafted out, and the boy clamped his nostrils.

Jayamma pointed to the floor of the room.

A triangle in white chalk had been marked inside a square in red chalk, dried coconut flesh crowned the points of the triangle. Withered, blackening flowers were strewn about inside the circle. A blue marble gleamed from its heart.

'It's for black magic,' she said, and the boy nodded.

'Spies! Spies!' Shaila stood athwart the door of the servant's room. She made a finger at Jayamma. 'You – you old hag! Didn't I tell you never to snoop around my room again?'

The old lady's face twitched. 'Brother!' she shouted. 'Did you see how this lower-caste speaks to us Brahmins?'

Karthik made a fist at the girl. 'Hey! This is my house, and I'll go wherever I want to, you hear!'

Shaila glared at him: 'Don't think you can treat me like an animal, okay . . .'

Three loud honks ended all the fighting. Shaila flew out to open the gate; the boy ran into his room and opened a textbook; Jayamma dashed around the dining room, laying down stainless-steel plates on the table in panic.

The master of the house removed his shoes in the entrance hall and threw them in the direction of the shoe rack. Shaila would have to rearrange them later. A quick wash in his private bathroom, and he emerged into the dining room, a tall, moustachioed man who cultivated flowing sideburns in the style of a previous decade. At dinner he was always bare-chested, except for the Brahmin caste-string winding around his flabby torso. He ate quickly and in silence, pausing once to stare at a corner of the ceiling. The house was put in order by the motions of the master's mandibles. Jayamma served. Karthik ate with his father. In the car shed, Shaila hosed down the master's green Ambassador and wiped it clean.

The advocate read the paper in the television room for an hour, and then the boy strolled and began searching for the black remote control in the mess of papers and books on

163

the sandalwood table in the centre of the room. Jayamma and Shaila at once scrambled into the room, and squatted in a corner, waiting for the television to come on.

At ten o'clock, all the lights in the house went out. The master and Karthik slept in their rooms.

In the darkness, a vicious hissing continued in the servants' quarters:

'Witch! Witch! Black-magic-making lower-caste witch!'

'Old hag! Mad old hag!'

A week of non-stop fighting followed. Each time Shaila passed by the kitchen, the old Brahmin cook showered vengeful deities by the thousand down on that oily lower-caste head.

'What kind of era is this when Brahmins bring lower-caste girls into their household?' she grumbled as she stirred the lentils in the morning. 'Where have the rules of caste and religion fallen today, O Krishna?'

'Talking to yourself again, old Virgin?' The girl had popped her head into the kitchen; Jayamma threw an unpeeled onion at her.

Lunch. Truce. The girl put out her stainless-steel plate outside the servant's living room and squatted on the floor, while Jayamma served out generous portions of the lentils over the mound of white rice on the girl's plate. She wouldn't starve anyone, she grumbled as she served, not even a sworn enemy. That's right: not even a sworn enemy. It wasn't the Brahmin way of doing things.

After lunch, putting on her glasses, she spread a copy of the newspaper just in front of the servants' quarters. Sucking air constantly, she read loudly and slowly, piecing letters into words and words into sentences. When Shaila passed by, she thrust the paper at her face.

'Here – you can read and write, can't you? Here, read the paper!'

The girl fumed; she went back to the servants' quarters and slammed the door.

'Do you think I've forgotten the trick you played on the advocate, you little lower-caste? He's a kind-hearted man, so that's why, one evening you go to him with your simpering lower-caste face and say, Sir, I can't read. I can't write. I want to read. I want to write. Doesn't he, immediately, drive out to Shenoy's Book Store in Umbrella Street and buy you expensive reading-and-writing books? And all for what? Were the lower castes meant to read and write?' Jayamma demanded of the closed door. 'Wasn't that all just a trap for the advocate?'

Sure enough, the girl lost all interest in her books. They lay in a heap in the back of her room, and one day when she was chatting up the thick-lipped Christian, Jayamma sold them all to the scrap-paper Muslim. Ha! Showed her!

As Jayamma narrated the story of the infamous reading-and-writing scam, the door to the servants' quarters opened; Shaila popped her face out, and screamed at the top of her voice.

That evening the advocate spoke up during dinner:

'I hear there's been some disturbance or the other every day in the house . . . it's important to keep things quiet. Karthik has to prepare for his exams.'

Jayamma, who had been carrying the lentil-stew away using the edge of her sari as a heat-pad, put the stew down on the table.

'It's not me making the noise, master – it's that Hoyka girl! She doesn't know our Brahmin ways.'

'She may be a Hoyka,' the advocate licked the rice-grains clinging to his fingers, 'but she is clean, and works well.'

As she cleaned the table after dinner, Jayamma trembled from the reproach.

Only once the lights were off in the house, and she lay in the prayer room with the familiar fumes of DDT about her, and opened the little black box, did she calm down. The baby God was smiling at her.

O, when it came to troubles and horrors, Krishna, who had seen what Jayamma had seen? She told the patient deity the story of how she came to Kittur; how her sister-in-law had commanded her – 'Jayamma, you have to leave us and go, the advocate's wife is in a hospital in Bangalore, someone has to take care of little Karthik' – that was supposed to be just a month or two. Now, it had been eight months since she had seen her little nephew Brijju, or held him in her arms, or played cricket with him. Oh yes, *these* were troubles, Baby Krishna.

The next morning, she dropped her ladle in the lentils again. Karthik had poked her midriff from behind.

She followed him out of the kitchen, and into the servants' room. She watched the boy as he looked at the diagram on the floor and the blue marble at the centre of it.

In his eyes the old servant saw the gleam – the possessive gleam of masters that she had seen so many times in the past forty years.

'Look at that.' Karthik said. 'The nerve of that girl, drawing this thing in my house . . .'

The crouching pair sat down by the yellow grille, and watched Shaila move along the far wall of the compound towards the Christian's house. A wide well, covered with green netting, made a bump in the back of the Christian's house. Hens and roosters, hidden by the wall, ran around the well and clucked incessantly. Rosie was at the wall. Shaila and the Christian talked for a while. It was a brilliant, flickering afternoon. As the light emerged and retreated at rapid intervals, the glossy green canopies of the coconut trees blazed and dimmed like bursts of fireworks.

The girl wandered aimlessly after Rosie left. They saw her bending by the jasmine plants to tear a few flowers off, and put them in her hair. A little while later, Jayamma saw Karthik begin to scratch his leg in long, shearing strokes, like a bear scratching the sides of a tree. From his thighs, his rasping fingers moved upward towards his groin. Jayamma watched with a sense of disgust. What would the boy's mother say, if she could see what he was doing right now?

The girl was walking by the clothesline. The thin cotton sheets hung out to dry turned incandescent, like cinema screens, when the light emerged from the clouds. Inside one of the glowing sheets, the girl made a round, dark bulge, like a thing inside a womb. A keening noise rose from the white sheet. She had begun singing:

*A star is whispering*
*Of my heart's deep longing*
*To see you once more,*
*my baby-child, my darling, my king.*

'I know that nursery rhyme . . . My brother's wife sings it to Brijju . . . my little nephew . . .'

'Quiet. She'll hear you.'

Shaila had re-emerged from the hanging clothes. She drifted towards the far end of the backyard, where neem trees mingled with coconut palms.

'Does she think about her mother and sisters often, I wonder . . .' Jayamma mumbled. 'What kind of a life is this for a girl, away from her family?'

'I'm tired of this waiting!' Karthik grumbled.

'Brother, wait!'

But he was already in the servant's room. A triumphant shriek: Karthik came out with the blue marble.

*

In the evening, Jayamma was on the threshold of the kitchen, winnowing rice. Her glasses had slid halfway down her nose, and her brow was furrowed. She turned towards the servants' room, which was bolted from the inside, and inside which someone was sobbing, and said:

'Stop crying. You've got to get tough. Servants like us, who work for others, have to learn to be tough.'

Swallowing her tears audibly, Shaila shouted back through the bolted door:

'Shut up, you self-pitying old hag! You told Karthik I had black magic!'

'Don't accuse me of things like that! I never told him you did black magic!'

'Liar! Liar!'

'Don't call me a liar, you lower-caste! Why do you draw triangles on the ground, if not to practice black magic! You didn't fool me for a minute!'

'Can't you see those triangles were just part of a game? Are you losing your mind, you old hag?'

Jayamma slammed the winnow down; the rice-grains were splattered about the threshold. She went into the prayer room, and closed the door.

She woke up and heard a sob-drenched monologue: it was coming from the servants' quarters, and it was so loud that it had penetrated the wall of the prayer room.

'I don't want to be here . . . I didn't want to leave my friends, and our fields, and our cows, and come here. But my mother said, "You have to go to the city and work for the Advocate Panchinalli, otherwise, where will you get the gold necklace? And who will marry you without a gold necklace?" But ever since I came, I've seen no gold necklace – just trouble, trouble, trouble!'

Jayamma shouted into the wall at once: 'Trouble, trouble, trouble – see how she talks like an old woman! This is nothing, your misfortune. I've seen real trouble!'

The sobbing stopped. Jayamma told the lower caste a few of her own troubles. At dinner, Jayamma came with the trough of rice to the servants' living room. She banged on the door, but Shaila would not open.

'Oh, what a haughty little miss she is!'

She kept banging on the door, until it opened. Then she served the girl rice and lentil-stew, and watched to make sure that it was eaten.

169

The next morning, the two servants were sitting at the threshold together.

'Say, Jayamma, what's the news of the world?'

Shaila was beaming. Flowers in her hair, and Johnson's powder on her face again. Jayamma looked up from the paper with a scornful expression.

'Oh, why do you ask me, you can read and write, can't you?'

'C'mon, Jayamma, you know we lower castes aren't meant to do things like that . . .' The little girl smiled ingratiatingly. 'If you Brahmins don't read for us, where will we learn anything . . .'

'Sit down,' the old woman said. She turned the pages over slowly, and read out from the news items that interested her.

'They say that in Tumkur District, a holy man has mastered the art of flying through willpower, and can go seventeen feet up in the air and bring himself down.'

'Really?' The girl was sceptical. 'Has anyone actually seen him do this, or are they simply believing him?'

'Of course they saw him do it!' Jayamma retorted, tapping on the news item as proof. 'Haven't you ever seen magic being done?'

Shaila giggled hysterically; then she ran into the backyard, and dashed into the coconut trees; and then Jayamma heard the song again.

She waited till Shaila came back to the house, and said: 'What will your husband think, if he sees you looking like a savage? Your hair is a mess.'

So the girl sat down on the threshold, and Jayamma oiled her hair, and combed it into gleaming black threshes that would set any man's heart on fire.

At eight o'clock the old lady and the girl went together to watch TV. They watched till ten, then came back to their rooms when Karthik switched off the TV.

Halfway through the night, Shaila woke up to see the door to her room pushed open.

'Sister . . .'

Through the darkness Shaila saw a silver-haired head peering in.

'Sister . . . let me spend the night here . . . there are ghosts outside the storage room, yes . . .'

Almost crawling into the servants' quarters, Jayamma, breathing hard and sweating profusely, propped herself against a wall of the room and sank her head into her knees. The girl went out to see what was happening in the storage room; she came back giggling.

'Jayamma . . . those aren't ghosts, those are just two cats, fighting in the Christian's house . . . that's all . . .'

But the old lady was already asleep, her silver hair spread out on the ground.

From then on, Jayamma began coming at regular intervals to sleep in Shaila's room, whenever she heard the two screeching cat-demons outside her room.

*

It was the day before the Navarathri festival. Still no word from home, or from the advocate, about when she was going home. The price of jaggery had gone up again. So had kerosene. Jayamma read in the papers that a holy man had learnt to fly from tree to tree in a grove in Kerala – but only if the trees were arecanut trees. There was going to be a partial solar eclipse the next year, and that might signal the end of the earth.

That night, after dinner, Jayamma proposed to the advocate that she take Karthik to the Kittamma Devi temple near the train station on the holy day.

'He should not fall out of the habit of prayer now that his mother is no more, should he?' she said meekly.

'That's a good idea . . .' the advocate picked up his newspaper.

Jayamma breathed in for courage.

'If you could give me a few rupees towards the rickshaw . . .'

She knocked on the little girl's room. She opened her fist triumphantly.

'Five rupees! The advocate gave me five rupees!'

Jayamma took a bath in the servants' toilet, lathering herself thoroughly in sandalwood soap. Changing from her vermilion sari into her purple one, she walked up to the boy's room relishing the fragrance of her own skin, feeling like someone important.

'Get dressed, brother – we'll miss the five o'clock pooja.'

The boy was on his bed, punching the buttons of a small handheld electronic game – Bip! Bip! Bip!

'I'm not coming.'

'Brother – it's a temple. We should go!'

'No.'

'Brother . . . What would your mother say . . .'

The boy put his game down for a second. He walked up to the door of his room, and slammed it in Jayamma's face.

She lay in the storage room, seeking comfort in the fumes of DDT and the sight of the Baby Krishna's silver buttocks. The door creaked open. A small black face, coated in Johnson's baby powder, smiled at her.

'Jayamma – Jayamma – take me to the temple instead of him . . .'

The two of them sat quietly in the autorickshaw.

'Wait here,' Jayamma said at the entrance to the temple. She bought a packet of flowers with fifty paise of her own money.

'Here,' she guided the girl to place the basket in the hands of the priest when they were in the temple.

A throng of devotees had gathered around the silver linga. Little boys jumped high to strike the temple bells around the deity. They struggled in vain, and then their fathers hoicked them up. Jayamma caught Shaila leaping high at a bell.

'Shall I lift you up?'

At five, the pooja got underway. Flames rose from camphor cubes. Two women blew giant conches; a brass gong was struck, faster and faster. Then, one of the Brahmins rushed out with a copper plate that burned at one end, and Jayamma dropped a coin in it, while the girl reached forward with her palms for the holy fire.

173

The two of them sat out on the verandah of the temple, on whose walls the giant drums that were played at weddings were strung up. Jayamma remarked on the scandal of a woman decked in a sleeveless blouse heading towards the temple gate. Shaila thought the sleeveless style was quite 'sporty.' A screaming child was being pulled along by her father to the temple door. She quietened down when Jayamma and Shaila both began petting her.

The two women left the temple reluctantly. Birds rose up from the trees as the two waited for a rickshaw. Bands of incandescent clouds piled up one above the other like military decorations as the sun set. Jayamma began fighting with the rickshaw-driver over the price to go home, and Shaila giggled by the side, the whole time, infuriating the old woman and the driver alike.

*

'Jayamma – have you heard the Big News?'

The old lady looked up from the newspaper spread out on the threshold. She removed her glasses and blinked at the girl.

'About the price of jaggery?'

'No, not that.'

'About the price of wild rice, then?'

'No, not that, either.' The girl grinned shyly. 'I'm getting married.'

Jayamma's lips parted. She turned her head down, took off her glasses, rubbed her eyes.

'When?'

'Next month. The marriage has been fixed. The advocate told me this yesterday. He will send my gold necklace directly to my village.'

'So you think you're a queen now, huh?' Jayamma snapped. 'Because you're getting hitched to some village bumpkin!'

She saw Shaila run to the wall to spread the tidings to the Christian. 'I'm getting married, I'm getting married,' the girl sung sweetly all day long.

Jayamma cautioned her from the kitchen:

'You think it's any big deal being married? Don't you know what happened to my sister, Ambika?'

But the girl was too full of herself to listen. She just sang all day:

'I'm getting married, I'm getting married!'

So at night, it was the Baby Krishna who got to hear the story of the luckless Ambika, punished for her sins in a previous life:

Ambika, the sixth daughter and the last to get married, was the family beauty. A rich doctor wanted her for his son. Excellent news! When the groom came to see Ambika, he left for the bathroom repeatedly. 'See how shy he is,' the women all giggled. On the wedding night, he lay with his back turned to Ambika's face. He coughed all night. In the morning, she saw blood on the sheets. He notified her that she had married a man with advanced tuberculosis. He had wanted to be honest, but his mother would not allow that. 'Someone has put black magic on your family, you wretched girl,' he said, as his body was wracked by fits of coughing. A month later, he was dead on a hospital bed. His mother told the village that the girl, and all her sisters, were cursed; and no one would agree to marry any of the other children.

'And that's the true story of why I'm a virgin,' Jayamma wanted the infant Krishna to know. 'In fact, I had such thick hair, such golden skin, I was considered a beauty, you know that?' She raised her eyebrows archly, like a film actress, feeling somehow that the little god did not believe her entirely. 'Sometimes I thank my stars I never married. What if I too had been deceived, like Ambika? Better a spinster than a widow, any day . . . And yet that little lower caste can't stop singing about it every minute of the morning . . .' Lying in the dark, Jayamma mimicked the little lower caste's voice for the baby god's benefit:

'I'm getting married, I'm getting married . . .'

The day came for Shaila's departure. The advocate said he would himself drive the girl home in his green Ambassador.

'I'm going, *Jayamma.*'

The old lady was brushing her silver hair on the threshold. She felt that Shaila was pronouncing the name with deliberate tartness. 'I'm going to get married.' The old lady kept brushing her hair. 'Write to me sometime, won't you, Jayamma? You Brahmins are such fine letter writers, the best of the best . . .'

Jayamma tossed the plastic comb to a corner of the storage room. 'To hell with you, you little lower-caste vermin!'

The weeks passed. Now she had to do the girl's work too. By the time dinner was served and the dishes cleaned, she was spent. The advocate made no mention of hiring a new servant. She understood that from now on, it was up to her to perform a lower caste's work too.

*

In the evenings, she took to wandering in the backyard with her long silver hair streaming down the sides. One evening, Rosie, the thick-lipped Christian, waved at her.

'What happened to Shaila? Did she get married?'

Thrown into confusion, Jayamma grinned.

She started watching Rosie. How carefree those Christians were – eating whatever they wanted, marrying and divorcing whenever they felt like it.

One night the two demons came back. She lay paralyzed for many minutes, listening to the screeching of the two spirits, which had disguised themselves as cats once again. She clutched the idol of Baby Krishna, rubbing its silver buttocks fervently while sitting on a bag of rice surrounded by the moat of DDT; she began singing:

*A star is whispering*
*of my heart's deep longing*
*To see you once more,*
*my baby-child, my darling, my king . . .*

That next evening, the advocate spoke to her at dinner. He had received a letter from Shaila's mother.

'They said they were not happy with the size of the gold necklace. After I spent two thousand rupees on it, can you believe it?'

'Some people are never satisfied, master . . . What can be done?'

He scratched his bare chest with his left hand and belched loudly. 'In this life, a man is always the servant of his servants.'

That night she could not go to sleep from anxiety. What if the advocate cheated her out of her pay too?

'For you!' One morning, Karthik tossed a letter on to the rice-winnower. Jayamma shook the grains of rice off it, and tore it open with trembling fingers. Only one person in the world ever wrote her letters – her sister-in-law in Salt Market Village. Spreading it down on the ground, she put together the words one by one.

'The advocate has let it be known that he intends to move to Bangalore. You, of course, will be sent back to us. Do not expect to stay here long; we are already looking for another house to dispatch you to.'

She folded the letter slowly, and tucked it into her sari at the midriff. It felt like a slap to her face: the advocate had not bothered telling her the news. 'Well, let it be, who am I to him, just another servant woman.'

A week later, he came into the storage room, and stood at the threshold, as Jayamma got up hurriedly, trying to put her hair in order. 'Your money has been sent already, to your sister-in-law in Salt Market Village,' he said.

This was the usual agreement anywhere Jayamma worked; the wages were never to come to her directly.

The advocate paused.

'The boy needs someone to take care of him . . . I have relatives in Bangalore . . .'

'I only hope for the best for you and for Master Karthik,' she said, bowing before him with slow dignity.

That Sunday, she had collected all her belongings over the past year into the same red suitcase with which she had come to the house. The only sad part was saying goodbye to the Baby Krishna.

The advocate was not going to drop her off; she would walk to the bus stand herself. The bus was not due till four o'clock, and she walked about the backyard, amidst the swaying garments on the clothesline. She thought of Shaila – that girl had been running around this backyard, her hair loose, like an irresponsible brat; and now she was a married woman, the mistress of a household. Everyone changed and moved up in life, she thought. Only I stay the same: a virgin. She turned to the house with a sombre thought:

'This is the last time I will see this house, where I have spent more than a year of my life.'

She remembered all the houses she had been sent to, these past forty years, so that she could fatten other people's children. She had taken back nothing from her time at all in those houses; she was still unmarried, childless, and penniless. Like a glass from which clean water had been drunk, her life showed no traces of the years that had passed – except that her body had grown ancient, her eyes were weak, and her knee joints ached. Nothing will ever change for me till I die, thought old Jayamma.

All at once, her gloom was gone. She had seen a blue rubber ball, half-hidden behind a hibiscus plant in the backyard. It looked like one of the balls Karthik played cricket with; had it been left out here because it was punctured? Jayamma brought it right up to her nose for a good examination. Although she could not see a hole anywhere, when she squeezed it next to her cheek, she felt a tickling hiss of air on her skin.

With a servant's instinct for caution, the old cook glanced around the garden. Breathing in deep, she tossed the blue ball to the side of the house; it smacked the wall and came back to her with a single bounce.

Good enough!

Jayamma turned the ball over and examined its skin, faded but still with a nice blue gloss. She sniffed it. It would do very nicely.

She came to Karthik, who was in his room, on the bed: Bip! Bip! Bip! She thought how much he resembled the image of his mother in photographs when he beetled his brow to concentrate on the game; the mark in his brow was like a bookmark left there by the dead woman.

'Brother . . .'

'Hm?'

'I'm leaving for my brother's home today . . . I'm going back to my village. I'm not coming back.'

'Hm.'

'May the blessings of your dear mother shine on you always.'

'Hm.'

'Brother . . .'

'What is it?' his voice crackled with irritation. 'Why are you always pestering me?'

'Brother . . . that blue ball out in the garden, the one that's punctured, you don't use it, do you?'

'No.'

'. . . Can I take that with me for my little Brijju? He loves playing cricket, but sometimes there's no money to buy a ball . . .'

'No.'

The boy did not look up. He punched the buttons on his game.

Bip!

Bip!

Bip!

'Brother . . . you gave the lower-caste girl a golden necklace . . . can't you give me just a blue ball for Brijesh?'

Bip!

Bip!

Bip!

Jayamma thought with horror of all the food she had fed this fat creature, how it was the sweat of her brow, dripping into the lentil-broth in the heat of that little kitchen, that had nourished him until here he was, round and plump, like an animal bred in the backyard of a Christian's house. She had a vision of chasing this fat little boy with a meat-cleaver; she saw herself catch him by the hair and raise the cleaver over his pleading head. Bang! She brought it down on him – his tongue spread out, his features bulged out, and he was . . .

The old lady shuddered.

'You are a motherless child, and a Brahmin. I don't want to think badly of you . . . farewell, brother . . .'

181

She went out into the garden with her red bag, shooting a final glance at the ball. She went to the gate, and stopped. Her eyes were full of the tears of the righteous. The sun jeered at her from between the trees.

Just then, Rosie came out of the Christian's house. She stopped and watched the bag in Jayamma's hand. She spoke. For a moment Jayamma couldn't understand a word, then the Christian's message sounded clear and loud in her mind.

*Take the ball, you Brahmin fool!*

Swaying coconut palms rushed past. Jayamma was on the bus back to Salt Market Village, sitting next to a woman who was returning from the sacred city of Benares. Jayamma could pay no attention to the holy lady's stories about the great temples she had seen . . . her thoughts were all on the thing she was concealing in her sari, tucked into her tummy . . . the blue ball with the small hole . . . the one she had just stolen . . . She could not believe that she, Jayamma, the daughter of good Brahmins of Salt Market Village, had done such a thing!

The holy woman next to her fell asleep after a while. Her snoring filled Jayamma with fear for her soul. What would the gods do to her, as the bus rattled on a mud road; what would she be in the next life? A cockroach, a silverfish that lived in old books, an earthworm, a maggot in a pile of cowshit, something even filthier.

Then she had a strange thought: maybe if she sinned enough in this life, she would be sent back as a Christian in the next one . . .

The thought made her feel light-headed with joy; she felt so good she dozed off at once.

## DAY FIVE (EVENING): THE CATHEDRAL OF OUR LADY OF VALENCIA

*It cannot be explained easily why the Cathedral of Our Lady of Valencia still remains incomplete, despite so many attempts and so much money being sent from expatriates working in Kuwait. The original baroque structure dating to 1691 was entirely rebuilt in 1890. Only one bell tower was left incomplete, and remains incomplete to the present day. Scaffolding has covered the north tower almost continuously since 1981; work resumes fitfully, and stops again, either because of the lack of funds, or the death of an important priest. Even in its incomplete state, the Cathedral is considered the most important tourist attraction of Kittur. Of particular interest are the frescoes of the miraculously preserved corpse of St. Francis Xavier painted on the ceiling of the central chapel, and the colossal mural entitled* An Allegory of Europe Bringing Science and Enlightenment into the East Indies *behind the altar.*

George D'Souza, the mosquito-man, had caught himself a princess. Evidence for this claim would be produced at sunset, when work ended on the Cathedral. Until then George was only going to suck on his watermelon, drop hints to his friends, and grin.

He was sitting on a pyramid-shaped mound of granite stones in the compound in front of the Cathedral, with his metal backpack and his spray-gun off to a side.

Mortar mixers were growling on both sides of the Cathedral, crushing granite stones and mud, and disgorging black mortar into a mound. On a scaffolding, bricks and cement were being taken up to the top of the northern bell tower. George's friends Guru and Keshav poured water from plastic one-litre bottles into the mortar mixer. As the machines dripped into the red soil of the compound, rivulets of blood-red water cascaded down from the Cathedral, as if it were a heart left on a piece of newspaper to drain out.

When he was done with his melon, George smoked beedi after beedi. He closed his eyes, and at once construction workers' children began spraying each other with pesticide. He chased them around, then he came back to the pyramid of stones and sat on it.

He was a small, lithe, dark chap who seemed to be in his early forties – but since physical labour accelerates aging, he might have been younger, perhaps only in his late twenties. He had a long scar under his left eye, and a pockmarked face which suggested a recent case of chickenpox. His biceps were slender and long: they were not the glossy rippling kind that had been bulked up in expensive gyms, but the hewed-from-necessity sinews of the working poor, stone hard and deeply etched out of a lifetime of having to lift things for other people.

At sunset, firewood was piled up in front of George's stone pyramid, a flame lit, and rice and fish curry cooked in a black pot. A transistor radio was turned on. Mosquitoes buzzed. Four men sat around the flickering fire, their faces burnished, smoking beedis. Around George were his old colleagues – Guru, James, and Vinay; they had worked with him on the construction site, before his dismissal.

Taking out his green notebook from his pocket, he opened it to the middle page, where he had kept something pink, like the tongue of an animal he had caught and skinned.

It was a twenty-rupee note. Vinay fingered the thing in wonder; even after it was gently prised away from him by Guru, he could not take his eyes off it.

'You got this for spraying pesticide in her house?'

'No, no, no. She saw me do the spraying, and I guess she was impressed, because she asked me to do some gardening work.'

'If she's rich, doesn't she have a gardener?'

'She does – but the fellow is always drunk. So I did his work.'

George described it – removing the dead log from the path of the gutter in the backyard, and carrying it a few yards away, removing the muck in the gutter, which was allowing the mosquitoes to breed. Then, trimming the hedges in the front yard with a giant clipper.

'That's all?' Vinay's jaw dropped. 'Twenty rupees for that?'

George blew smoke into the air with a luxuriant wickedness. He put the twenty-rupee note back in the notebook, and the notebook in his pocket.

'That's why I say: she's my princess.'

'The rich own the whole world,' said Vinay, with a sigh that was half rebellion and half acceptance of this fact. 'What is twenty rupees to them?'

Guru, who was a Hindu, generally spoke little, and was considered 'deep' by his friends. He had been as far as Bombay, and could read signs in English.

'Let me tell you about the rich, let me tell you about the rich.'

'All right, tell us.'

'I'm telling you about the rich. In Bombay, at the Oberoi Hotel in Nariman Point, there is a dish called a "Beef Vindaloo" which costs Rs. 500.'

'No way!'

'Yes, five hundred! It was in the English newspaper on Sunday. Now you know about the rich.'

'What if you order the dish, and then you realize you made a mistake and you don't like it? Do you get your money back?'

'No, but it doesn't matter to you if you're rich. You know what the biggest difference is, between being rich and being like us? The rich can make mistakes again and again. We make only one mistake, and that's it for us.'

Dinner ended. George took everyone else out to drinks at the arrack shop. He had drunk and eaten off their generosity since being fired from the construction site: the mosquito-spraying, which Guru had arranged for him through a connection in the city Corporation, was only a once-a-week job.

'Next Sunday,' Vinay said, as they headed out of the arrack shop at midnight, dead drunk, 'I'm coming to see your fucking princess.'

'I'm not telling you where she lives,' George shouted. 'She's my secret.' The others were annoyed, but didn't press the issue. They were happy enough to see George in a good mood, which was a rare thing, since he was a bitter man.

They went to sleep in the tents at the back of the Cathedral construction site. Since it was September, there was still the danger of rain, but George slept out in the open, looking at the stars, and thinking of the generous woman who had made this day a happy one for him.

*

The next Sunday, George strapped his metal backpack on, connected the spray gun to one of its nozzles, and walked out into Valencia. He stopped at every house along his route, and wherever he saw a gutter, puddle, and every sewage hole he found, he fired his gun: Tzzzk . . . Tzzzk . . .

He walked the half-kilometre from the Cathedral and then turned left, into one of the alleys that slide downhill from Valencia; then he took the route down, firing his gun into the gutters by the side of the road: Tzzk . . . Tzzk . . . Tzzk . . .

The rain had ended, and muddy raucous torrents no longer gushed downhill from the main road, but the twinkling branches of roadside trees and the sloping tiled roofs of the houses still dripped into the road, where the loose stones braided the water into shining rivulets that flowed into the gutters with a soft music. Thick green moss coated the gutters like sediment of bile, and reeds sprouted up from its bedrock, and small swampy patches of stale water gleamed out of nooks and crannies like liquefied emeralds.

A dozen women in colourful saris, each with a green or mauve bandana around her head, were cutting the grass from the sides of the road. Swaying in concert as they sang strange Tamil songs, the migrant workers were down in the gutters, where they scraped the moss, and pulled the weeds out from between the stones with violent tugs, like something being taken back from children, while others scooped out handfuls of black gunk from the bottom of the gutters, which they heaped up in dripping mounds.

He looked at them with contempt, and he thought: but I have fallen to the level of these people myself!

He grew moody; he began spraying carelessly; in some cases he avoided spraying a few puddles deliberately.

By and by, he got to 10 A, and realized that he was outside his princess' house again. He unlatched the red gate and went in.

The windows were closed; when he got near he could hear the sound of water hissing inside. She is taking a shower in the middle of the day, he thought. Rich women can do things like this.

He had guessed, immediately upon seeing the woman last week, that her husband was away. You could tell, after a while, with these women whose husbands work in the Gulf: they have an air of not having been around a man a long time. Her husband had left her compensated for his absence: the only chauffeur-driven car in all of Valencia, a white Ambassador in the driveway, and the only air conditioner in the lane, which jutted out of her bedroom and over the jasmine plants in her garden, rumbling and dripping water.

The driver of the white Ambassador was nowhere around.

'He must be off drinking somewhere again,' George thought. He had seen an old cook somewhere in the back last time. An old lady and a derelict driver – that was all this lady had in the house with her.

A gutter led from the garden into the backyard, and he followed its path, spraying into it: Tzzzk . . . Tzzzk . . . The gutter was blocked again. He got down into the filth and muck of the blocked gutters, carefully applying his gun at different angles, pausing to examine his work periodically. Locating the largest patch of slush on the gutter, he pressed the mouth of the spray gun against the side of the gutter. The spraying sound stopped. A white froth, like the one formed when a snake bites on a glass to release its venom, spread over the mosquito larvae. Then he tightened a knob on his spray gun, clicked it into a groove on his backpack canister, and came to her once again with the book she had to sign.

'Hey!' a woman peeped out of a window. 'Who are you?'

'I'm the Mosquito Man! I was here last week!'

The window closed. Sounds came from various parts of the house. Things were unbolted, slammed, and shut, and then she was before him again – his princess. Mrs. Gomes, the woman of house 10 A, was a tall woman, approaching her forties now, who wore bright red lipstick and a Western-style gown that exposed her arms nine-tenths of the way up her shoulder. Of the three kinds of women in the world – 'traditional,' 'modern,' and 'working' – Mrs. Gomes was an obvious member of the 'modern' tribe.

'You didn't do a good job last time,' she said, and showed him red welts on her arms, then stepped back and lifted up the edge of her long green gown to expose her ravished ankles. 'Your spraying didn't do any good.'

He felt hot with embarrassment, but he did not dare take his eyes off what he was being shown.

'The problem is not my spraying, but your backyard,' he retorted. 'Another twig has blocked the gutters, and I think there's a dead animal of some kind, a mongoose maybe, blocking the flow of water. That's why the mosquitoes keep breeding. Come and see if you don't believe me,' he suggested.

She shook her head. 'The backyard is filthy. I never go there.'

'I'll clean it up again,' he said. 'That will get rid of the mosquitoes better than my spray gun.'

She frowned. 'How much do you want to do this?'

Her tone annoyed him, and he said: 'Nothing.'

He went around to the backyard, got into the gutter, and began attacking the gunk. How the rich think they can buy us like cattle! – he thought. How much do you want to do this?

Half an hour later, he rang the bell with blackened hands; after a few seconds there was a shout: 'Come over here.'

He followed the voice to a closed window.

'Open it!'

He put his blackened hands on a small crack in the partition, between the two wooden shutters of the window, and ripped them apart. Mrs. Gomes was reading in her bed.

He stuck his pencil into the book and held it out.

'What should I do with the book?' she asked, bringing the smell of freshly washed hair with her to the window.

He held his thumb on one line. House 10 A: Mr. Roger Gomes.

'Do you want some tea?' she asked, as she forged her husband's signature on his book.

He was dumbfounded; he had never been offered tea before on his job. Mostly out of fear of what this rich lady might do if he refused, he said yes.

An old servant, perhaps the cook, came to the backdoor, and regarded him with suspicion as Mrs. Gomes asked her to get some tea.

The old cook came back a few minutes later, with a glass of tea in her hand; she looked at the mosquito-man with scorn, and put the glass down on the threshold of the house for him to pick up.

He came up the three steps, took the cup, and then went back down three steps, and took three steps further back, before he began sipping.

'How long have you been doing this job?'

'Six months.'

He sipped the tea. Seized by a sudden inspiration, he said:

'I have a sister in my village whom I have to support. Maria. She is a good girl, madam. She can cook well. Do you need a cook, madam?'

The princess shook her head. 'I've got a very good cook. Sorry.'

191

George finished his tea, and put the glass down by the base of the steps, holding it an extra second, to make sure it didn't totter over as he left it.

'Will the problem in my backyard start again?'

'For sure. A mosquito is an evil thing, madam. It causes malaria and filaria,' he said, telling her of Sister Lucy in his village, who got malaria of the brain. 'She said she was going to flap-flap-flap her wasted arms like a hummingbird until she got to Holy Jerusalem' – using his arms, and gyrating around the parked car, he showed her how.

She let out a sudden wild laugh. He seemed a grave and serious man, so she had not expected this burst of levity from him; she had never heard a person of the lower classes be so funny before. She looked him over from head to toe, feeling she was seeing him for the first time.

He noticed that she laughed heartily, and snorted, like a peasant woman. He had not expected this either; women of good breeding were not meant to laugh so crudely and openly, and her behaviour confused him, coming from such a rich, well-off woman.

In a weary voice, she added:

'Matthew is supposed to clean the backyard. But he's not even here often enough to do the driving, forget about the backyard. Always out, drinking.'

Then her face lit up with an idea:

'You do it.' she said. 'You can be a part-time gardener for me. I'll pay you.'

George was about to say 'yes,' but something within him resisted, disliking the casual way the job had been offered.

'That's not the kind of work for me to do. Taking shit out of backyards. But I will do it for you, madam. I will do anything for you, because you are a good person. I can see into your soul.'

She laughed again.

'Start next week,' she said, vestiges of the laugh still rippling on her face, and closed the door.

When he was gone, she opened the door to her backyard. It was not a place she went out much: strong with the smell of fecund black soil, overgrown with weeds, the sewage-tinged air. She smelled the pesticide; it drew her out of the house. She heard the sound, and recognized that the mosquito-man was still somewhere in her neighbourhood.

Tzzk . . . Tzzzk; in her mind she followed it as it sounded from the various parts of the neighbourhood – first going to the Monteiros's house; then to Dr. Karkada's compound; then to the Valencia Jesuit Teacher's College and Seminary: tzzzk . . . tzzzk . . . tzzzk – before she lost track of it.

*

George was on the pile of stones, waiting till other men who felt about their work as he did, joined him, and then they would move together to an arrack shop close by, to start drinking.

'What's got into you?' the other guys asked him later that evening, at the arrack shop. 'Hardly a word out of you.'

After an initial hour of raucousness, he had become sullen. He was thinking of that man and woman – the ones he had seen on the cover of his princess' novel. They were

193

in a car; the wind was blowing through the woman's hair, and the man was smiling. In the background, there was a plane. Words in English, the title of the novel, in silver letters, hovered over the scene, like a benediction from the God of good living.

He thought of the woman who could afford to spend her days reading such books, in the comfort of her home, with an air conditioner kept on at all times.

'The rich abuse us, man. It's always, here, take twenty rupees, kiss my feet. Get into the gutter. Clean my shit. It's always like that.'

'There he goes again,' Guru chuckled. 'It was this talk that got him fired from the construction site, but he hasn't changed one bit. Still so bitter.'

'Why should I change? Am I lying?' George shouted back: 'The rich lie in bed reading books, and live alone without families, and eat five-hundred rupee Vindaloos!'

At night he could not sleep. He walked out of the tent, and went to the construction site, staring at the unfinished Cathedral for several hours, and thinking about that woman in 10 A.

The next week it was clear to him she had been waiting for him. When he came to her house, she stuck her arm out at him, rotating it from side to side until he had seen the flesh from 360 degrees.

'No bites,' she said. 'Last week was much better. Your spray is finally working.'

He took charge of her backyard. First, walking with his spray gun out and his left hand adjusting a knob on his backpack canister, he went down on his knees, and drizzled germicide over her gutters. Then, as she watched, he put some order into her long-neglected backyard: he dug, and sprayed, and cut, and cleaned it for an hour.

That evening, the guys at the construction site could not believe the news.

'It's a full-time job now,' George said. 'The Princess thinks I'm such a good worker she wants me to stay there, and sleep in a shed in the backyard. She's paying me double what I get now. And I don't have to be a Mosquito Man anymore. It's perfect.'

'We'll never see you again, I bet,' Guru said, flicking his beedi to the ground.

'That's not true,' George protested. 'I'll come down to drink every evening.'

Guru snorted. 'Yeah, right.'

And it was true: they did not see much of George after that evening.

\*

Every Monday, a white woman dressed in North Indian salwar kameez came to the gate, and asked him, in English: 'Madam is in?'

He opened the gate, and bowed, and said: 'Yes. She is in.'

She was from England; she had come to teach yoga and breathing to madam. The air conditioner was turned off, and George heard the sound of deep breathing from the bedroom. Half an hour later, the white woman came out and said:

'It's amazing, isn't it? I have to teach you yoga.'

'Yes, it's sad. We Indians have forgotten everything about our own civilization.'

Then the white woman and madam walked around the garden for a while. On Tuesday mornings, Matthew, his eyes red and breath full of arrack, drove madam to the Lion Ladies' meeting at the club on Rose Lane. That seemed to be the extent of Mrs. Gomes's social life. When they drove out, George held the gate open: as the car passed him, he saw Matthew turn and glare.

'He's frightened of me,' George thought, as he got back to trimming the plants in the garden. 'Does he think I will try to take over from him as driver one day?'

It was not a thought he had entertained until then.

When the car came back, he looked at it with disapproval: its sides were filthy. He hosed the car down, and then wiped the outsides with a dirty rag, and the insides with a clean rag. The thought came to him as he was doing it that cleaning the car was not his job, as gardener, he was doing something extra – but of course madam wouldn't notice. They never have any gratitude, the rich, do they?

'You've done a very good job with the car,' Mrs. Gomes said in the evening. 'I am grateful.'

George was ashamed of himself. He thought: this rich woman really was different from other rich people.

'I'll do anything for you, madam,' he said.

He kept a distance of about seven or ten feet between them whenever he talked; sometimes, in the course of movement, the distance contracted, perfume made his nostrils expand, and he would automatically, with small backward steps, re-establish the radius between mistress and servant.

The cook brought him tea in the evenings, and chatted for hours. He had not yet gone inside the house, but through chatting with the old cook he came to realize that the house's share of wonders went far beyond an air conditioner. That enormous white thing he saw whenever the backdoor opened was a machine that did washing – and drying – automatically, the old cook said.

'Her husband wanted to use it, and she didn't. They never agreed on anything. Plus,' she said in a conspiratorial whisper, 'no children. That always causes problems.'

'What drove them apart?'

'That way she laughs,' the old woman said. 'He said she laughed like a devil.'

He had noticed it, too: high-pitched, savage, like the laugh of a child or an animal, gloating and wanton. He always stopped work to listen when it ricocheted out of her room; and he often heard it even in the creak made by the opening of a door, or the particular cadence of an unusual bird-cry.

'Are you educated, George?' Mrs. Gomes asked one day, in a surprised voice. She had found him reading the newspaper.

'A little bit. I did the tenth standard, madam, but I failed the SSLC.'

'Failed?' She asked with a smile. 'How can anyone fail the SSLC? It is such a simple exam . . .'

'I could do all the sums, madam. I passed Mathematics with sixty marks out of hundred. I only failed Social Studies, because I could not mark Madras and Bombay on the map of India that they gave me. What could I do, madam – we had not studied those things in class. I got 34 in Social Studies – one mark fail!'

'Why didn't you take the exam again?' she asked.

'Take it again?' He uttered the words as if he did not understand them. 'I began working,' he said, because he did not know how to answer her. 'I worked for six years, madam. The rains were bad last year, and there was no agriculture at all. We heard there were jobs for Christians at the site, and we came up here. I was working as a carpenter there, madam. Where was the time to study?'

'Why did you leave the construction site?'

'I have a bad back,' he said.

'Should you be doing this kind of work, then?' she asked. 'Won't it hurt your back? And then you'll say that I broke your back, and make a fuss about it!'

'My back is fine, madam. My back is fine. Don't you see me bent over and working every day?'

'So why did you say your back was bad?' she demanded. He said nothing, and she shook her head and said: 'O, you villagers are impossible to understand!'

The next day he was waiting for her. When she came out into the garden after her bath, wiping her wet hair dry with a towel, George came to her and said:

'He slapped me, madam. I slapped him back.'

'What are you talking about, George? Who slapped you?'

He explained: he had got into a fight with his foreman, because of a woman. George pantomimed the exchange of palms, hoping to impress upon her how fast it had been, how reflexive.

'He said I was making eyes at his wife, madam. But that was untrue. We are honest people in my family, madam. We used to plough in the village, madam,' he said. 'And we would find copper coins. These are from the time of Tippu Sultan. They were over one hundred years old. They were beautiful to look at once you washed them. I loved those coins very much! And those coins were taken from me, and melted down for copper. I wanted so much to keep them, but I handed them over to the landowner at once. I am not dishonest. I do not steal, or look at another man's woman. This is the truth.'

She smiled at this; like all villagers, his manner of defending his character was naive, circuitous, and endearing.

'I trust you,' she said, and went in, without locking the door. He peered into the house, and saw clocks, red carpets, wooden medallions on the walls, potted plants, things of bronze and silver. Then the door closed again.

She brought tea out herself this day. She put it down at the top of the steps, and he scampered up with a bowed head, picked it up, and scampered back down the steps.

'Ah, madam, but you people have it all, and we people have nothing. It's just not fair,' he said, sucking on the tea.

She let out a little laugh. She did not expect such directness from the lower classes; it was charming.

'It's just not fair, madam,' he said again. 'You even have a washing machine that you never use. That's how much you have.'

199

'Are you asking me for more money?' she arched her eyebrows.

'No, madam, why should I? You pay very well. I don't do things in a roundabout way,' he said. 'If I want it, I'll ask for money.'

'I have problems you don't know about, George. I have problems too.' She smiled and went in. He stood outside, hoping vainly for an explanation.

A little later it began raining. The foreign yoga teacher came, with an umbrella, through the thick rain; he ran up to the gate to let her in, and then sat in the garage, by the car, eavesdropping on the sound of deep breathing from madam's bedroom. By the time the yoga session was over, the rain had ended, and the sun was sparkling in the garden. The two women seemed excited by the sun – and the garden's carefully tended condition. Mrs. Gomes talked to her foreign friend with an arm on her hip; George noticed that unlike the European woman, his employer had retained her maidenly figure. He supposed it was because she did not have any children.

The lights came on at around six-thirty in her bedroom, and then the noise of water began flowing. She was taking a bath; she took a bath every night. It was not necessary, since she bathed again in the morning, and anyway she smelled of wonderful perfume, yet she bathed twice – in hot water, he was sure, coating herself in lather, and relaxing her body. She was a woman who did things just for her pleasure.

On Sunday, George walked uphill to attend mass at the Cathedral on Sunday; when he came back, the air conditioner was still purring. 'So she does not go to church,' he thought.

Every alternate Wednesday afternoon, the Ideal Mobile Circulating Library came to the house on a Yamaha motorbike; the librarian-cum-driver of the bike, after pressing the bell, would untie a metal box of books strapped by ropes to the back of his motorbike, and place it on the back of the car for her to inspect. Mrs. Gomes squinted over the books, and picked out a couple. When she had made her selection, and paid, and gone back in, George went up to the librarian-cum-driver, who was retying the box with ropes to the back of his Yamaha, and tapped him on the shoulder.

'What sort of books does madam take?'

'Novels.'

The librarian-cum-driver stopped his work and winked. 'Dirty novels. I see dozens like her every day: women with their husbands abroad.'

He bent his finger and wiggled it.

'It still scratches, you know——. So they have to read the books to get rid of it.'

George grinned. But when the Yamaha, kicking up a cloud of dust, turned in a circle and went out of the garden, he ran to the gate and shouted:

'Don't talk of madam like that, you bastard!'

At night he lay awake; he wandered about the backyard quietly, making no noise. He was thinking. It seemed to him, when he looked back on it, that his life consisted of things that had not said 'yes' to him, and things that he could not say 'no' to. The SSLC had not said 'yes' to him, and his sister he could not say 'no' to. He could not imagine, for instance, abandoning his sister to her own fate and trying to go back and complete his SSLC examination a second time.

He went out, he walked up the lane and went along the main road. The unfinished Cathedral was a giant black mass against the blue coastal night sky. Lighting a beedi, he walked in circles about the mess of the construction site, looking at familiar things in an unfamiliar way.

The next day, he was waiting for her with an announcement:

'I've stopped drinking, madam,' he told her. 'I made the decision last night – never another bottle of arrack.'

He wanted her to know; he had the power, now, to live any way he wanted. That evening, as he was out in the garden, trimming the leaves on the rose plant, Matthew unlatched the gate and came in. He glared at George, then he walked away to the backyard, to his quarters.

Half an hour later, when Mrs. Gomes needed to be driven to the Lion Ladies' meeting, Matthew did not turn up in front of the car, even after she yelled into the backyard six times.

'Let me drive, madam,' he said in a soft voice.

She looked at him sceptically: 'Do you know how to drive?'

'Madam, when you grow up poor, you have to learn to do everything, from farming to driving. Why don't you get in and see for yourself how well I drive?'

'Do you have a licence? Will you kill me?'

'Madam,' he said, 'I would never do anything to put you in the least danger.' A moment later he added: 'I would even give my life for you.'

She smiled at what he said; then she saw that he was saying it in earnest, and she stopped smiling. She got into the car, and he started the engine, and he became her driver.

'You drive well, George. Why don't you work as my driver from now on?' she asked him at the end.

'I'll do anything for you, madam.'

Matthew was dismissed that evening. The cook came up to George and said: 'I never liked him. I'm glad you're staying, though.'

George bowed to her. 'You're like my elder sister,' he said, and watched her beam with happiness.

In the mornings he cleaned and washed the car, and sat on Matthew's stool, his legs crossed, humming merrily, and waiting for the moment madam would command him to take her out. When he drove her to the Lion Ladies' meetings, he wandered about the flagpole in the front of the Club, watching the buses go by around the municipal library. He looked at the buses and the library differently: not as a wanderer, a manual worker who got down into gutters and scooped earth out – but like someone with a stake in things. He drove her down to the sea once. She walked out, and sat by the rocks, watching the silver waves, while he waited by the car, watching her.

As she got out of the car, he coughed.

'What is it, George?'

'My sister Maria.'

She looked at him with a smile, encouraging him.

'She can cook, madam. She is clean, and hard-working, and a good Christian girl.'

'I have a cook, George.'

'She's not good, madam. And she's old. Why don't you get rid of her, and have my sister over from the village?'

203

Her face darkened.

'You think I don't know what you're doing? Trying to take over my household! First you get rid of my driver, and now my cook!'

She walked in, and slammed the door. He smiled; he was not worried. He had planted the seed in her mind; it would germinate, in a little time. He knew now how this woman's mind worked.

\*

That summer, during the water-shortage, George showed Mrs. Gomes he was indispensable. He was up at the top of the hill, waiting for the water-tanker to come along; he brought the buckets down himself, filling up her flush and commodes so she did not have to go through the humiliation of rationing her flushes, like everyone else in the neighbourhood. As soon as he heard a rumour, anywhere in the neighbourhood, that the Corporation was going to release water through the taps for a limited time (they gave half an hour of water every two or three days), he would come rushing into the house, shouting: 'Madam! Madam!'

She gave him a set of the keys to the backdoor, so that he could come into the house anytime he heard that the water was being released in the taps, and fill up the buckets.

Thanks to his hard work, at a time when most people couldn't bathe even once every other day, madam was still taking her twice-a-day pleasure baths.

'What absurdity,' she said, one evening, coming to the backdoor with her hair wet, and falling down her shoulders, which she was rubbing vigorously with a white cloth. 'That in this country, with so much rain, we still run water shortages. When will India ever change?'

He smiled, averting his eyes from her figure and her wet hair.

'George, your pay will be increased,' she said, and went in, closing the door firmly.

There was more good news for him too, a few evenings later. He saw the old cook walking out, with a bag under her arm. She looked at him with baleful eyes as their paths crossed, and hissed:

'I know what you're trying to do to her! I told her you'll destroy her name and reputation! But she's fallen under your spell.'

A week after Maria joined the household of 10 A, Mrs. Gomes came up to George when he was tinkering with the inside the engine of the car.

'Your sister's shrimp curry is excellent.'

'Everyone in our family is hard-working, madam,' he said, and got so excited he jerked his head up and whacked it against the bonnet. It stung, but Mrs. Gomes had begun to laugh – that sharp, high-pitched animal laugh of hers – and he tried to laugh along with her, while rubbing the red bump on his skull.

Maria was a small, frightened girl who came with two bags, no English, and no knowledge of life beyond her village. Mrs. Gomes had taken a liking to her, and allowed her to sleep in the kitchen.

'What do they talk about, inside the house, madam and that foreign woman?' George asked her in the evenings, when Maria came to his one-room quarters with his evening food.

'I don't know,' she said, ladling him out his fish curry.

'Why don't you know?'

'I wasn't paying attention,' she said, her voice small, scared, as always, of her brother.

'Well, pay attention! Don't just sit there like a doll, saying Yes Madam and No Madam! Take some initiative! Keep your eyes open!'

On Sundays, he took Maria along to Mass at the Cathedral; construction stopped in the morning, to let people in, but as they came out, they could see the contractors getting ready to resume work in the evening.

'Why doesn't madam come to Mass like other Christians?' Maria asked, as they were leaving church.

He took in a deep breath. 'The rich do as they want. It's not for us to question them.'

He noticed Mrs. Gomes talking to Maria; with her open, generous nature, which did not distinguish between rich and poor, she was becoming more than just a mistress to Maria, but a good friend. It was exactly as he had hoped.

In the evenings he missed his drink, but he filled it in by walking about, or by listening to a radio, and letting his mind drift. He thought: Maria can get married next year. She had a status now as a cook in a rich woman's house. Boys would line up for her back home in the village.

After that, he figured, it would be time for his own marriage, which he had put off so long, out of a mixture of bitterness, poverty, and shame. Yes, time for marriage, and children. Yet the regret still gnawed at him, created by his contact with this rich woman, that he could have done so much more with his life.

'You're a lucky man, George,' Mrs. Gomes said one evening, watching him rub the car with a wet cloth. 'You've got a wonderful sister.'

'Thank you, madam.'

'Why don't you take Maria around the city? She hasn't seen anything in Kittur, has she?'

He decided that this was a clear opportunity for some initiative. 'Why don't we all three go together, madam?'

The three of them drove down to the beach. Mrs. Gomes and Maria went for a walk along the beach. He watched from a distance. When they came back, he was waiting with a paper cone filled with roasted groundnuts for Maria.

'Aren't I going to get some too?' Mrs. Gomes demanded, and he hurried to spill some to give her, which she took from his hands, and that was how he touched her for the first time.

*

It was raining again in Valencia, and he knew he had been at the house almost a year. One day, the new mosquito-man came for the backyard. Mrs. Gomes watched, and George directed the fellow around the gutters and canals in the back, to make sure not a spot was missed.

That evening, she called him to the house and said: 'George, you've got to do it yourself. Please put the spray in the gutter yourself, like last year.'

Her voice became sweet, and though it was the same voice she had used to make him move mountains for her, this time he stiffened. He was offended that she would still ask him to do a task like this.

'Why not?' she raised her voice, angrily. She shrieked. 'You work for me! You must do what I say!'

The two of them stared, and then, grumbling and cursing her, he walked out of the house. He wandered aimlessly for some time, then decided to go visit the Cathedral again, to see how the old fellows were doing.

Nothing much had changed in the field by the Cathedral. The construction had been held up, he was told, because of the Rector's death. It would start again soon.

His other friends were missing – they had left the work and gone back to the villages – but Guru was there.

'Now that you're here, why don't we—' Guru made the gesture of a bottle being emptied down a throat.

They went to an arrack shop, and there was some fine drinking, as in old times.

'So how are things with you and your princess?' Guru asked.

'Oh, these rich people are all the same,' George said, bitterly. 'We're just trash to them. They'll just use us and throw us out. A rich woman can never see a poor man as a man. Just as a servant.'

He remembered his carefree days, before he was tied down to a house, and to madam – and he became resentful of having lost his freedom. He left early, a little before midnight, saying that he had something to take care of, at the house. On the way back, he staggered drunkenly, singing a Konkani song; but another pulse had started throbbing underneath the light-hearted film number.

As he drew near the gate, his voice dropped down and died out, and he realized he was walking with exaggerated stealth. He wondered why, and felt frightened of himself.

He came into the house, opened the latch soundlessly, and walked towards the backdoor. He had been holding the key in his hand for some time; bending down to the lock, and squinting at the keyhole, he inserted it in. Opening it carefully and quietly, he walked into the house. The heavy washing machine lay in the dark, like a nightwatchman. In the distance, wisps of cool air escaping from a crack in its closed door, was her bedroom.

George breathed slowly. His one thought, as he staggered forward, was that he must avoid hitting the washing machine.

'O God,' he said, suddenly. He realized that he had banged his knee into the washing machine, and the damn machine was giving off a reverberating noise.

'O God,' he said again, with the dim, desperate consciousness that he had spoken too loudly.

There was a movement; a door opened, and a woman with long loose hair came out of a room.

A cool air-conditioned breeze thrilled his entire body. The woman pulled the edge of a sari over her shoulder.

'George?'

'Yes.'

'What do you want?'

He said nothing. As he saw her, the answer to the question was at once vague, and full of substance, like her half-obscure but all too present. He almost knew what he wanted to say; she said nothing. Perhaps she wanted it too.

He felt that it was now only a matter of saying it, or even of moving. Just do *something*. It will happen.

'Get out,' the woman said.

He had waited too long.

'Madam, I—'

'Get out.'

It was too late now; he turned around and walked fast.

The moment the backdoor closed on him, he felt foolish. He thumped it with his fist so hard that it hurt. 'Madam, let me explain!' He pounded the door harder and harder. She had misunderstood him – completely misunderstood!

'Stop it,' came a voice. It was Maria, looking at him with fear through the window. 'Please stop it at once.'

At that moment, the immensity of what he had done hit George. He was conscious the neighbours might be watching. Madam's reputation was at stake.

He dragged himself up to the construction site, and fell down there to sleep. The next morning, he discovered he had lain, as he had done months before, on top of a pyramid of crushed granite stones.

He came back in, slowly. Maria was waiting for him by the gate.

'Madam,' she went into the house, shouting, and Mrs. Gomes came out, her finger deep in a copy of the latest novel.

'Maria, go to the kitchen,' Mrs. Gomes ordered, as he walked into the garden. He was glad of that; so she wanted to protect Maria from what was coming. He felt gratitude for her delicacy. She was different from other rich people; she was special. She would spare him.

He put the key on the slab of the house.

'It's okay,' she said. Her manner was cool. He understood now that the radius had expanded; it was pushing him back every second he stood. He did not know how far back to go; it seemed to him he was already as far back as he could be and hear what she was saying. Her voice was distant and small and cold. For some reason, despite all that he had to do, he could not take his eyes off the cover of her novel; a man was driving a red car, and two white women in bikinis were sitting inside.

'It's not anger,' she said. 'I should have taken greater precautions. I made a mistake.'

'I've left the key out here, madam,' he said.

'It doesn't matter,' she said. 'The lock is being changed this evening.'

'Can I stay, until you find someone else?' he blurted out. 'How will you manage the garden? And what will you do for a driver?'

'I'll manage,' she said.

Until then, all his thoughts had been for her – her reputation in the neighbourhood, her peace of mind, the sense of betrayal she must feel – but now he understood: she was not the one who needed taking care of.

He wanted to speak his heart out to her, and tell her all this, but she spoke first.

'Maria has to leave as well.'

He stared with an open mouth.

'Where will she sleep tonight?' His voice was thin, and desperate. 'Madam, she left everything she had in our village and came here to live with you.'

'She can sleep in the church, I suppose,' Mrs. Gomes said calmly. 'They let people in all night, I've heard.'

'Madam,' he folded his palms. 'Madam, I'm begging you in the name of Christian Charity, please leave Maria out of—!'

She closed the door; then he heard the sound of it being latched, and double-latched.

He waited at the top of the road, and looked in the direction of the unfinished Cathedral.

## DAY SIX: THE SULTAN'S BATTERY

*The Sultan's Battery, which appears on the way towards Salt
Market Village, is one of the prime tourist attractions of Kittur.*

He walked fast towards the white dome of the Dargah, a
fold-up wooden stool under one arm, and in the other a red
bag with his album of photographs and seven bottles full of
white pills. When he got to the Dargah, he walked along the
wall, without paying any attention to the long line of beggars
along the wall: the lepers who were sitting on rags, the men
with mutilated arms and legs, the men in wheelchairs and
the men with bandages covering their eyes, and the one
creature, with little brown stubs like a seal's flippers where
he should have had arms, a normal left leg, and a soft brown
stump where he should have had a second leg, who lay on
his left side, twitching his hip continuously, like an animal
getting galvanic shocks, and intoning, with blank,
mesmerized eyes: 'Al-lah! Al-laaaah! Al-lah! Al-laaah!'

He walked past this sorrowful parade of humanity, and
went behind the Dargah.

Now he went between the vendors squatting on the
ground in a long line that extended for half a mile. He passed
rows of baby shoes, bras, T-shirts bearing the logo 'New York
Fucking City,' fake Ray-Ban cooling glasses, fake Nike shoes
and fake Adidas shoes, and piles of Urdu and Malayalam

magazines. He spotted an opening in between a counterfeit shoe-seller and a counterfeit bra-vendor, and unfolded his stool there, and put a glossy black sheet of paper with gold lettering on the stool.

The golden words read:

RATNAKARA SHETTY
SPECIAL INVITEE
FOURTH PAN-ASIAN CONFERENCE ON SEXOLOGY
HOTEL NEW HILLTOP PALACE NEW DELHI
APRIL 12-14 1987

The young men who had come to pray at the Dargah, or to eat lamb kebabs in one of the Muslim restaurants, or simply to watch the sea, began making a semi-circle around Ratna, watching, as he put down on the stool, a mauve photo album, and the seven bottles of white pills. With grave ceremony, he then rearranged the bottles, as if their position had to be exactly right for his work to begin. In truth, he was waiting for more onlookers.

They came. Standing in pairs or alone, the crowd of young men had now taken on the look of a human Stonehenge; some with their hands folded on a friend's shoulder; some standing alone; and a few crouched by the ground, like fallen boulders.

All at once, Ratna began to talk. Young men came quicker, and the crowd became so thick that it was two- or three-persons deep at each point; and those at the back had to stand on their toes to get a partial glimpse of the sexologist.

He opened the album, and let the young men see the photos in plastic folders inside. The onlookers gasped.

Pointing to his photographs, Ratna spoke of abominations and perversions. He described the consequences of sin: he demonstrated the passage of venereal germs up the body, touching his nipples, his eyes, and then his nostrils, and then closing his eyes. The sun climbed the sky, and the white dome of the Dargah shone more brightly. The young men in the semi-circle pressed against each other, straining to get closer to the photographs. Then Ratna went in for the kill: he closed the book, and held up a bottle of white pills in both of his hands. He began shaking the pills.

'With each bottle of pills you will receive a certificate of authenticity from Hakim Bhagwandas of Daryaganj in Delhi. This man, an experienced old doctor, has brought wisdom from Egypt, and has used his scientific equipment to create magnificent white pills that will heal all your ailments. Each bottle costs just four rupees and fifty paise! Yes, that is all you pay to atone for sin and earn a second chance in this life! Four rupees and fifty paise!'

In the evening, dead-tired from the heat, he got on to the 34 B bus with his red bag and fold-up stool. It was packed full at this hour: so he held on to a strap hanging from the ceiling of the bus and breathed in and out slowly. He counted to ten, to get his strength back, then put a hand into the red bag, and took out four green brochures, each of which had an image of three large rats on the cover. He held the brochures up high in one hand, in the manner of a gambler holding up his cards, and spoke at the top of his voice:

'Ladies and gentlemen! All of you know that we live in a rat race, where there are few jobs, and many job applicants. How will your children survive, how will they get the jobs you have? For life in this day and age is a veritable rat race. Only in this booklet will you find thousands of useful general knowledge data, arranged in question and answer form, that your sons and daughters need to pass the civil service entrance examination, the bank entrance examination, the police entrance examination, and many other exams which are needed to win the rat race. For instance' – he took a quick breath –

'The Mughal Empire had two capitals; Delhi was one of them. Which was the other? Four capital cities of Europe are built on the banks of one river. Name that river. Who was the first king of Germany? What is the currency of Angola? One city in Europe has been the capital of three different Empires. Which city? Two men were involved in the assassination of Mahatma Gandhi. Nathuram Godse was one of them. Name the other man. What is the height of the Eiffel Tower in metres?'

Holding the pamphlets up with his right hand, he staggered forward, bracing himself as the bus bumped over the potholes of the road. One passenger asked for a pamphlet, and handed him over a rupee. Ratna walked back, and waited near the exit door; when the bus slowed down, he dipped his head in silent thanks to the conductor, and got off.

Seeing a man at the bus stand, he tried to sell him a collection of six coloured glass pens, at a rupee a pen; then at two pens a rupee; finally offering three for a rupee.

Although the man said he would not buy, Ratna could see the interest in his eyes; he also took out a large spring that could give much amusement to children, and a geometrical set that could make wonderful designs on papers. The man bought one of the geometrical sets for three rupees.

Ratna walked the opposite way from the Sultan's Battery, taking the road towards Salt Market Village.

Once he got to the village, he went to the main market, took a clump of change and sorted it out on the flat of his palm as he walked; he left it on the counter of a shop, and took in exchange a packet of Engineer beedis, which he put into his suitcase.

'What are you waiting for?' The boy in charge of the shop was new to the job. 'You got your beedis.'

'I usually get two packets of lentils too, included in the price. That's the way it's done.'

Before entering his house, Ratna ripped open one plastic packet of lentils with his teeth, and poured its contents out into the ground near his door. At once seven or eight of the neighbourhood dogs came running to his feet, and he watched them crunch the lentils loudly. When they began digging the earth, he ripped the second packet of lentils open with his teeth, and scattered their contents on the ground.

He walked into his house without waiting to see the dogs devour this pack. He knew they would still be hungry even after eating these lentils; he could not afford to buy them a third pack every day.

He hung his shirt on a hook next to the door, kicked the door open, and walked in scratching his armpits and hairy chest. He sat down on a chair, exhaled, said 'O Krishna, O

Krishna,' and stretched his legs out; even though they were in the kitchen, his daughters knew at once that he had come in – a powerful odour of stale feet went through the house like a warning canon shot. They dropped their women's magazines, and rushed at once to their work.

His wife came out from the kitchen with a tumbler of water. He had begun smoking the beedis.

'Are they working in there – the maharanis?' he asked her.

'Yes,' the three girls, his daughters, shouted back from the kitchen. He did not trust them, so he went in to check.

The youngest, Aditi, crouched near the gas stove, wiping the leaves of the photo album clean with a corner of her sari. Rukmini, the older sister, sat beside a mound of white pills, which she was counting off and pouring into a bottle; Ramnika, who would be married after Rukmini, pasted a label on each bottle. The wife was making noise with some plates and pots.

After he had smoked his second beedi, and his body had visibly relaxed, she built up the courage to come near:

'The astrologer said he would come at nine.'

'Uhm.'

He burped, and then lifted a leg and waited for a fart to come out. The radio was turned on; he put it on his thigh, and slapped his palm on his other thigh to the beat of the music, humming constantly, and singing the words whenever he knew them.

'He's here,' she whispered. He turned the radio off, as the astrologer came into the room and folded his palms in a namaste.

Sitting down on his chair, he took off his shirt, which Ratna's wife hung for him on the hook next to Ratna's own shirt. While Ratna's wife and the girls waited in the kitchen, the astrologer showed Ratna the choice of boys.

He opened an album, in which he had black and white photos; he gazed at the faces of boy after boy, who looked back at them in tense, unsmiling portraits. Ratna scraped one with his thumb. The astrologer slid it out of the album.

'Boy looks okay,' Ratna said, after a moment's concentration. 'The father does what for a living?'

'Owns a firecracker shop in Car Street. A very good business. Boy inherits it.'

'His own business,' Ratna exclaimed, with genuine satisfaction. 'It's the only way ahead in the rat race: being a salesman is a dead end.'

His wife dropped something in the kitchen; then coughed; then dropped something else.

'What's going on?' he shouted.

A timid voice said something about 'horoscopes.'

'Shut up!' Ratna shouted. He jerked the photo at the kitchen – 'I have three daughters to marry off, and this damn bitch thinks I can be choosy?' – and he threw the photo back into the astrologer's lap.

The astrologer drew an 'X' across the back of the photo.

'The girls' parents will expect something,' he said. 'A gesture.'

'Dowry,' Ratna gave the evil its proper name in a soft voice. 'Fine. I've saved money up for this girl.' He breathed out. 'Where I'll get dowry for the next two, though, God alone knows.'

Gritting his teeth in anger, he turned to the kitchen and shouted.

The next Monday, the boy's party turned up. The younger girls were made to go around with a tray full of lemon juice, while Ratna and his wife sat in the drawing room. Rukmini's face was whitened by a thick layer of Johnson's baby powder, and streams of jasmine ran through her hair; she plucked the strings of a veena and recited a religious song, while looking out the window at something far away.

The prospective groom's father, the firecracker merchant, was sitting on a mattress directly opposite Rukmini; he was a huge man in a white shirt and a white cotton sarong, with thick tufts of glossy, silvery hair sticking out of his ears. He moved his head to the rhythm of the song Rukmini was playing, which Ratna took as an encouraging sign. The prospective mother-in-law, another enormous fair-skinned creature, looked around at the ceiling and the corners of the house. The groom-to-be had his father's fair skin and features, but he was much smaller than either his father or his mother, and seemed more the family's domestic pet than the scion. Halfway through the song, he leaned over and whispered something into his father's hairy ears.

The merchant nodded. The boy got up and left. The father held up a small finger and showed it to everyone in the room.

Everyone giggled.

The boy came back, and squirmed into place between his fat father and fat mother. The two younger girls came with a second tray of lemon juice, and the fat firecracker merchant and his wife took glasses; as if only to follow them, the boy also took a glass and sipped. Almost as soon as the fluid touched his lips, he tapped his father and whispered into his hairy ear again. This time the old man grimaced; but the boy ran out.

Perhaps to distract attention from his son, the firecracker merchant asked, in a raspy voice: 'Do you have a beedi, my good man?'

Searching in the kitchen for his packet of beedis, Ratna saw, through the grille in the window, the bridegroom-to-be, urinating furiously into the trunk of an Ashoka tree that grew in the backyard.

Nervous fellow, he thought, grinning. But that's only natural, he thought, feeling a little affection already for this fellow who was going to be part of his family soon. All men are nervous before their weddings. The boy appeared to have done with his piddle; he shook his penis, and stepped back from the tree. But instead of walking away, he stood frozen. After a moment he craned his head back and gasped for air, like a man drowning.

The matchmaker returned in the evening to report that the firecracker merchant seemed satisfied with Rukmini's singing.

'Get the date fixed up soon,' he told Ratna. 'In a month, the rental rates for the wedding halls will start to—' he made an upward gliding motion with his palms.

Ratna nodded, but seemed distracted.

The next morning, he took the bus to Umbrella Street, walking past the furniture and fan shops until he found the firecracker-owner's shop. The fat man with the hairy ears sat on a high stool, in front of a wall full of paper bombs and rockets, like an emissary of the God of Fire and War. The groom-to-be was also in the shop, down on the floor, licking his fingertips and turning the pages of a ledger.

The fat man give his son a light kick.

'This man is going to be your father-in-law, aren't you going to say hi?' He smiled at Ratna: 'The boy is a shy one.'

Ratna sipped tea, chatted with the fat man, and kept an eye on the boy all the time.

'Come with me, son,' he said, 'I have something to ask you in private.'

The two walked down the road, neither saying a word, till they got to banyan tree growing near the side of a Hanuman temple. Ratna indicated that they should sit down in the shade of the tree. He wanted the boy to turn his back to the traffic, so they were staring at the temple.

For a while Ratna let the young man talk, doing nothing except observe his eyes, ears, nose, mouth, and neck.

All at once, he seized the fellow's wrist.

'Where did you find this prostitute that you sat with?'

The boy wanted to get up, but Ratna increased the pressure on his wrist to indicate there would be no escape. The boy turned his face to the road, as if pleading for help.

Ratna increased the pressure on the boy's wrist.

'Where did you sit with her? By the side of a road, inside a hotel, or at the back of a building?'

He twisted harder.

'By the side of a road,' the boy blurted out; then turned to Ratna with a face about to burst into tears. 'How do you know?'

Ratna closed his eyes; breathed out; let go of the boy's wrist. 'A truckers' whore.' He slapped the boy on the head.

The boy began crying. 'I only sat with her once,' he said, fighting back his sobs.

'Once is enough. Do you burn when you pass urine?'

'Yes, I burn.'

*'Nausea?'*

The boy asked what that English word meant, and said 'yes' when he understood.

'What else?'

'A feeling that there is something large and hard – like a solid rubber ball between my legs all the time. And then dizziness, sometimes sickness.'

'Can you get erect?'

'Yes. No.'

'Tell me what your organ looks like. Is it black? Is it red? Are the lips of your penis swollen?'

Half an hour later, the two men were still at the base of the banyan tree, facing the temple.

'I beg you . . .' The boy folded his palms. 'I beg you.'

Ratna shook his head.

'I have to cancel the wedding, what else can I do now? How can I let my daughter get this disease too?'

The boy stared hard at the earth, as if he had simply run out of ways to beg. A drop of moisture on the tip of his nose gleamed like silver.

'I'll ruin you,' he said quietly.

Ratna wiped his hands on the back of his sarong. 'How?'

'I'll say that the girl has slept with someone. I'll say that she's not a virgin. That's why you had to cancel the wedding.'

In one swift motion, Ratna seized the boy's head, yanked it back, held it for a moment like that, and then slammed it against the tree. He got up and spat on the boy.

'I swear by the god who sits in the temple before us, I will kill you with my own hands if you do that.'

He was in fiery form that day in front of the Dargah; thundering, as the young men gathered around, about sin, and disease, and about how germs rise from the genitalia, through the nipples, into the mouth, and eyes, and ears, until they reach the nostrils. Then he showed them his photos: images of rotted, red genitalia, some gone black, some distended, some charred, as if acid-burnt. Above each rotted organ was the face of the victim, his eyes covered by a black rectangle, as if he were a victim of torture or rape. These were the consequences of sin, Ratna explained: and expiation and redemption came only in the form of a bottle of magic white pills.

Three months or so passed. One morning, he was back at his spot behind the white dome, shouting at the Stonehenge of worried young men, when he saw a face that made his heart stop.

Afterwards, when he was done with his talk, he saw the face again, in front of him.

'What do you want?' he hissed. 'It's too late. My daughter's married now. Why have you come here now?'

Ratna folded his stool under his arm, dropped his medicines into his red bag, and walked fast. A flurry of footsteps followed him. The boy – the firecracker merchant's son – panted as he spoke.

'Things are becoming worse by the day. I can't pass urine without my penis burning hard. You must do something for me. You must give me your pills.'

Ratna gnashed his teeth. 'You sinned, you bastard. You sat with a prostitute. Now pay for it!'

He walked faster, and faster, and then the footsteps were gone and he was alone.

But the next evening, he saw the face again: then the quick steps followed him all the way to the bus stand, and the voice said, again and again, 'help me,' but Ratna did not turn around.

He got on to the bus, counted to ten, then took out the brochures with the image of rats on them and spoke to the passengers of the rat race. Then the dark outline of the fort appeared in the distance; the bus slowed down and stopped. He got off. Someone else got off with him. He walked. Someone else walked behind him.

Ratna spun around and seized his stalker by his collar.

'Didn't I tell you, leave me alone? What has got into you?'

The boy pushed Ratna's hands away, and straightened his collar, and whispered: 'Help me. I think I'm dying. Help me.'

'Look here, I can't. None of those young men is going to be cured by anything I sell. Don't you get it?'

There was a moment of silence, and then the boy whispered: 'But you were at the sexology conference . . . the sign in English says so . . .'

Ratna raised his hands to the sky.

'I found that sign on the ground.'

'But the Hakim Bhagwandass of Delhi . . .'

'Hakim Bhagwandass, my arse! Those are white sugar pills that I buy wholesale from a chemist in Karwar; then my daughter bottles them and sticks labels on them at my house!'

To prove his point, he opened his leather case, popped a bottle open, and scattered the pills across the ground, as if broadcasting seed on the earth. 'They do nothing! I have nothing for you, son!'

The boy sat down, picked up a white pill from the earth, and swallowed it. He got down on all fours, and scrambled about the black mud for the white pills, which he began swallowing in a frenzy along with any dirt attached to them.

'Are you mad?'

Getting down on his knees, Ratna gave the boy a good shake, and asked the same question again and again.

And then, at last, he saw the boy's eyes. They had changed since he had last seen them; teary and red, they were like pickled vegetables of some kind. Individual blood vessels bulged and swelled large.

His grip on the boy's shoulder slackened.

'You'll have to pay me, understood, for my help? I don't do charity.'

Half an hour later, the two men got off a bus near the railway station. They walked together through streets that got progressively narrower and darker, until they reached a store whose awning was marked with a large red medical cross. From inside the store, a radio was blaring a popular Kannada film song.

'Buy something here, and leave me alone.'

Ratna tried to walk away, but the boy clutched on to his wrist.

'Wait. Pick the right medicine for me and then go.'

Ratna began walking fast to the place where the bus would stop, but again he heard footsteps. He turned around, and there the boy was, following with his hands full of green bottles.

Regretting that he had ever agreed to bring him here, Ratna walked faster. He heard the light, desperate footsteps again, like a ghost following him.

For several hours that night Ratna stayed awake, wriggling in his bed, and disturbing his wife. He had soliloquies with the boy, who seemed to be somewhere around his bed.

The next day, in the evening, he took the bus into the city, back into Umbrella Street. When he got to the firecracker shop he stood at a distance, with his arms folded, until the boy saw him. The two of them walked together in silence for a while, until they came to a sugarcane juice stand. As the machines turned and crushed the raw cane, Ratna said:

'Go to the hospital. They'll help you.'

'I can't go to the hospital. They know me. They'll tell my father.'

Ratna had a vision of that immense man with the tufts of white hair growing out of his ears, sitting in front of his arsenal of firecrackers and paper bombs.

The next day, as Ratna was folding up his wooden stand and suitcase, he saw a shadow on the ground in front of him. He went around the Dargah; he walked past the long line of pilgrims going in to pray at the tomb, and past the rows of lepers, and past the man with one leg who was lying on the ground, twitching from the hip and chanting: 'Al-lah! Al-laaaah! Al-lah! Al-laaah!'

He looked up at the white dome and stared for a moment.

He went down to the sea, and the shadow followed him. A low stone wall ran around the edge of the land, and he put his right foot on it, and looked out at the sea. The waves were coming in violently; now and then there was a big crash of water against the wall, and thick white foam rose up into the air and spread out, like a peacock's tail coming up from the sea. Ratna turned around.

'What choice do I have? If I don't sell them those white pills, how will I marry my daughters off?'

The boy, avoiding his glances, stared at the ground, and shifted his weight about uncomfortably.

The two of them caught the no. 5 bus and took it all the way to the heart of the city, getting off near the Angel Talkies. The boy carried the wooden stool, and Ratna searched up and down the main road, until he found a large billboard of a husband and a wife standing together in wedding clothes:

HAPPY LIFE CLINIC
Consulting Specialist: Doctor M. V. Kamath
M.B.B.S. (Mysore), B. Mec (Allahabad), D.B.B.S
(Mysore), M.Ch (Calcutta), G.Com (Varanasi).
SATISFACTION GUARANTEED

'You see those letters after his name?' Ratna whispered into the boy's ear. 'That's the man for you. He's a *real* sexologist.'

In the waiting room, they saw a half dozen lean, nervous men sitting on black chairs, and one married couple, in a corner. Ratna and the boy sat down in between the single men and the couple. Ratna looked curiously at the men; all of them avoided his glance. These were the same fellows who came to him – older, sadder versions; men in whom venereal disease had taken a deep bite, who had thrown bottle after bottle of white pills at it, to find no improvement – who were now at the end of a long journey of despair, that led from his booth at the Dargah, through a long trail of other hucksters, to this doctor's clinic, where they would be told the truth at last.

One by one, the lean men went into the doctor's room, and the door shut behind them. Ratna looked at the married couple, and thought – at least they are not alone in this ordeal. At least they have each other.

Then the man got up to see the doctor; the woman stayed back. She went in later, after the man had left. Of course they are not husband and wife, Ratna told himself. When he gets this disease, this disease of sex, every man is alone in the universe.

'And who are you in relation to the patient?' the doctor asked.

They had taken their seats, at last, at his consulting desk. There was a giant chart showing a cross-section of a man's urinary and reproductive organs on the wall behind the doctor, and Ratna looked at it for a moment, and then said:

'His uncle.'

The doctor made the boy remove his shirt; then he sat

next to him, made him put his tongue out, peered into his eyes, and put his stethoscope to the boy's chest, moving it from nipple to nipple.

Ratna thought: to get a disease like this, on his very first time! Where was the justice in that?

After examining the boy's genitals, the doctor moved to a washbasin with a mirror attached over it; he pulled a cord, and a tube-light flickered to life over the mirror.

Letting the water run in the basin, he gargled and spat, and then turned the light over the basin off. He took care of janitorial duties around his office – wiping a corner of the basin with a palm, then lowering a blind over a window, casting a glance into the state of his green plastic waste-basket.

When he ran out of things to do, he returned to his desk, looked at his feet, and practised breathing for a while.

'His kidneys are gone.'

'Gone?'

'Gone,' the doctor said.

He turned to the boy, who was trembling so hard that his seat had begun to titter.

'Are you a homosexual?'

The boy covered his face in his hands. Ratna answered for him.

'Look, he got it from a prostitute, there's no sin in that. He's not an unnatural fellow. He just didn't know enough about this world we live in.'

The doctor nodded. He turned around, to the image of the male reproductive system behind him, and put his finger on the kidneys, and said:

'Gone.'

Ratna and the boy came together to the bus station the next day, at six in the morning, to catch the bus to Manipal, to see if there was a good doctor at the Medical College who might help them out. A man in a blue sarong, sitting on the bench in the station, told them that the bus to Manipal was always delayed by a few minutes, maybe fifteen, maybe thirty, maybe more. 'Everything's been falling apart in this country since Mrs. Gandhi got shot,' the man said, and kicked his legs about merrily. 'Buses are coming late. Trains are coming late. Everything's falling apart. We'll have to hand this country back to the British or the Muslims or the Russians or someone, I tell you. We're not meant to be masters of our own fate, I tell you.'

Telling the boy to wait for a moment in the bus stand, Ratna came back with some peanuts in a paper cone that he had bought for twenty paise, and said: 'You haven't had breakfast, have you? Take some.' But the boy reminded him that the doctor had warned against eating anything spicy; it would irritate his penis. So Ratna went back to the vendor and exchanged the peanuts for the unsalted kind. They munched them together for a while, until the boy ran to the wall and began throwing up. Ratna stood over him, patting his back, while he retched again and again. The man in the blue sarong watched with greedy eyes; then he came up to Ratna and whispered into his ear: 'What's the kid got? He's dying, isn't he?'

'Nonsense; he's just got a flu,' Ratna said. The bus came to the station an hour late.

It was late on the way back as well. The two of them had to stand in the midst of the thick crowd returning to Kittur for over an hour, until a pair of seats emptied near them. Ratna slid into the window seat and motioned for the boy to sit down next to him. 'We got lucky, considering how packed the bus is,' Ratna said with a smile.

Gently, he disengaged his hand from the boy's.

The boy understood too; he nodded, and took out his wallet, and threw five-rupee notes, one after the other, on Ratna's lap.

'What's this for?'

'You said you wanted something for helping me.'

Ratna thrust the notes into the boy's shirt-pocket. 'Don't go and get an attitude now. I have helped you out so far; and what did I have to gain from it? It was pure public service on my part, remember that. We aren't related: there's no blood in common between us.'

The boy said nothing.

'Look! I can't keep coming around with you as you go from doctor to doctor. I've got my daughters to marry off, I don't know where I'll get the dowry for—'

The boy turned, plunged his face into Ratna's collar-bone and burst into sobs; his lips rubbed against Ratna's clavicles, and began sucking on them. The passengers stared at them, and Ratna was too bewildered to say anything.

It took another hour before the outline of the black fort appeared on the horizon. The man and the boy got off the bus together. He stood on the main road and waited, while the boy blew his nose and shook off the phlegm to the ground. Ratna looked at the black rectangle of the fort, and felt a sense of despair: how had it been decided, and by whom, and when, and why, that Ratnakara Shetty was responsible for helping this firecracker merchant's son fight his disease? Against the black rectangle of the fort, he had a vision, momentarily, of a white dome, and he heard a throng of mutilated beings chanting in unison. He put a beedi in his mouth, struck a match and inhaled.

'Let's go,' he told the boy. 'It's a long walk from here to my house.'

## DAY SIX (EVENING): BAJPE

*Bajpe, at the edge of the last patch of forested land in Kittur, was marked out by the founding fathers as one of the 'cleansing lungs' of the town, and for this reason had been protected for thirty years from the avarice of real estate developers. The great forest of Bajpe, which stretched from Kittur right up to the Arabian Sea, was bound on the town side by the Ganapati Hindu Boys' School and the small adjacent temple of Ganesha. Next to the temple ran Bishop Street, the only stretch in the neighbourhood where houses could be built. Beyond the street stood a large rectangle of wilderness, and beyond that began a dark lattice of trees – the forest. When relatives from the heart of town visited, the residents of Bishop Street were usually up in their terraces or balconies, enjoying the cool breezes that blew from the forest in the evening. Guests and hosts together watched as herons, eagles, and kingfishers flew into and out of the darkening mass of trees, like ideas circulating around an immense brain. The sun, which had plunged into the forest, burned orange and ochre through the interstices of the foliage, as if it were peering out of the trees, and the observers had the distinct impression that they were being observed in return. At such moments, the guests declared that the inhabitants of Bajpe were the luckiest people on earth. At the same time, it was assumed that if a man built a house on*

*Bishop Street, there was a reason for him to want to be far from civilization.*

Giridhar Rao and Kamini, the childless couple on Bishop Street, were one of the hidden treasures of Kittur, all their friends declared. Weren't they a marvel? All the way out in Bajpe, at the very edge of the wilderness, this barren couple kept alive the all-but-dead art of Brahmin hospitality.

It was another Thursday evening, and the half-a-dozen or so members of the Raos' circle of *intimates* were making their way through the mud and slush of Bishop Street for the weekly get-together. Ahead of the pack, moving with giant strides, came Mr. Anantha Murthy, the philosopher. Behind him was Mrs. Shirthadi, the wife of the Life Insurance Company of India man. Then Mrs. Pai, and then Mr. Bhat, and finally, Mrs. Aithal, always the last to get down from her green Ambassador.

The Raos' house was all the way down at the end of the slushy part of Bishop Street, just a few steps away from where the thick clump of trees began – the last bit of virgin forest in Kittur, which stretched from the town's edge right up to the shore of the Arabian Sea. Sitting at the forest's edge, the house had the look of a fugitive, ready to spring into the wilderness at a moment's notice.

'Did everyone hear that?'

Mr. Anantha Murthy turned around. He put a hand to his ear, and raised his eyebrows.

Cool breezes were blowing in from the forest. The *intimates* stopped mid-track, trying to hear what Mr. Murthy had heard.

'I think it's a woodpecker, somewhere in the trees!'

An irritated voice boomed down:

'Why don't you get up here first, and listen to the woodpeckers later! The food's been prepared with a lot of care, and it's cooling down!'

It was Mr. Rao, leaning out of the balcony of his house.

'Okay, okay,' Mr. Anantha Murthy grumbled, picking his way through the slush again. 'But it's not every day a man gets to hear a woodpecker.' He turned around to Mrs. Shirthadi. 'We forget everything that's important when we live in towns, don't we, madam?'

She grunted. She was trying to make sure she didn't get mud on her sari.

The philosopher led the *intimates* to the house. When they had done scraping their chappals and shoes on the coconut-fibre mat placed on the doorway to the house, the visitors entered to find old Sharadha Bhatt squinting at them. She was the proprietor of the place, a widow whose only son lived in Bombay. It was understood that the Raos stayed on in that cramped apartment, so far from the heart of town, partly out of concern for Sharadha Bhatt – she was a distant relative. A suggestion of intense religiosity clung to the old lady's person. The visitors heard the drone of M.S. Subbalakshmi singing 'Suprabhata' from a small black tape recorder in her room. Sitting with folded legs on a wooden bed, she was slapping her thighs alternately with the front and back of her left palm while following the rhythm of the holy music.

Some of the visitors remembered her husband, a celebrated teacher of Carnatic music who had performed on radio, and paid their respects: a nod of the head.

Done with their obligation to the ancient one, they hurried up a wide stairwell to the Raos' quarters. It was a crushingly small space that the childless couple occupied. Half the living area was a single drawing room, cluttered with sofas and chairs. In a corner, a sitar was propped up against the wall, its shaft having slid down to a 45 degree angle.

'Ah! It's the *intimates* again!'

Giridhar Rao's appearance was neat, modest, and unpretentious. You could tell at once that he worked in a bank. Since his transfer from Perur – his hometown – he had been the deputy branch manager at the Karnataka Bank's Cool-Water Well Branch for nearly a decade now. (The *intimates* knew that Mr. Rao could have risen much higher within the bank had he not repeatedly refused to be transferred to Bombay.) The wavy spread of his hair was flattened with coconut oil, and parted at the side. A handlebar moustache – the one anomaly in the demure appearance – was neatly combed and curled at its ends. Mr. Rao had now thrown a half-sleeved shirt over his singlet. The fabric of the shirt was thin: inside its dark, silken spread, the thick singlet glowed like a skeleton in an X-ray.

'How are you, Kamini?' Mr. Anantha Murthy shouted out in the direction of the kitchen, which was hidden behind a blue screen.

The furniture in the drawing room was a motley mix – green metal seats discarded from the bank, a torn old sofa, and three fraying cane chairs. The *intimates* pounced on their favourite pieces of seating. The conversation started haltingly. The people gathered sensed that they were as haphazard a

237

collection as the furniture. None was aware of any blood relation to the other. By day, Mr. Anantha Murthy was a chartered accountant to Kittur's rich. In the evenings he became a committed philosopher of the Advaita school. He found Mr. Rao a willing (but silent) listener to his theories of the Hindu life – and that was how he became part of the circle. Mrs. Shirthadi, who usually came without her busy husband, had been educated in Madras and espoused several 'liberated' opinions. Her English was exceptionally fine, a marvel to listen to. Mr. Rao asked her to speak on Charles Dickens at the bank a few years ago. Mrs. Aithal and her husband had met Kamini at a musical concert last May. The two of them were originally from Vizag.

The *intimates* knew that the Raos had picked them for their distinction – for their delicacy. They bore a responsibility upon entering that cosy little garret. Certain topics were taboo. Within the wide circumference of acceptable conversation – world news, philosophy, bank politics, the relentless expansion of Kittur, the rainfall this year – the *intimates* had learnt to meander freely. Forest breezes fluttered in from a balcony, and a transistor radio balanced precariously on the edge of the parapet emitted a steady patter of the BBC's evening news service.

A late arrival – Mrs. Karwar, the teacher of Victorian literature at the University – threw the house into chaos. Her vivacious five-year-old, Lalitha, charged up the stairs shrieking.

'Look here, Kamini' – Mr. Rao shouted at the blue screen – 'Mrs. Karwar has smuggled your secret lover into the house!'

Kamini came rushing out of the kitchen. Fair-skinned and shapely, she was almost a beauty. (The forehead was protuberant, and the hair thinnish up the front.) She was famous for her 'Chinese' eyes: wide thin slits that were half-closed under the curve of heavy eyelids, like lotus buds prematurely opened. Her hair – she was known to be a 'modern' woman – was tied up in a Western-style 'bob.' Ladies admired her hips, which, never having been burst wide by childbirth, still sported a girlish slimness.

She rushed at once at Lalitha. The little girl was hoisted into the air and kissed several times.

'Look, let's wait till my husband's back is turned, and then we'll get on my moped and drive away, huh? Let's leave the evil man behind us and go away to my sister's house in Bombay, okay?'

At this, Giridhar Rao put his hands on his waist and made large eyes at the giggling girl.

'Are you planning on stealing my wife? Are you really her "secret lover?"'

'Hey, keep listening to your BBC,' Kamini retorted, leading Lalitha by the hand into the kitchen.

The *intimates* acknowledged their keen delight in this pantomime. The Raos certainly did not lack the skill to keep a child happy.

The drone of the BBC continued from the outside radio – a gravy of words that the *intimates* dipped into when their conversation ran dry. Mr. Anantha Murthy broke one long pause by declaring that the situation in Afghanistan was getting out of hand. One of these mornings Soviets would come streaming over Kashmir with their red flags. Then the country would regret having missed its chance to forge an alliance with America back in 1948.

'Don't you feel this way, Mr. Rao?'

The host had never anything more to express than a grin. Mr. Murthy did not mind. Mr. Rao was not a 'man of many words,' he acknowledged – but he was a 'deep' fellow all the same. If you ever wanted to know little details about world history – like for instance, who was the American president who dropped the bomb on Hiroshima – not Roosevelt, but the little man with round glasses – then you turned to Giridhar Rao. He knew everything; he said nothing. That kind of fellow.

'How is it you stay so calm, Mr. Rao, despite all this chaos and killing that the BBC is always telling you about? What is your secret?' Mrs. Shirthadi asked, as she did often.

The bank manager smiled.

'When I need peace of mind, madam, I just go to my private beach.'

'Are you a secret millionaire?' Mrs. Shirthadi demanded. 'What's this private beach you keep talking about?'

'Oh, nothing, really.' He gestured towards the distance. 'Just a little lake, with some gravel around it. It's a very soothing place.'

'And why haven't we all been invited there?' Mr. Murthy demanded.

The guests sat up. A triumphant Mrs. Rao entered the drawing room with a plastic tray whose multiple compartments brimmed with the evening's first offerings.

The stuff in each compartment was a marvel – dried walnuts (which looked like little shrunken brains), juicy figs, sultana raisins, diced almonds, chips of desiccated pineapples . . .

Before the guests had recovered, they were hit by the next assault:

'Dinner is ready!'

They went into the dining room – the only other room in the house (a little kitchen led out on one side, and a toilet was built into the kitchen). An enormous bed, plump with cushions, lay flat in the middle of the room. There was no pretending not to see the conjugal site. It lay there, brazenly open to the view. A small table was pulled up right next to it, and three of the guests, hesitantly took their seat there. Their embarrassment disappeared in a moment. The informality of their hosts, the voluptuous softness of the bedding beneath them – these things soothed their nerves. Then dinner rolled out of Kamini's little kitchen. Course after course of fine saaru, idli, and dosas flowed out of that factory of gustatory treats.

'This kind of cooking would amaze people even in Bombay,' proposed Mr. Anantha Murthy, when the pièce de résistance – fluffy North Indian rotis, lined on the inside with chilli powder – arrived on the table. Kamini beamed at his remarks, and protested, he was all wrong, she had so many inadequacies as a cook and a housewife!

When the guests rose, they noticed that their buttocks had left wide, warm, and deep, markings on the bed, like elephant's footprints on clay. Giridhar Rao brushed aside their apologies:

241

'Our guests are like gods to us; they can do no wrong. That's the philosophy in this house.'

They stood in line outside the washroom, where the water flowed down from a green rubber pipe twisted into a loop over the faucet. Then back to the drawing room for the highlight of the evening – almond kheer.

Kamini brought out the dessert in breathtakingly large tumblers. The shake – served warm or cold, according to each guest's pleasure – was so full of almonds that the drinkers protested they had to *chew* the drink! When they looked into their cups, they held their breath in wonder: shiny flecks, strands of real saffron, floated about the chunks of almond.

They walked out of the door wordlessly, heeding Mr. Rao's request not to disturb the sleeping Sharadha Bhatt. (The old lady turned restlessly on her wooden bed as they departed; in the background the religious music droned on.)

'Remember to come next week!' Mr. Rao had said from the terrace. 'It's the week of the Satya Narayana Pooja! I'll make sure Kamini does a good job with the cooking next week, unlike tonight's disaster!' He turned around into the house and raised his voice: 'Did you hear that, Kamini? The food had better be good next time, or you're divorced.'

There had been a laugh, and a high-pitched scream from inside: 'You'll be the one to get divorced, unless you shut up at once!'

Once at a safe distance, the *intimates* broke out into talk.

What a pair! Man and woman such complete opposites! He was 'bland'; she was 'spicy.' He was 'conservative,' she was 'modern.' She was 'quick,' he was 'deep.'

Still picking their way through the muddy road, they began discussing the forbidden topic, with all the excitement and eagerness of people who were discussing it for the first time.

'It's obvious—' one of the women, Mrs. Aithal or Mrs. Shirthadi, said, 'Kamini is the one "at fault." She wouldn't get *the operation* done. No wonder her life is racked by guilt. Don't you see how she throws herself on any available child in a storm of frustrated maternity, showering them with kisses and blandishments and caramel chocolates? What does that signify to you, if not guilt?'

'And why does she refuse the operation?' Mr. Anantha Murthy demanded.

Obstinacy. The women were sure of it. Kamini simply refused to acknowledge that the fault was hers. Some of Kamini's stubbornness, to be sure, came straight from her privileged background. She was the youngest of four sisters, all fair as buttermilk, the darling children of a famous eye-surgeon in Shimoga. How she must have been spoilt as a child! The other sisters had married well – a lawyer, an architect, and a surgeon, and all lived in Bombay. Giridhar Rao was the poorest of the brothers-in-law. You could be sure that Kamini was not the kind of woman to let him forget this. Didn't you see how defiantly she rode about town in her Hero Honda moped, as if she were the lord of their household?

Mr. Anantha Murthy raised several objections. Why were all the womenfolk so suspicious of Kamini's 'sportiness'? How rare to find such a free-thinking woman! The fault was *his*.

Didn't you see him refusing promotion after promotion just because he would have to move to Bombay? What did that tell you? The man was *lethargic*.

'If only he would show . . . some more *initiative* . . . the problem of childlessness could be solved . . .' Mr. Murthy said, giving his bald head a sad philosopher's shake.

He even claimed to have given Mr. Rao the names of doctors in Bombay who could solve the lack of 'initiative.'

Mrs. Aithal reacted indignantly. Mr. Rao had more than enough 'spunk' in him! Didn't he have such dense facial hair? And didn't he ride a manly red Yamaha motorcycle to the bank every morning?

The women enjoyed romanticizing him. Mrs. Shirthadi irritated Mr. Murthy by suggesting that the modest little bank manager, too, was in secret 'a philosopher.' Once she had caught him reading the 'religious issues of the day' column on the last page of *The Hindu*. He seemed embarrassed at this discovery, and parried her inquiries with jokes and puns. Still, the feeling had grown that beneath all his joking, he was undeniably 'deep.'

'How can he be so calm all the time, even without having children?' Mrs. Aithal demanded.

'He has a secret of some kind, I'm sure,' Mr. Murthy suggested.

Mrs. Karwar coughed and said:

'Sometimes I fear that she might be thinking of divorcing him' – and everyone looked worried. The woman certainly was 'modern' enough to think of things like that . . .

But they had reached their cars now, and broke up into groups, and drove away one after the other.

Later in the week, they saw the Raos as they circled the Cool-Water Well Junction on his Yamaha bike. Kamini was on the backseat holding on tightly to her husband, and the watchers were always surprised to see how the two of them looked like a real couple just then.

Next Thursday, when the intimates came back to the Rao residence, they were surprised to see Sharada Bhatt herself opening the door for them. The old woman's silver hair was disarrayed, and her eyes glared at her tenants' guests.

'She's having some trouble with Bobby – you know, her architect son in Bombay. She's asked him again if she can come stay with him, but his wife won't allow it,' Kamini whispered, as she led them up the stairs.

Because of the anticipation of an extraordinary meal this evening, Mr. Shirthadi, the Life Insurance Company of India man, was putting in a rare appearance alongside his wife. He spoke passionately about the ingratitude of today's children, and said he sometimes wished he had stayed childless. Mrs. Shirthadi watched nervously – her husband had almost crossed the invisible line

Then Mrs. Karwar came with Lalitha, and there was the usual shouting and shrieking between Kamini and the 'secret lover.'

After the sherbet was presented, Mr. Anantha Murthy asked Mr. Rao to confirm a piece of gossip – had he turned down another offer to be posted to Bombay?

Mr. Rao confirmed this with a nod.

'Why don't you go, Giridhar Rao?' demanded Mrs. Shirthadi. 'Don't you want to rise in the bank?'

'I'm happy out here, madam,' Mr. Rao said. 'I have my private beach, and my BBC in the evenings. What more does a man need?'

'You are the perfect Hindu man, Mr. Giridhar,' said Mr. Anantha Murthy, who was growing restless for dinner. 'Which is to say, you are almost completely contented with your fate on earth.'

'Well, would you still be contented if I ran away with Lalitha?' Kamini shouted out from the kitchen.

'My dear, if you ran away, then I'd be truly contented,' he retorted.

She shrieked out in mock outrage, and the *intimates* applauded the joke.

'Well, what about this private beach that you keep talking about, Mr. Rao – when are we going to see it, exactly?' Mrs. Shirthadi asked.

Before he could reply, Kamini came scampering out of the kitchen, and leaned over the stairs.

A stertorous breathing grew louder. Sharadha Bhatt's face slowly emerged into the upper quarters, as she limped up, one stair at a time.

Kamini was agitated.

'Should I help you up the stairs? Should I do something?'

The old woman shook her head. Half out of breath, she stumbled onto a chair at the top of the steps.

The conversation stopped. This was the very first time the old woman had joined the weekly diners.

In a few minutes the *intimates* learned to ignore her.

Mr. Anantha Murthy clapped his hands when Kamini came out with the appetizer tray.

'So, what's this I hear about your taking up swimming?'

'And if I am?" she snapped, putting a hand on her waist. 'What's wrong with that?'

'I hope you are not going to wear a bikini like Western women?'

'Why not? If they do it in America, why can't we? Are we less than them in any way?'

And Lalitha, giggled furiously, while Kamini announced plans for the two of them to buy the scandalous swimsuits right away.

'And if Mr. Giridhar Rao doesn't like it – then the two of us are going to run away and live together in Bombay, aren't we?'

Giridhar Rao glanced nervously at the old woman, who had her gaze fixed on her toes.

'All this "modern" talk isn't getting you upset, is it, Sharadha-amma?'

The old lady breathed heavily. She curled her toes up and stared at them.

Mr. Anantha Murthy ventured a comparison between the barfi that Kamini had put out on the appetizer tray and the barfi served in the best café in Bombay.

Then the old lady spoke in a hoarse voice:

'It is written in the Scriptures . . .' she paused for a long time. The room went silent.

'. . . that a man . . . a man who has no son may not aspire to enter the gates of Heaven.' She breathed out. 'And if a man doesn't enter Heaven, neither can his wife. And here you go about talking of bikinis and wikinis, and cavorting with "modern" people, instead of praying to God to forgive your sins!'

She breathed heavily for another moment, then got up and hobbled down the stairs.

When the *intimates* left – it was a truncated evening – they found the old lady outside the house. Sitting on a suitcase bursting with clothes, she was bellowing out to the coconut grove.

'Yama Deva, come for me! Now that my son has forgotten his mother, what more is there for me to live for?'

As she called out to the Lord of Death, she struck her forehead with the stems of her fists, and her bangles jangled.

Feeling Giridhar Rao's hand on her shoulder, the old woman burst into tears.

The *intimates* saw Giridhar Rao gesturing for them to leave. The old lady had exhausted her histrionics. Her head sunk into Kamini's breast, and she convulsed with sobbing.

'Forgive me, mother . . . The gods have given us each our punishment. They gave you a uterus of stone, and they have smashed the heart in my son's chest . . .'

After they put the old lady to sleep together, Mr. Rao let his wife walk up the stairs first. When he got up, she was lying on the bed, turned away from him.

He walked into the verandah and turned the radio off.

She said nothing while he picked up his helmet and headed down the stairs. The kick-starting of his engine rent the quiet of Bishop Street.

*

In a few minutes, he was on the road that went through the forest to the sea. On either side of the speeding bike, the serried silhouettes of coconut palms bristled against the blue coastal night. Hanging low over the trees, a bright moon had the look of something cleaved by an axe. With its top right corner sliced off, it hung in the sky like an illustration of the idea of 'two-thirds.'

The sound of waters brimming excited the air after several minutes. The Yamaha bike swerved off the road into a mud path, and thundered over stones and gravel. Then its engine went dead.

A lake, a small inland waterway inside the forest, came into view, and Giridhar Rao stopped his bike and left his helmet on the seat. A small shore had been cleared by some fishermen around the lagoon, which was sealed off on the far side by more coconut trees. At this hour, there would be nets all over the lake, but there was not a soul about. A heron, walking through the shallow water at the edge of the lake, was the only other living thing in sight. Giridhar had stumbled upon his lake years ago, on a night-drive through the forest. He had no idea why no one came here; but a small town is like that, full of hidden treasures. He walked along the lake for a few minutes, then sat down on a rock.

The water in the lake, glossy, and rippled by black waves, had the look of sheets of molten glass settling on top of one another.

The heron flapped its wings and rose from the lake. Now he was all alone. He hummed softly, a tune from his bachelor days in Bangalore. A yawn expanded his face. He looked up. Three stars had emerged from the tatters of a grey cloud; together with the lopped-off moon they composed a quadrilateral. Mr. Rao admired the structure of the night sky. It pleased him to think that the elements of our world were not cast about at random. Something stood behind them: an order.

He yawned again and stretched his legs from the rock.

His peace was broken. It had begun to drizzle on him. At once he wondered: had he remembered to fasten the windows above their bed? The rain might hit her face.

Leaving his private beach behind him, he sprinted to his motorbike, put his helmet on, and kicked the machine to life.

*One morning in 1987, all of Bishop Street woke up to hear the dull thack-thack-thack of axes hacking away at the trees. In a few days, chain-saws were buzzing, and cranes were scooping up giant portions of black earth. And that was the end of the great forest of Bajpe. In its place, the inhabitants of Bishop Street now saw a giant pit filled with cranes, lorries, and an army of bare-chested migrant workers carrying stacks of bricks and cement bags on their head like ants moving about grains of rice. A giant sign in Kannada and Hindi proclaimed this the future site of 'Sardar Patel Iron Man of India Sports Stadium.' The racket was incessant, and dust swirled up from the pit like steam from a geyser. Outsiders who came to Bajpe thought the neighbourhood had become a dozen degrees warmer.*

## DAY SEVEN: SALT MARKET VILLAGE

*If you want a servant you can trust, a cook who won't steal sugar, a driver who won't drink, you go to Salt Market Village. Although a part of Kittur Corporation since 1988, Salt Market is still largely rural and much poorer than the rest of the town.*

*If you are here in March or April, you must stay to watch the local festival known as the 'rat hunt' – a nocturnal event in which the women of the suburb march through the rice fields with a burning torch in one hand, while pounding the earth with pestles, hockey sticks, or cricket bats with the other hand, shouting all the time at the top of their voices. The rats, mongooses, and shrews, terrified by the sound, run into the centre of the field; the women start to pound the encircled rodents to death with their sticks.*

*The only tourist attraction of Salt Market Village is an abandoned Jain basadi, where some early Kannada epics were written by the poets Harihara and Raghuveera. In 1990, a portion of the Jain basadi was purchased by the Mormon Church of Utah, USA, and turned into an office for its evangelists.*

Murali, waiting in the kitchen for the tea to boil, took a step to his right and peeped.

Comrade Thimma, who was sitting beneath the framed Soviet poster, had begun grilling the old woman.

'Do you understand the exact nature of the doctrinal differences between the Communist Party of India, the Communist Party of India (Marxist), and the Communist Party of India (Marxist-Maoist).'

Of course she doesn't know, Murali thought, taking a step back to the left, and turning the kettle off.

No one on earth did.

He put his hand into a tin box full of sugar biscuits. In a moment, he was out in the reception holding a tray with three cups of tea and a sugar biscuit by the side of each cup.

Comrade Thimma was looking at the point high up on the wall opposite him, which was pierced by a grilled window. The evening light illuminated the grille; a few feet away, a block of light glowed on the floor, like the tail of an incandescent bird perched in the grille.

The Comrade's manner strongly hinted that the old woman, considering her state of utter doctrinal ignorance, was unworthy of receiving assistance from the Communist Party of India (Marxist-Maoist), Kittur unit.

The woman was frail and haggard; her husband had hanged himself two weeks ago from the ceiling of their house.

Murali placed the first tea cup before Comrade Thimma, who picked it up and sipped it at once. This improved his mood.

Once again looking high up at the glowing grille, the Comrade said: 'I will have to tell you our *dialectics*; if they are acceptable to you, we can talk about help.'

The farmer's wife nodded, as if the word 'dialectics,' in English, made perfect sense to her.

Without taking his eyes off the grille, the Comrade bit into one of the sugar biscuits Murali had left for him; the crumbs fell down near his chin, and Murali, after handing the old woman her tea, went back to the Comrade, and wiped the crumbs off his chin with his fingers.

The Comrade had small, sparkling eyes, and a tendency of looking high up, and far away, as he delivered his words, which he always did with a feeling of suppressed excitement. All this gave him the air of a prophet. Murali, as sidekicks to a prophet often are, was physically the superior specimen: taller, broader, with a large forehead, creased heavily, and a kind smile.

'Give the lady our brochure on *dialectics*,' the Comrade said, speaking straight to the grille.

Murali nodded, and moved purposefully towards one of the cupboards. The reception of the Communist Party of India (Marxist-Maoist) consisted of an old tea-stained table, a few decrepit cupboards, and a desk for the secretary-general, behind which was a giant poster from the early days of the Soviet Revolution, in which a group of proletarian heroes were climbing a ladder up into heaven with mallets and sledgehammers, while a group of oriental gods cowered at their advance. After digging into two of the cupboards, Murali found a brochure with a big red star on the cover that he brushed with a corner of his shirt and brought to the old woman.

'She can't read.'

The soft voice came from the woman's daughter, who was sitting in the chair next to her, holding on to her tea

253

cup and untouched sugar biscuit. After a moment's hesitation Murali let the daughter have the brochure. Keeping the tea cup in her left hand, she held the brochure between two fingers of her right, as if it were a soiled handkerchief.

The Comrade smiled at the window grille; it was not clear if he was reacting to the events of the past few minutes. He was a thin, bald, dark-skinned man with sunken cheeks and gleaming eyes. He kept his eyes on the grille, moving them for relief to a patch of sunlight on the ground.

'In the beginning we had only one party in India, and it was the true party. It made no compromise. But then the leaders of this true party were seduced by the lure of bourgeois democracy; they decided to contest the elections. That was the first mistake and the fatal one. Soon the one true party had split. New branches came up, trying to regain the original spirit. But they too got corrupted.'

Murali wiped the cupboard, and tried to realign the loose hinge of its door as well as he could. He was not the peon; there was no peon, Comrade Thimma would not allow the exploitative hiring of proletarian labour. Murali was certainly not proletarian – he was the scion of a major landowning Brahmin family of Kittur – so it was okay for him to do any kind of menial work.

The Comrade took a deep breath, took off his glasses and rubbed them clean with a corner of his white cotton shirt.

'We alone have kept the faith – we, the members of the Communist Party of India (Marxist-Maoist). We alone stay true to the dialectics. And do you know what the strength of our membership is?'

He put his glasses back on, and inhaled with satisfaction. 'Two. Murali and me.'

He stared at the grille with a wan smile. He appeared to be done; so the old woman put her hands on her daughter's head. 'She is unmarried, sir. We are begging of you some money to marry her off, that is all.'

Thimma turned to the daughter and stared; the girl looked at the ground. Murali winced. 'I wish he'd have more delicacy sometimes,' he thought.

'We have had no support,' the old woman said. 'My family won't even talk to me. Members of our own caste won't—'

The Comrade slapped his thigh with his palm.

'This caste question is only a manifestation of the class struggle: Mazumdar and Shukla have definitely established this in 1938. I refuse to accept the category of "caste" in our discussions.'

The woman looked at Murali. He nodded his head, as if to say: 'Go on.'

'My husband said, the Communists were the only ones who cared about people like us. He said if the Communists ruled the earth there would be no hardships for the poor, sir.'

This seemed to mollify the Comrade. He looked at the woman and the girl for a moment, and then sniffed. His fingers seemed to want something. Murali understood. As he went to the pantry to make another cup of tea, behind him, he heard the Comrade's voice go on:

'The Communist Party of India (Marxist-Maoist) is not the party of the poor – it is the party of the proletariat. This distinction has to be understood, before we talk about assistance or resistance.'

After turning on the kettle once more, Murali was about to toss the tea leaves in; then he wondered why the daughter had not touched her tea. He was seized by the suspicion that he had thrown too much tea into the kettle – and that the way he had been making tea for nearly twenty-five years might have been wrong.

\*

Murali got off the no. 67 C bus at the Salt Market Village stop, and walked down the main road, picking his way through a bed of muck, while hogs sniffed the earth around him. He kept his umbrella up on his shoulder, like a wrestler keeps his mace, so that its metal point wouldn't be sullied by the muck. Asking a group of boys playing a game of marbles in the middle of the village road for directions, he found the house: a surprisingly large and important-looking structure, with rocks placed on the corrugated tin roof to stabilize it during the rains.

He unlatched the gate and went in.

A handspun cotton shirt hung on a hook on the wall next to the door; the dead man's, he assumed. As if the fellow were still inside, taking a nap, and would come outside and put it on to greet his visitor.

At least a dozen multi-coloured framed images of gods had been affixed to the front wall; one of a potbellied local guru with an enormous nimbus affixed to his head. There was a bare cot, with fraying fibres, for visitors to sit down on.

Murali left his sandals outside, and wondered if he should knock on the door. Too intrusive for a place like this – where death had just entered – so he decided to wait until someone came out.

Two white cows were squatting in the compound of the house. A bell on their neck tinkled during their rare movements. In front of them was a puddle of water in which straw had been soaked to make a gruel. A black buffalo, with snippets of fresh green all over on its moist nose, stood looking at the opposite wall of the compound, and chewing on a large sack of grass that had been emptied on the ground in front of it. Murali thought: these animals have no concern in the world. Even in the house of a man who has killed himself, they are still fed and fattened. How effortlessly they rule over the men of this village, as if human civilization had mixed up masters and servants. Murali was transfixed. His eyes lingered on the fat body of the beast, its bulging belly, its glossy skin. He smelled its faeces, which had caked on its backside; it had been lying in puddles of its own refuse.

Murali had not been to Salt Market Village in decades. The last time was twenty-five years ago, when he had come searching for visual details to enrich a short story on rural poverty that he was writing. Not too much had changed in a quarter century; only the buffaloes had grown fat.

'Why didn't you knock on the door?'

The old woman had come out of the backyard; she walked around him with a big smile and went into the house and shouted: 'Hey, you! Get some tea!'

In a moment the girl came out with a tumbler of tea, which Thimma took, touching her wet fingers as he did so.

The tea, after his long trip, felt like heaven. He had never mastered the art of tea, even though he had been making it for Thimma for nearly twenty-five years now. Maybe it was one of those things that only women truly can get right, he thought.

'What do you need from us?' the old woman asked. Her manner had become more servile; as if she had guessed the purpose of his visit only now.

'To find out if you are telling the truth,' he replied, calmly.

She called in the neighbours so he could interview them. They squatted around the cot; he insisted they sit level with him but they stayed where they were.

'Where did he hang himself?'

'Right here, sir!' one old villager with broken, paan-stained teeth said.

'What do you mean right here?'

The old fellow pointed to the beam of the roof. Murali could not believe it: In full public view, he had killed himself? So the cows had seen it; and the fat buffalo too.

He heard about the man whose shirt still hung from the hook. The failure of his crops. The loan from the moneylender. Three per cent per month, compounded.

'He was ruined from the first daughter's wedding. Then he knew he had one more to marry off – this girl you see inside.'

The daughter had lingered in a corner of the front yard the whole time. He saw her turn her face away, in slow agony.

As he was leaving, one of the villagers came running after him: 'Sir . . . sir . . . I mean, an aunt of mine committed suicide two years ago . . . I mean, just a year ago, sir, and she was virtually a mother to me . . . can the Communist Party . . .'

Murali seized the man's arm, and pressed his fingers deeply into his flesh. He peered into his eyes:

'What is the name of the daughter?'

With slow steps he walked back to the bus station. He let the tip of his umbrella trail along the earth. The horror of the dead man's story, the sight of those fat buffaloes, the pain-stricken face of that beautiful daughter – these details kept churning over and over in his mind.

He thought back twenty-five years, when he had come to this village with a notepad and dreams of becoming an Indian Maupassant. As he walked down the twisting streets, crowded with streetchildren playing their violent games, fatigued day-labourers sleeping under the shade of trees, and with thick, still, shiny pools of effluent lying everywhere, he remembered that strange mixture of the unbelievably beautiful and filthy which is the nature of every Indian village – and the simultaneous desire to admire and to castigate that they had inspired in him from the time of his first visits.

He felt the need, once again, to take down notes. To make observations.

Back then, he had come each day to Salt Market Village for a week, jotting down painstakingly detailed descriptions of farmers, roosters, bulls, pigs, piglets, hogs, sewage, children's games, religious festivals, in order to juggle them into a series of short stories that he finished in the reading room of the municipal library at night. He was not sure if the party would approve of his stories, so he sent a bundle of them under a nom de plume – 'The Seeker of Justice' – to the editor of a weekly magazine in Mysore.

After a week, he got a postcard from the editor, summoning him from Kittur for an interview. He took the train to Mysore and waited half a day for the editor to call him into his office.

'Ah, yes . . . the young genius from Kittur.' The editor searched around his table for his glasses, and pulled out the folded bundle of Murali's stories from their envelope, while the young author's heart beat violently.

'I wanted to see you . . .' the editor let the stories drop down on the table, 'because there is talent in your writing. You have gone into the countryside, and seen life there, unlike 90 per cent of our writers.'

Murali glowed. It was the first time anyone had mentioned 'talent' and him in the same sentence.

The editor went silent, and scanned the pages again.

'Who is your favourite author?' he asked, biting the stem of his glasses.

'Guy de Maupassant.' Murali corrected himself: 'After Karl Marx.'

'Let's stick to literature,' the editor retorted. 'Every character in Maupassant is like this . . .' he bent his index finger, and wiggled it. 'He wants, and wants, and wants. To the last day of his life he wants. Money. Women. Fame. More women. More money. More fame. Your characters—' he unbent his finger, 'want absolutely nothing. They simply walk through accurately described village settings, and have deep thoughts. They walk around the cows and trees and roosters and think, and then walk around the roosters and trees and cows and think some more. That's it.'

'They do have thoughts of changing the world for the better. . .' Murali protested. 'They desire a better society.'

'They *want* nothing!' the editor shouted. 'I can't print stories of people who want nothing!'

He threw the bundle of short stories back at Murali. 'When you find people who want something, come back to me!' He had shouted.

Murali had never rewritten those stories. Now, as he waited for the bus to take him back to Kittur, he wondered if he still had that bundle of stories with him somewhere in his house.

*

When Murali got off the bus and walked back to the office, he found Comrade Thimma with a foreigner. It was normal to find strangers in the office; lean, fatigued men with paranoid eyes who were on the run from nearby states that were going through one of their routine purges of radical Communists. In those places radical Communism was still a threat to the state. The fugitives would sleep and take tea at the office for a few weeks, until things cooled down and they could go home.

But this man was not one of those hunted ones; he had blonde hair and an awkward European accent.

He sat next to Thimma, and the Comrade was pouring his heart out, while staring at the distant light in the grille

261

high up on the wall. Murali sat down and listened to him. He was magnificent for the next half an hour. Trotsky had not been forgiven, nor had Bernstein been spared. Thimma was trying to show the European student that even in a small town like Kittur people were up to date with the theory of dialectics.

The foreigner had nodded a lot, and written down everything. At the end, he capped his ballpoint pen and asked:

'I find that the Communists have virtually no presence in Kittur.'

Thimma slapped his thigh. He glared at the grille. The Socialists had had too much influence in this part of India, he said. The question of feudalism in the countryside had been solved; big estates had been broken up and distributed among farmers.

'The Socialists and the Congress have created a revolution here,' Thimma sighed. 'Just a pseudo-revolution, naturally. The falsehood of Bernstein once again.'

Murali's own land had been taken by the Socialist policies of the Congress government. His father had lost his land; in return, the government had allocated compensation. His father went to the municipal office to get his compensation, but he found that someone, some bureaucrat, had forged the signature and run away with his money. When Murali heard this, he had thought: my old man deserves this. I deserve this. For all that we have done to the poor, this is fit retribution. Of course, he realized, his family's compensation had not been stolen by the poor, but by some corrupt civil servant. Nevertheless it was justice of a kind.

Murali went about his regular end-of-day tasks. Sweeping the pantry came first. As he reached with his broom under the sink, he heard the foreigner say:

'I sometimes wonder if the problem with Marx is that he doesn't assume human beings are too . . . decent. He doesn't accept the idea of original sin. The irrationality of wanting that is in all of us.'

Murali crawled under the sink to get to the hard-to-reach places; Thimma's voice resonated strangely in the small space of the sink:

'You have completely misunderstood the dialectical process!'

He paused, and waited under the sink for a better response from Comrade Thimma.

He swept the floor, closed the cupboards, turned off the unwanted lights to save on the electricity bill, tightened the taps to save on the water bill, and went to the bus station for the number 56 B to take him home.

Home. A blue door, one fluorescent lamp, three bare electric bulbs, ten thousand books. The books were all over; waiting for him like faithful pets by the side of the door when he walked in, coated in dust on the dinner table, filling the sides of the old walls like buttressing the structure of the house. They had taken the best space in the house, and had left him a little rectangle for his cot.

He opened the bundle that he had brought home with him.

'Is Gorbachev straying from the True Path? Notes by Thimma swami, B.A. (Kittur), M.A. (Mysore), secretary-general, Kittur regional politburo, Communist Party of India (Marxist-Maoist)'

Aravind Adiga

He would add them to the notes he was collecting about Thimma's thoughts. The idea was to publish them, and hand them out to the workers as they left the factories.

This evening, Murali could not write for long; the mosquitoes bit him and he swatted. He lit a coil to keep the mosquitoes away. Even then he could not write; and then he realized it was not the mosquitoes disturbing him.

The way she had averted her face. He would have to do something for her.

What was her name? – Ah, yes. Sulochana.

He began searching in the mess around his bed, until he found the old collection of short stories, which he had written all those years ago. He blew the dust off the pages, and began reading.

*

The photograph of the dead man was up on the wall, beside the portraits of the gods who had failed to save him. The guru with the big belly, perhaps taking all the blame, had now been dismissed from the wall.

Murali stood at the door, waited, and knocked slowly.

'They're working in the fields,' the old neighbour with the broken red teeth shouted.

The cows and the buffalo were missing from the courtyard; sold for money, no doubt. Murali thought it was appalling. That girl, with her noble looks, working in the fields like a common labourer?

'I've come just in time,' he thought.

264

'Run out and get them!' he shouted at the neighbour. 'At once!'

The state government had a scheme for money for the widows of farmers who had killed themselves under duress, Murali explained to the widow, making her sit down on the cot. It was one of those well-intentioned rural improvement schemes that never got to anyone, because no one knew about them – until people from the city, like Murali, spread the word.

The widow was leaner, and sunburnt; she sat wiping her hands constantly against the back of her sari; she was ashamed of the dirt on them.

Sulochana brought out the tea. He was amazed that this girl, who had been working out in the fields, had still found time to make him tea.

When he took the cup from her, touching her fingers, he quickly admired her features. Having just come from a day's hard labour in the fields, she still looked beautiful – in fact, more beautiful than ever before. There was that simple, unpainted elegance to her face. None of the make-up, lipstick or false eyelashes you see in cities these days.

How old is she? he wondered.

'Sir . . .' the old woman folded her hands. 'Will the money really come?'

'If you sign here,' he said. 'And here. And here.'

The old lady held the pen and grinned idiotically.

'She can't write,' Sulochana said; so he put the letter on his thigh, and he signed for her.

He explained that he had brought another letter, one to be delivered to the police in Kittur, demanding a prosecution

265

of the moneylender for his role in instigating the man's death through usury. He wanted the old woman to sign that too, but she folded her palm.

'Please, sir, don't do that. Please. We don't want any trouble.'

Sulochana stood by the wall, looking down, silently doubling her mother's plea.

He tore the letter up. As he did so, he realized that he was now the arbiter over this family's fate; he was the patriarch here.

'And her marriage?' he said, pointing to the girl leaning against the wall.

'Who will marry this one? And what am I to do?' the old woman wailed while the girl retreated into the dark of the house.

It was on the way back to the bus station that the idea came to him.

He touched the metal tip of his umbrella to the ground, and trailed a long, continuous line through the mud.

And then he thought, Why Not?

She had no other hope, after all . . .

He got on the bus. He was still a bachelor, at the age of fifty-five. After his stint in jail his family had disowned him, and none of his aunts or uncles had tried to fix him up with an arranged marriage. Somehow, in the midst of distributing pamphlets and spreading the word to the proletariat and collecting Comrade Thimma's speeches, he had never found time to marry himself off. There had not been much desire to do so, either.

Lying in bed, staring at the fan that was turning slowly overhead, he thought: But this is no habitation for a girl. It is a filthy house, filled with old editions – books by veterans of the Communist party and nineteenth-century European short-story writers – that no one reads anymore.

He had not until now realized how badly he had been living all these years. But things would change; he felt a great hope. If she came into his life everything could be different. He lay down on his cot, and stared at the ceiling fan. It was switched off; he rarely turned it on, except in the most awful summer heat, so that he wouldn't have to spend more on the electricity bill.

All his life he had been dogged by a restlessness, a feeling that he was meant for some greater endeavour than could be found in a small town. After his law degree from Madras, his father had expected him to take over his law practice. His father had been in the Congress; he had gone along to meetings. Perhaps Murali had been too easily swayed by what he heard; the boy took to wearing a Nehru cap and keeping a photo of Gandhi on his desk. His father noticed. One day there was a confrontation, and shouting, and Murali had left his father's house, and joined the Congress as a full-time member. He knew what he wanted to do with his life already: there was an enemy to overcome. The old, bad India of caste and class privilege – the India of child marriage; of ill-treated widows; of exploited subalterns – it had to be overthrown. When the state elections came, he campaigned with all his heart for the Congress candidate.

After the candidate won, he saw two of his fellow Congress workers sitting outside the party office every morning. He saw men approaching them with letters meant for the candidate: they took the letters, and a dozen rupees from each supplicant.

Murali threatened to report them to the candidate. The two men turned very grave. They stepped aside, and invited Murali to go right in.

'Please complain at once,' they said.

As he went and knocked on the candidate's door, he heard laughter growing behind him.

Murali tried out the Communists next, having heard that they were incorruptible. There were various factions among the Communists, and he changed his membership from one Communist party to the other, until one day he entered the dim office and saw, under the giant poster of heroic Proletarians climbing up to heaven to knock out the gods of the past, the small, dark figure of Comrade Thimma. At last – an incorruptible. Back then Comrade Thimma had seventeen member-volunteers; they ran women's education programmes, library programmes, population control campaigns, and proletarian radicalization drives. With a group of volunteers, Murali went to the factories near the port, distributing pamphlets with the message of Marx and the advantages of sterilization. As the membership of the party dwindled, he found himself going alone; it made no difference to him. The cause was a good one. He was never strident like the workers from the other Communist parties; quietly, and with great perseverance, he stood by the side of the road, holding out the pamphlets to the workers, and repeating the message that so few of them ever took to heart:

'Don't you want to find out how to live a better life, brothers?'

He thought his writing too, would contribute to that cause – although he was honest enough to admit that perhaps only his vanity made him think so. The word 'talent' was lodged in his mind, and gave him hope; but even as he was wondering how to shape his writing, he was sent to jail.

The police came for Comrade Thimma one day. This was during the Chinese war.

'You are right to arrest me,' Thimma had said, 'as I freely and openly support the Communist invasion of India.'

Murali was in the party headquarters, and he asked the policemen: 'Would you mind arresting me as well?'

Jail had been a happy time for him. He washed Thimma's clothes and hung them to dry in the mornings. He had hoped all the free time in jail would concentrate his mind, and help him reshape his fiction, but he had no time to write down his own ideas. In the evenings, he took notes as Thimma dictated. Thimma's responses to the great questions of Marxism. The apostasy of Bernstein. The challenge of Trotsky. A justification for Kronstadt.

He collected the responses faithfully until it was time to sleep; then he pulled a blanket over Thimma's body, leaving his toes out in the cool air.

He shaved him in the morning, as Thimma thundered to the mirror about the problems with Khrushchev's defiling of the legacy of Comrade Stalin.

It was the happiest period of his life. But then he had been released.

Aravind Adiga

With a sigh, Murali got off his bed. He walked around the dark house, looking at the mess made by the books, and saying to himself again and again: What do I have to show for my life? Just this broken-down house . . .

Then he saw the face of the girl again, and his whole body lit up with hope, and joy. He took out his short stories, and read them again. With a red-ink pen he began to scratch out details of his characters and quicken their motives, their impulses.

*

It came to Murali one evening, on his way to Salt Market Village: 'They're avoiding me. Both mother and daughter.'

Then he thought: 'No, not Sulochana – it's only the old woman who's gone cold.'

For two months now, he had been catching the bus and going to Salt Market Village on a variety of fictitious premises, only to see Sulochana's face again, only to touch her fingers again when she brought him the cup of scalding-hot tea.

He had tried to put it to the old lady that they should marry – hints could be delivered, and the topic would insinuate itself into the lady's mind. That had been his hope. Then, out of sheer social responsibility, he would agree, despite his advanced age, to marry her.

But the old lady had never divined his desire.

'Your daughter is excellent in the household. I am happy to observe that,' he had said once, thinking that enough of a hint.

270

The next day, when he came, a strange young girl came out to meet him. The widow had moved up in life; she had now hired a servant.

'Is madam in?' he asked. The servant nodded.

'Will you go get her?'

A minute passed. He thought he heard the sound of voices behind the door; then the servant came out and said, 'No.'

'No what?'

She turned her eyes into the house again. "They . . . are not here. No.'

'And Sulochana? Is she in?'

The servant girl shook her head.

Why shouldn't they avoid me, he thought, trailing his umbrella on the ground as he returned to the bus station. He had done his work for them; he was not needed any more. This is how people in the real world behaved. Why should he be hurt?

In the evening, walking around his gloomy home, he felt he had to agree with the old woman's judgment: surely this is no fit habitation for a young girl like Sulochana. How could he bring a woman to it? He had never thought how poorly he lived, until he tried imagining living with someone else.

Yet the next day, he was back on the bus to Salt Market Village, where, once again, the servant girl told him that no one was home.

On the way back, he rested his head against the grille of the bus and thought; the more they snub me, the more I want to fall down before that girl and propose marriage.

271

At home he tried writing a letter. 'Dear Sulochana: I have been searching for a way to tell you. There is so much to speak . . .'

He went back every day for a week, and was refused entry every day. 'I will never come back,' he promised himself on the seventh evening, as he had for six evenings before. 'I really will never come back. This is disgraceful behaviour. I am exploiting these people.' But he was also angry with the old woman and Sulochana for treating him like this.

On the journey back, he got up and shouted to the conductor: 'Stop! Stop!' He had remembered, out of the blue, a story he had written twenty-five years ago, about a matchmaker who worked in the village.

He asked the children playing marbles for the matchmaker; they directed him to the shopkeepers. It took an hour and a half to find the house.

The matchmaker was an old, half-blind man sitting on a chair and smoking a hookah; his wife brought a chair for the communist to sit down on.

Murali cleared his throat, and cracked his knuckles. He wondered what to say, what to do. The hero in his story had walked around the matchmaker's house and gone back; he had never come this far.

'There is a friend of mine who wishes to marry that girl. Sulochana.'

'The daughter of the fellow who . . .' The matchmaker pantomimed a hanging.

Murali nodded.

'Your friend is too late, sir. She has money now, and so she has a hundred offers,' the matchmaker said. 'That is the way of life.'

'But . . . my friend . . . my friend has set his heart on her . . .'

'Who is this friend?' the matchmaker asked, with a dirty, omniscient gleam in his eyes.

He caught the bus in the morning, as soon as his work was over at the party, and waited for her in the markets. From then on, he began waiting for her in the market, when she was buying her vegetables in the evening. He would follow her slowly. He looked at the bananas, at the mangoes. He had been buying fruit for Comrade Thimma for decades. He was an expert at so many women's tasks; his heart skipped a beat when he saw her pick an over-ripe mango; when the vendor tricked her, he wanted to run over and yell at him and protect her from his avarice.

In the evenings, he stood waiting for the bus back to Kittur. He observed the way people lived in villages. He saw a boy cycling furiously, with a block of ice strapped to the back of his bicycle. He had to make it in time before the ice melted; it was already half gone, and he had no aim in life but to deliver the rest of the ice in time. A man came with bananas in a plastic bag and looked around; there were large black spots on the bananas already, and he had to sell them before they rotted. All these people gave Murali a message. To want things in life, they were saying, is to recognize that time is limited.

He was fifty-five years old.

He did not take the bus back that evening; he walked to the house. Instead of going in the front door, he walked in through the back. Sulochana was winnowing rice; she looked at her mother and went in.

The servant went in to bring a chair, but the old woman said: 'Don't.'

'Look here; you want to marry my daughter?' she asked.

So she had found out. It was always like this; you make an effort to conceal desire and it is out in the open. The greatest fallacy; that you can hide from others what you want from them.

He nodded, avoiding her eyes.

'How old are you?' she asked.

'Fifty.'

'Can you give her children at your age?'

He tried to respond.

The old woman said:

'Why would we want to get you into our family, in any case? My late husband always told me, the Communists are trouble.'

He dropped his jaw. Was this the same husband who had praised the Communists? Had this woman just made all that up?

Murali understood now; her husband had said nothing about the Communists. In their wanting they became so cunning, these people!

He said: 'I bring many advantages to your family. I am a Brahmin by birth; a graduate of the . . .'

'Look here!' the woman got up. 'Please leave – or there will be trouble.'

'Why not? Maybe I can't give her children, at my age, but I can make her happy, certainly,' he thought, on the bus back home. 'We can read Maupassant together.'

He was an educated man, a graduate of the Madras University; this was no way to treat him. Tears flooded his eyes.

He sought out books of fiction and poetry, but it was the words of a film song he had heard on the bus which seemed to express his feelings best. So this is why the proletariat went to the cinema, he thought. He bought a ticket himself.

'How many?'

'One.'

The ticket-seller grinned. 'Don't you have any friends, old man?'

After the movie, Murali wrote a letter, and posted it to her.

The next morning he woke up wondering if she would ever read it. Even if it got to the house, wouldn't her mother throw it away? He should have hand-delivered it!

It is not enough to make an honest attempt. That was enough for Marx and Gandhi – to have tried. But not for the real world, in which he suddenly found himself.

After considering the matter for an hour, he wrote the letter again. This time he paid an urchin three rupees to take the message straight to the girl's hands.

*

'She knows you come to look for her,' the vegetable-seller said, the next time he came to the market. 'You've scared her away.'

275

Aravind Adiga

*She is avoiding me* – his heart felt a pang. Now he understood so many more film songs. This is what they meant, the humiliation of being avoided by a girl you have come a long way to see . . .

He thought the vegetable-sellers were all giggling at him.

Even ten years ago – in his forties – there would have been nothing unseemly about approaching a girl, he thought, on the way back. Now he was a dirty old man; he had become a figure whom he had worked several times into his short stories – the lecherous old Brahmin, preying on the innocent girl of a lower caste.

But those fellows were just caricatures, class-villains; *now* he could flesh them out so much better. When he got into bed at night, he took a piece of paper and wrote:

'Some thoughts that a lecherous old Brahmin might *actually* have.'

'Now I know enough,' Murali thought, looking at the words on the page. 'I can become a writer at last.'

The next morning there was order and reason once more. There was the comb on his hair, the breathing exercises before the mirror, the slow steady gait out the front door, the business of cleaning the party headquarters and making tea for Thimma.

But by afternoon, he was on the bus to Salt Market Village again.

He waited for her to come to the market, and then walked behind her, examining potatoes and brinjals and stealing glances at her. All the time he could see the vendors mocking him: dirty old man, dirty old man. He thought with regret

276

of a man's traditional prerogative in India – in the old, bad India – to marry a younger woman.

The next morning, back at the pantry of the headquarters, boiling tea for Thimma, everything around him seemed dingy, and dark and unbearable – the old pots and pans, the filthy spoons, the dirty old tub out of which he scooped sugar for the tea: the embers of a life that had never flared, never flamed.

'You've been fooled,' everything in the room said to him. 'You've wasted your life.'

He thought of all the advantages in life; his education, his sharper wit, his brains, his gift for writing. And 'talent' – as that Mysore editor had said.

All of that, he thought as he brought the tea out into the reception, wasted in the service of Comrade Thimma.

Even Thimma had wasted himself. He had never remarried after his wife's early death; he had dedicated himself to his life's goal – uplifting the proletariat of Kittur. Ultimately it was not Marx; it was Gandhi and Nehru to blame. Murali was convinced of that. A whole generation of young men, deluded by Gandhianism, wasting their lives by running around organizing free eye clinics for the poor and distributing books for rural libraries, instead of seducing those young widows and unmarried girls. That old man in his loincloth had turned them mad. Like Gandhi you had to withhold all your lusts. Even to know what you wanted in life was a sin; desire was bigotry. And look where the country was, after forty years of idealism? A total mess! Maybe if they had all become bastards, the young men of his generation, the place would be like America by now!

277

That evening he forced himself not to take the bus to the village. He stayed on, cleaning the party headquarters twice over.

No – he thought, as he strained to clean under the sink the second time – it was not a waste! The idealism of young men like him had changed Kittur and the villages around it. Rural poverty was halved, smallpox had been eradicated, public health was a hundred times improved, literacy was up. If Sulochana could read, it was because of volunteers like him, because of the free library projects . . .

He paused in the darkness under the sink. A voice growled inside him: 'Fine, she can read – and what does that do for you, you idiot?'

He rushed back into the light, into the reception.

The poster now came to life. The proletarians climbing up to heaven to overturn the gods began to melt and change form. He saw them for what they were: a subaltern army of semen, blood, and flesh rebelling inside him. A revolution of the body proletariat, long suppressed, but now turning articulate, saying, *We want!*

The Communists were finished. The European visitor had said as much; and all the newspapers were saying the same thing. The edifice of Marx and Lenin was collapsing. The Americans had somehow won. Comrade Thimma would talk on and on. But there would soon be nothing to talk about; because Communism was dead. Dialectics had become Dust. So had Gandhi; so had Nehru. Out in the streets of Kittur, the young people were driving brand-new Suzuki cars, blaring pop music from the West; they were licking ice-cream cones with red tongues and wearing shiny metal watches.

He picked up the brochure and threw it at the Soviet poster, startling a gecko that had been hiding behind it.

*

Do you think intelligence has no place in Indian life? Do you think a Madras University man – a Brahmin – is tossed aside so lightly?

In his hand, as the bus rocked, Murali held a letter from the Government of Karnataka that announced another instalment of the money was due to arrive for the widow of the farmer Arasu Deva Gowda, provided she signed. Eight thousand rupees.

Asking for directions, he found the house of the moneylender. He saw it: the biggest thing in the village, with a pink façade and pillars up the front supporting a portico – the house that 3 per cent interest, compounded monthly, had built.

The moneylender, a fat, dark man, was selling grain to a group of farmers; by his side, a fat, dark boy, probably his son, was making a note in a book. Murali stopped to admire it all: the sheer genius of exploitation in India. Sell a farmer his grain. Get rid of your bad stock this way. Then charge him a loan for it. Make him pay it back at 3 per cent a month. Thirty-six per cent a year! – how diabolical, how brilliant! And to think, Murali smiled, that he thought that mastering dialectics was a sign of intelligence.

When Murali went up to him, the moneylender was sticking his palm deep into the grain; when he brought it out, the chocolate-colour skin was coated with a fine yellow dust, like a bird's pollen-covered beak.

Without wiping his arm, he took the letter from Murali. Behind him, on an alcove on his front wall, sat a giant red statue of the potbellied Ganesha. A fat wife, with fat children around her, was sitting on a charpoy. And from behind them wafted the smell of a feeding, defecating beast: a water-buffalo, without doubt.

'Did you know that government money has paid the widow another eight thousand rupees?' Murali told him. 'If you have debts outstanding, you should collect them now. She is in a position to pay.'

'Who are you?' the moneylender asked, with small suspicious eyes.

Hesitating for a moment, Murali said, 'I am the fifty-five-year-old communist.'

He wanted them to know. The old woman and Sulochana. They were both in his power now. They had been in his power from the day they had walked into his office.

When he went back to his house, there was a letter from Comrade Thimma under the door. Probably hand-delivered, since there was no one else to deliver anything now.

He tossed it away. He realized, as he did it, that he was casting away his lifelong membership in the Communist Party of India (Marxist-Maoist). Comrade Thimma, his lips thirsty for tea, would deliver lectures alone, in that dim hall, denouncing him. He joined Bernstein and Trotsky and the long line of apostates.

At midnight he was still awake. He was staring at the ceiling fan, whose fast-rotating blades were chopping the beam of light from the halogen streetlamps outside the bedroom into sharp white glints: they showered down on Murali like the first particles of wisdom he had received in his life.

He stared at the shining edges of the fan's blades for a long time; then, with a jerk, got up from the bed.

# CHRONOLOGY

*31 October 1984*
News reaches Kittur via the BBC that Mrs. Indira Gandhi, prime minister of India, has been assassinated by her bodyguards. The town closes for two days. Mrs. Gandhi's cremation, telecast live, leads to a jump in the number of TVs sold in Kittur.

*November*
General elections. Anand Kumar, the Congress (I) candidate and a junior minister in Indira Gandhi's cabinet, wins. His lead of 45,457 votes over Ashwin Aithal, his BJP rival, is the largest in Kittur's history.

*1985*
As a result of the growing interest in the stock market, *The Dawn Herald* begins publishing a daily report on the activities of the Bombay Stock Exchange on page 3.

   Dr. Shambhu Shetty opens HAPPY SMILE CLINIC, Kittur's first orthodontic clinic.

*1986*
A giant rally held by the Hoyka community in Nehru Maidan pledges to build the first temple 'for, by, and of Backward Castes' in Kittur.

   The first video lending library opens in Umbrella Street.

   Construction of the northern bell tower, delayed for over a century, is resumed at the Cathedral of Our Lady of Valencia.

1987

The Cricket World Cup is held in India and Pakistan. Interest in cricket leads to a major hike in the demand for colour TVs.

Riots break out between Hindus and Muslims in the Bunder. Two people are killed. Dawn-to-dusk curfew in the port.

Kittur is reclassified by the state government of Karnataka from 'town' to 'city,' and the town municipality is now a 'corporation.' The first act of the new corporation is to authorize the tearing down of the great forest of Bajpe.

The arrival of migrant Tamil workers, drawn by the construction boom in Bajpe and Rose Lane, is believed to be the cause of a severe outbreak of cholera.

1988

Mabroor Engineer, believed to be the richest man in town, opens the first Maruti Suzuki car showroom in Kittur.

The Rashtriya Swayamsevak Sangh (RSS) holds a march from Angel Talkies to the Bunder. Marchers call for the declaration of India as a Hindu nation, and a return to traditional social values.

Elections are held to the city corporation. The BJP and the Congress split the seats almost evenly.

St. Alfonso announces that it will admit girls into the college (but not into the high school or junior school).

Construction of the northern bell tower, delayed for a year by the death of the Rector, recommences at the Cathedral of Our Lady of Valencia.

**1989**

Elections held to India's parliament. Ashwin Aithal, BJP candidate, upsets union minister and Congress candidate Anand Kumar to become the first non-Congress candidate ever to win the seat of Kittur.

The Sardar Patel Iron Man of India Stadium opens in Bajpe. The construction of houses continues rapidly, and by the year's end the old forest is almost entirely gone.

**1990**

A bomb explodes during a class in St. Alfonso Junior College, leading to closure of classes. *The Dawn Herald* runs a front page editorial asking: 'Do we need martial law in this country?'

The first computer lab in Kittur is opened in January in St. Alfonso High School. Other schools follow within the year.

The Gulf War breaks out, leading to the loss of expatriate remittances from Kuwait. A severe economic crisis follows. However, the telecast of the war on CNN, available only to those TVs with a dish antenna, leads to a great jump in the sales of satellite TV dish antennas.

With its funding frozen, construction work on the northern bell tower of the Cathedral stops again.

*21 May 1991*

News reaches Kittur via CNN of the assassination of Rajiv Gandhi. The town is closed for two days.